OPAL EGGS OF FIRE

Opal Eggs of Fire

James Calderwood

Library of Congress Control Number: 2013908023
ISBN: Hardcover   978-1-4836-3579-8
               Softcover   978-1-4836-3578-1
               Ebook   978-1-4836-3580-4

This is a work of fiction. Names, characters, places and incidents either are the product of the author's imagination or are used fictitiously, and any resemblance to any actual persons, living or dead, events, or locales is entirely coincidental.

Rev. date: 05/03/2013

To order additional copies of this book, contact:
Xlibris Corporation
1-800-618-969
www.Xlibris.com.au
Orders@Xlibris.com.au
503471

Chapter 1

The coppery sun shone down on the dusty paddock. A cold breeze pushed the thin dust before it as it blew lazily across the barren landscape. Patches of ice still lay on the ground, left over from the previous night's frost—a typical day in a drought. John was just leaving the house with his son Tony when Helen called, 'Stop, John, you are wanted on the phone. It's the bank.' John's shoulders dropped as he turned back to the kitchen. Tony followed with a look of gloom. He pulled out one of the kitchen chairs from the table and sat down.

This phone call was not unexpected as the bank overdraft was getting out of hand. The high interest rates and the bad season on the farm surely did not help. John answered the phone and spoke briefly to the teller and made an appointment to see the manager. 'The bank. 10.30. Tuesday,' said John.

'Did you speak to the manager?'

'No, only Debbie.' Debbie was the teller in the small bank.

'Well, that's that, I suppose. Where can we get some extra money?' John was evidently upset as he left with Tony following him. *Bloody Lizard!* John thought. He had no love for the manager of the local bank and referred to him as the Lizard. Most of the previous managers in the bank had joined in with local community events and played some sort of sport. This man had no friends or even acquaintances in the district. His wife did have a couple of friends in the school council.

John and Tony got into the battered farm's four-wheel drive utility and drove it to the grain silo, where a full bin of oats on a trailer waited. Tony alighted and hooked the bin to the utility and got in. John drove off to feed the sheep.

It was halfway along the lane before John spoke. He had evidently been doing a lot of thinking. *I wish we didn't have this blasted bank problem. Where in God's name are we going to get any money to pay the bank?*

The battered old four-wheel drive stopped halfway along the lane way whilst Tony opened the wire gate. John then drove out of the lane way into the adjoining paddock next to the lane way. Behind it in the dusty paddock, a mob of skinny sheep ran back and forth, trying to eat as much of the oats which had been let out in a trail behind the bin.

The occasional sheep would have an altercation with its neighbour, and a bunting match would ensue. Both sheep would back off and charge each other head first. They would meet together with a sickening thud as their heads banged together. They would back up and charge again until one sheep gave in and turned away. This sheep usually got a bunt in the ribs or the bum to send it on its way.

A few of the greedier sheep followed the trailer to the open gate, hoping for an extra feed of the precious oats. One of the sheep ran past the ute and on to the lane way.

Tony was just getting out to shut the gate as they left the paddock, when a sheep veered past him. 'Here, Laddie, fetch him back,' he said softly to the sheepdog sitting on the tray of the ute. The black-and-white border collie jumped out of the ute tray and ran up the lane way, passing the sheep, heading the escapee off, ran after the escapee, and then turned the runaway back down the lane towards the gate. Tony ran out into the lane to direct the sheep back into the paddock. Laddie trotted back to the ute and then walked over, puffing lightly, and muzzled at Tony's hand. Tony crouched down and patted Laddie's faithful head. 'Good boy' he crooned to the dog.

Tony shut the wire gate and got into the ute. Laddie jumped up on to the ute tray. 'Well, it looks as if it's going to be another prick of a day. It would not surprise me if the damned wind sprung up and started to blow from the north and start a dust storm,' grunted John, as he let the clutch out, and the ute rattled on its way. 'There's lots of other places I'd rather be at the present time than trying to farm in this dust bowl'.

The ute drove along the laneway back towards the homestead, which shimmered in the distance against the cloudless sky. Dust billowed out from behind the ute. Usually this time of the year, the potholes in the lane were full of water.

A group of crows took it in turns to pick at a dead sheep in the paddock. The crows flew off a short distance and sat in a small mallee tree, which was growing out of a stone heap.

'Bloody bastards. They are the only ones who will do any good out of this farm this year,' growled John. 'Remind me to put the rifle in the ute. At least, some of the bludgers might have to pay.' The crows were a bad enemy in times of drought because they picked the eyes out of any poor hapless sheep which could not get to their feet in the morning and join the mob. The only thing to do then was to cut the sheep's throat to put it out of its misery.

John stopped by one of the wheat paddocks. Both the men got out of the ute and climbed through the fence to look at the water-stressed wheat. The plants were stunted and were quickly, day by day, turning blue. A few small area on the stony rises had already turned brown and died.

Tony dug out some plants and then dug down into the sandy soil, looking for any sign of moisture. He let the dry soil run through his fingers and blew away in the breeze. 'Dry as a bloody lime burner's boot.' The men walked further out into the crop. The story was the same. The soil was extremely dry. The crop must be living on the memory of the earlier thunder storms after which it had been sown.

'Well, let's go. We aren't doing much good here. Must be getting close to smoko time.' The men walked back to the ute and drove off towards the house, which shimmered in the distance at the end of the lane way.

There was a cattle grid in the road with an old worn-out tractor tyre on each side to stop the stock from passing the barrier. Next to the grid was a large wire gate, which could be opened to allow farm machinery and livestock into the house and shed yard. The grid was just before the house. The ute rumbled over this and then entered a small bare area, which was surrounded by a house on one side, then a large implement shed, and a hay shed, which by now was nearly empty. Most of the hay that was left in the shed was poor-quality hay, which had been rained on soon after it had been baled some years before and had gone mouldy. There were a large assortment of grain silos for seed grain and. A small shearing shed which was raised off the ground on piles . . . this allowed the sheep manure and urine to drop through the grating on the floor There was a small, oil-cum-chemical shed with diesel and petrol tanks next to it. A large scrap heap of old, definitely dead pieces of machinery was heaped up behind the implement shed.

John pulled up outside the double car shed behind the house. They got out and walked through the gate along the concrete path towards the verandah. The washing machine could be heard thumping away in the laundry at the back of the shed. Rows of newly washed clothes swung in the light breeze on the rotary clothes hoist a short distance from the laundry.

The house was a mismatch of materials surrounded by an iron fence. The front section of the house was built out of the local limestone, whilst the rear was corrugated roofing iron, which was laid on horizontally. The whole lot was covered by a bungalow roof and a wide verandah. The poor house was desperately in need of a good coat of paint. The old paint was peeling off in places, leaving the remnants of the old, previous paint colours showing through. Looking at the paint brought back memories of the previous colours used in the past painting exercises.

In the front of the house, there was a series of garden beds marked out with the local limestone used as borders. A few straggly flowers struggled to survive the dry in the garden. These were mainly daisies and a rockery of succulents, which seemed as if they could almost live without water. At the rear of the house though, there was a vegetable garden. It was watered by the washing and shower water, which was directed on to the different beds by a thick hose led from the sink and shower drain.

The flower garden, in better times, had been Helen's hobby, but as money was very tight, the water had to be saved for the necessities, such as the livestock, and the used shower water was for the vegetable patch.

As they walked past the vegetable garden, John bent down and pulled a few weeds out from between the rows of vegies. They took their dirty boots off, then opened the rear fly screen door of the house, and then walked into the kitchen. Laddie, the dog, had followed them into the verandah and settled himself close to the door on an old grain bag, which was his bed.

Helen looked up from the timber table on which she had some bread dough rolled out. She brushed a strand of blonde hair out of her eyes with a flour-covered hand. Some of the flour stuck to the side of her face, leaving a white mark. 'Smoko time already. Don't just stand there. Shut the door, Tony. The flies are getting in!' Tony quickly shut the door to keep the small, sticky bush flies out of the house. 'How time flies when you are having fun,' said Helen as the two men sat down at the table.

Helen got three mugs out of the kitchen dresser and put coffee and sugar in them. She then put them on the table, then walked over to the large, slow combustion stove, got the kettle which had been simmering on the side of the hot plate, and filled the mugs with hot water 'What are things like out in the paddock?' she asked, with a worried look on her face, as she topped the mugs up with milk from a small jug.

'The crops look as if they can only last another week or two before they die, and there were two more dead sheep. The bloody crows got to them.'

Helen shook her head. *What are we going to do about the bank?* She had not asked John before because he was a deep thinker and would have spent some time remonstrating. To wait was the best way with John. Helen knew that he and Tony would have discussed this in John's own time.

John pushed his chair back from the table. It made a screeching sound as the legs dragged over the lino. In the silence which ensued, the tick-tock of the old Ansonia mantle clock, which sat on the smoky mantle piece above the combustion stove, was the only noise in the kitchen. As if to break the silence, the old clock cranked up and started to chime its brassy clang. The ten chimes seemed to bring John and the others back to the real matters at hand. John let out a sigh. 'Urgh! Well, I was expecting that. We've had nearly no income for the last three years, thanks to this bloody drought.' John sat down at the table and sipped his coffee, evidently deep in thought. 'What did the miserable little prick have to say for himself? Going to give us a few thousand out of the goodness of his heart, I suppose,' he stated sarcastically.

John had been worried about the bank loan for some time. He had tried to get some off-farm work, but all farmers in the district had tightened their belts financially because of the droughts. The phone call from the Lizard had been expected for some time.

John and Helen had bought the farm cheaply some twenty years before. John had been share farming and shearing in the district since his teens. John had a reputation as a tough football player. Many an opponent left the field with a black eye when standing against John. In all fairness, John copped his fair share back. John had amassed a small amount of cash for the deposit on the farm. They bought it two years after he had married Helen.

Helen's grand father and grand mother had come to the district from the Barossa Valley in the 1920s as a young married couple and had amassed a large holding of land. Her father was from tough German stock and definitely was not afraid of work. The 1930 depression had cost the grand parents most of the land, leaving them with just enough land to survive. Helens father was the eldest son. Big Herman was his nick name. He was ready to help all and sundry in the district. The family had ten children. Helen was the youngest.

John and Helen's farm was only partly cleared when they purchased it. They had put very long hours in dusty hard conditions, chaining and ploughing the new land each year, spending many weeks picking stumps and stones by hand to bring the land into production. A lot of the farm income during the good years was ploughed back into the property to improve the land and build fences.

When the children were born, they had spent a fair amount of their time, being pushed around the dusty paddocks in a pram or stroller as Helen toiled in the paddocks.

John had kept his shearing round to help with the finances. Eventually, Tony had joined him, after leaving school. The other two children had gone out of the district. David had an apprenticeship in Adelaide, whilst Emma worked at a supermarket at Whyalla.

Through hard work and persistence, the farming venture had started to pay off. They had been able to upgrade their old, worn-out plant with a reasonable second-hand assortment of implements. John had gone to a government auction a few years previously and had purchased an old Caterpillar D7 bulldozer. This had been invaluable in digging some large dams for water for the livestock, prior to the reticulated piped water being laid to the farm, and, finally, in clearing the last of the large stumps and stones from the land. This old dozer was John's pride and joy, mainly for the hard work it had saved them in finishing the clearing work.

A few years back, the farm was made more viable with the reticulated water being connected This allowed them to run more sheep, as they were not solely reliant on the dam water. The dams had dried up during the last summer and were still dry as there had been no decent rains, causing water run off to fill them. This would have meant that they would have had to sell all of their livestock prior to having the reticulated water being laid on. There was only rain water in the house and shed tanks for their use.

The last three years had been a nightmare. Three years ago, they had only received half of their annual rainfall. Consequently, their crop and wool yields were cut by about half. This had happened before, and as they lived in a marginal area, they were used to such events.

The next year had been worse with them, only reaping enough grain for seed, having to cut the remaining flock by another half, and selling the excess sheep for almost nothing as there was no demand for skinny sheep because of the drought.

John had borrowed carry-on finance, but the factors of the bad season and the drastically rising interest rates had compounded, leaving them in a bad situation. As was usual in a drought situation, the land values had dropped very low as there would be no local buyers looking to buy a property in the middle of a drought.

To make matters worse, there were only about a third of the sheep left in the district, and most farmers were shearing their own sheep to save on costs.

John had been talking to a few neighbours who had informed him that the bank was getting tough and threatening to start selling some farmers' land up to recover costs.

John and Tony rose from the table and then walked out into the cold sunshine. 'What do you think we should do about the dead sheep lying around?' Up until now there had only been a few, but as the feed situation worsened, both men could see the situation worsening. John felt a sense of guilt over the plight of the poor, skinny sheep.

John got into the ute and drove it over to the large silo which contained the precious oats they were feeding. Tony had walked over in anticipation of having to unhitch the grain feeder. He unhitched the trailer and left the bin and trailer sitting under the grain auger ready for the next load of precious oats. John walked over to the silo and tapped at the wall of the silo, trying to tell from the noise on the iron as to where the level of the oats had descended to.

Tony had been pondering John's conversation about the dead sheep. 'Why don't we get the dozer going and dig trench for the dead sheep? At least, it will keep the flies down and make us feel a bit better if we don't have to see them when we drive out in the paddock. I feel as if it's my fault that they are dying.' They both agreed the sheep could be buried to keep the crows and foxes away.

Tony walked over to the large skillion-roofed shed, which held most of the farming plant. John slid in to the worn seat of the ute, drove it over to the shed, and parked in front of the old Caterpillar D7. He turned the rattling diesel motor off. 'Get the battery out of the Chamberlain tractor, whilst I check the oil and water in the dozer'. Tony climbed up and undid the tractor's bonnet and started to remove the battery. Laddie noticed that John was checking the dozer. This was usually a good source of sport, as, like the header, it was usually the home of some rats.

Tony carried the battery over and put it into the battery box on the dozer. 'I'll go and let the pup go. May as well let him have a bit of fun too.' Tony walked off around the corner and unleashed the young sheepdog from its running lead from the kennel, which was under a mallee tree behind the shed. The dog was pleased to be set free and jumped at Tony, licking his hands, and then ran back and forth, yipping. 'Calm down, you silly young bugger.' Laughed Tony.

The D7 had not been started for two years. John filled the petrol tank for the pilot motor from a plastic can, then turned the petrol on, and then turned the starter key. The petrol-starting motor spluttered to life, shooting loose black soot out of the small exhaust poking out of the bonnet. It settled down to a steady roar. John pulled the hand clutch on the side of the motor in and started the main motor, turning with the compression lift on. He watched the oil pressure gauge. When the oil pressure rose, he dropped the compression lift and pulled the throttle out. The big motor roared to life, tossing more loose soot towards the shed rafters. John then released the hand clutch of the pilot motor and then turned the petrol tap off. Finally, he turned the key off, and the roaring pilot motor stopped. The big diesel idled steadily, its turbocharger making a whistling noise.

The dogs, who had been quivering in anticipation, jumped on the first hapless rat which ran from its dozer fortress. John climbed up on to the machine and sat in the seat. He opened the throttle, pulled the gearshift lever, and then drove the dozer out of the shed. The dogs were dispatching almost every rat which ran out with a quick nip to the back of the head. The occasional one had the good fortune to escape and climb up under the truck header or the tractor.

Tony walked over and opened the gate in the fence by the shed so John could drive over next to a stone heap in the paddock and dig the grave.

Tony then started the ute and drove over, pulled a bale of hay from the hay shed, and tossed it on to the tray of the ute. He took it to a small mob of sheep which had been put into a holding paddock by the shearing shed. This was the hospital paddock where any sheep which had gone down were brought to be cared for. There were around twenty sheep in this small paddock, which was usually used for a holding paddock at shearing time, either for the woolly sheep waiting for their turn in the shearing shed or for the freshly shorn sheep waiting to be let out into the paddock at the end of the day.

John stopped about two hundred metres from the sheds next to a large heap of limestone, which both he and Helen had picked off the farming land when they had first bought the farm. These rocks had been thrown into the tray of an old tip dray, which had been converted to be pulled by a tractor.

The heavy dozer had rattled the accumulation of dust and rats' nests from under the tracks on the way. The dozer tracks were rusty and squealed in protest when John turned a corner. John lined the machine up, then dropped the heavy rippers into the stony ground, and drove forward. The extra effort caused the exhaust manifold to get hotter. The smell of cooking rat manure and urine was overpowering. Finally, after a couple of rips, the smell started to abate.

John had scooped a hole about five metres long and two metres deep, the width of the blade. There was not a sign of moisture even at this depth. This was the legacy of the three dry years. *The usual subsoil moisture, which helped the crops to grow in a normal drought, was all but gone, a bit like the money in the bank account.* John thought as he turned the machine on its axis and then drove the dozer back to the shed.

John was not looking forward to the trip to town. Helen carefully packed the eggs into the baskets, placing a sheet of newspaper between each layer to make sure that none broke on the trip to town on the rough, dirt road. To have eggs break and leak on to the floor of the car was not a good idea as the smell was almost impossible to remove, as they had found from a previous occasion. These eggs were used in part to swap for some of the groceries. These were the basics such as flour, sugar, soap powder, and other items of daily use. John butchered their own sheep, and Helen had a pretty little jersey cow, which she milked daily for their milk and butter. The cow was housed in a small paddock adjoining the house yard. During the night, the cow's calf was allowed to drink from her. It was shut away during the day so the cow could be milked at night.

All three were very on edge all the way to Kimba. They were definitely not looking forward to the meeting with the Lizard.

They had all talked long into the night about the problem they had in the previous evening, but they could not come up with any answers. The machinery was certainly not worth a lot of money, and owing to the drought, it would only bring half of its value. After going to bed, John and Helen had cuddled for a while. This had helped to take their minds off the daily problems. They had talked well into the night between themselves, being too keyed up to sleep.

Selling the plant was not really an option as if they could survive this year. It would be needed the next year. There were definitely no luxuries. They were living on the bare minimum.

They approached the small town. The large concrete grain silos were the most prominent structure on the skyline. The silos would hardly be used this year, which would be another detrimental blow to the town as a lot of the town's people relied on this seasonal work for a living.

John drove through the nearly deserted streets, turned the car into the curb, and stopped in front of the small bank building. They got out of the car and walked inside. The young girl Debbie, the teller, asked them to take a seat as Mr Wilson was busy and would be with them in about ten minutes.

A heated discussion was taking place in the manager's office. After half an hour, a red-faced man walked out. 'Bloody little turd,' he said almost inaudibly. He turned to John and grimaced. 'G'day, John, bloody hard times. I hope you do a bit better than I did with the little shit. He threatened to sell me up.' The man stormed out through the bank door, muttering to himself.

Debbie walked into the manager's office with a sheaf of papers in a folder. 'Mr Wilson will see you now.' She went back to working behind the counter.

They walked into the office. The Lizard was shuffling the papers on his desk. He rose and shook John's and Helen's hands. He omitted to acknowledge Tony. John always thought that his hand felt like a cold dead fish, soft and slimy.

'Ah, Mr and Mrs Nickols. Take a seat, please whilst I sort some of these papers.' The manager had a superior smile on his face. He sat back down on his chair, then leaned back, and surveyed the trio sitting in front of him, looking over the top of his bifocal glasses.

The name Lizard was almost true to label. The man had a thin, pinched-in face, which always seemed to be in need of a shave. He wore thin steel-rimmed glasses, which covered the small beady eyes, which seemed to be darting back and forth around the room. 'Looking for flies to eat,' John had always joked. His lips were just like a pencil line on his face. He was almost completely bald, having just a thin ring of black hair around the sides of his head, a very unattractive man. His voice had a nasal squeak to it.

The Lizard leaned towards the desk again. 'We seem to have a large problem at the moment regarding your overdraft. What do you expect to do about it?' squeaked the Lizard. He shuffled through the papers some more. He then looked up and stared at John with the reptilian eyes.

'I think that you should know our position better than most. We have tried almost everything. What would you suggest?' said John, his face getting red from the effort to contain himself.

'It's not for me to suggest anything at the moment. This is your problem.'

John leaned forward. 'I beg to differ. This is also the bank's problem. If you rotten cows had not raised the interest rates to nearly 20 per cent, most of us would not be in this mess. You did not even have the good sense to keep the extra money you earned. Your bloody bank nearly broke the state's finances because of the airy-fairy investments it made.'

The Lizard took offence at these remarks and sat upright and informed them that if there was not a reduction to the overdraft in the next month, there would be actions taken by the bank to recoup moneys owed to it.

The discussion became more heated with both Tony and Helen having their say. This was unusual for Helen as she was not usually the type to become belligerent.

The meeting ended as the previous one evidently had, with a lot of yelling and nothing resolved. The Nickolses walked out. John, as the previous man, muttered under his breath, then stopped, and greeted the next customers waiting. 'Hi, Fred, hope you have better luck with the little arsehole than we did.' He was still muttering as he walked out through the door.

'I reckon the little prick gets off on stirring everyone up. Pity help his bloody wife if he is that big an arsehole at home,' Tony added as they got into the old car and then reversed back into the near deserted street.

The three were still stirred up when they stopped out in front of the local supermarket where Helen was going to swap the eggs. Under normal conditions, they would have had a counter meal at the hotel and a couple of beers with the local patrons of the hotel before travelling home. The hotel trade had dropped off drastically since the drought had taken hold on the district. John and Tony walked over to the stock and station agents, Elders. John was interested in what had been happening to some of the other farmers in the district. Tony's interests were more in the pretty girl who served behind the counter. The news was not good. The Lizard had woven his ways throughout the district. Most farmers were upset. 'Billy Franklin offered to punch his nose for him. Bloody lucky for him, he didn't. He's a real scrapper when he gets going. The manager was going to get the police on to him.'

'I think the boy fancies your counter staff,' John joked to the stock agent. They both had a laugh. Tony was trying really hard to make a good impression. 'You've kept the poor young bugger out in the bush too long. He looks as if he is egg-bound,' said the manager laughing. The only news that John had found out was bad. There was not any money around to buy farms. No one in their right mind was going to borrow money at the exorbitant interest rates to buy a farm in the middle of a drought. It was a buyer's market if they were silly enough.

'Come on, Tony, we had better go and get mum and shoot through.' Tony reluctantly left the pretty girl.

'Stuff the bloody droughts and farming,' he mumbled as he walked out the door, reluctant to leave the pretty girl.

As they drove back to the farm, John was deep in thought. He was trying hard to take his mind off the problems with the bank. 'I reckon that if we could control those bloody crows, we might have a bit better chance of bringing a few of the weaker sheep home to the hospital paddock. I think we ought to build a crow trap when we get home.'

Tony had never heard of a crow trap and asked a lot of questions during the trip home. At least, it took their minds off the real problem, the bank, and the lack of money. 'I think you are trying to pull my leg. Those crows are that cunning that all you have to do is pick up the gun in the workshop and they're gone before you poke it out of the door. Those mongrels have sixth sense. I've walked out of the shed with a broom and pointed it at the tree with the crows in it, and they just laughed at me. But the minute you pick up a gun, that's different. They fly away before you can poke a bullet into its breech.'

'Well, have it your way, but most of the cunning animals or birds have a foible. It is usually greed.'

John carried the scant groceries into the house, whilst Helen pushed the kettle further on to the hot plate of the stove so it would boil for a coffee. Tony got some cold roast mutton, bread, and chutney out to prepare some late lunch. The mutton was lean and stringy as there were no decent fat sheep on the farm to slaughter for food.

After lunch, John and Tony drove to the back of the machinery shed to get ready for the crows.

They loaded some old, rusty wire netting and some fence droppers on to the ute and set out down the lane to the dead sheep near the lane way, which the crows had been hanging around. Tony opened the gate, and John drove the short distance over to the dead sheep. The crows flew off, cawing in protest at the disturbance of their feast.

Tony threw the fencing materials off the tray of the ute, whilst John selected six of the straightest used steel fence droppers.

John hammered six fence droppers into the ground with the light sledge hammer to form a circle three metres across around the dead sheep. The crows sat in the mallee trees and still cawed their disapproval at having their feast interrupted. They watched the proceedings with much interest. 'Never mind, boys, you can have all you like soon. Just wait for a while,' John chuckled. Getting some sort of revenge against such cruel birds as the crows was going to be sweet justice.

Tony pulled the netting tight around the circle and tied the ends. 'Ow, I always do that with this blasted stuff.' Tony had pushed one of the sharp, recently cut netting ends into his finger, up under his finger nail. He gave it a quick pull to get it out; bright red blood squirted out of the puncture. Tony reached into his trouser pocket and got his handkerchief, which he wrapped around his finger, and went on working. John pulled a couple of pieces of netting over the top, then twirled the edges together, and then cut a hole the size of a small hat brim into the middle of the top. 'They're all finished. Let's drive off a bit and see what happens.'

They drove back down the lane for about 150 metres and waited. 'I still reckon that this is all bullshit,' chided Tony as they sat and watched. After about five minutes, one of the hungrier crows flew down and sat on top of the trap. He walked around on the netting, protesting loudly. He cocked his head from side to side as he studied the trap. He was soon followed by more of his mates.

One of the gamer crows was not going to be done out of a meal by this cage with a hole in the top. He had worked out that he could drop down inside quite easily. Crows were notorious for finding their way into the fowl run and stealing eggs if there was a hole in the netting.

The crow dropped down and started to feed. He was soon followed by some more. 'Now this is the funny part. The greedy bludgers can drop through the hole with their wings shut but cannot fly out with their wings open. See.' One of the crows had eaten enough and had tried to fly out and could not manage it. It flapped its wings against the sides of the trap as it tried to escape. Still more crows landed on the trap and, upon seeing so many inside, must have thought that they were missing out on something really good. They too jumped down and feasted off the dead sheep. 'Right, let's go. We'll clean it out tomorrow morning. You can give mum a hand and milk Daisy when you get home. She is still pretty upset today after the bloody visit to the Lizard.'

Tony had just finished separating the milk in the laundry to get thick farm cream and was cleaning the cream separator, which was always a bit of a chore as there were lots of pieces to wash and dry. He was just walking out of the iron laundry at the back of the shed with the skimmed milk for the four small pigs, which they were fattening up to eat, when an old Land Cruiser rattled over the cattle grid and pulled up at the back fence.

The door of the ute swung open. 'cripes, things must be bloody bad on this farm if you have to eat bloody crows.' One of the men yelled as he half-fell and got out of the ute. The other man climbed out of his side with effort. The two men were as skinny as rakes, and their skin was weather-beaten and lined. Their skin was burnt by the sun so much that they were both nearly black. The Kelly boys Bert and Harry, two bachelor brothers who lived two farms up the road. 'Put the milk down and give us a hand.' Bert handed Tony a carton of beer. 'Got this for your mum.' He showed Tony a bottle of Irish cream, Helen's favourite. Helen and John came out to see what the noise was all about. 'Something for you, m'lady.' Bert gave a mock bow as he handed Helen the small bottle of Irish cream.

'Come in and take a seat,' offered Helen 'Oy, Tony, bring the booze. Don't try to sneak off with it,' joked Harry. Tony carried the beer inside and then walked back out to finish the job of feeding the milk to the little pigs.

Harry and Bert were evidently a bit worse for wear already. Tony gratefully accepted the cold beer which was thrust into his hand as he walked through the door with the bowl of cream. 'We've come to celebrate with our friends. We have just got rid of the debt at the bank. You should have seen the look on the rotten Lizard bastard's face when we paid him off with new hundred-dollar bills. Here, have another beer.' More beers were handed around.

'What have you guys been doing? Growing whoopee weed?' asked John.

'Nah, better than that. This is legal. We've been to Coober Pedy and found some opal. Sixty thousand bucks. You should have seen the Lizard when we put the forty thousand dollars on his desk. He almost smiled. We told him we had just reaped out marijuana crop.' Bert had another drink from the beer can. 'He said he was not worried as to where the money had come from. We'll probably have the local cop out to check us over. I wouldn't put anything past that devious little prick.'

'You're going to stay for a meal?' asked Helen.

'Nah, we had better get going soon. We have got some stew on the stove ready to warm up for tea. Thanks anyway, Helen.' This was a bit of a game by now, the Kellys always stayed. 'Hey, Tony, how about going out and getting the other carton of beer out of the ute. Some rotten cows drank all of this one.' Tony went out to fetch the beer. Helen busied herself and took a frying pan from the cupboard, then put the frying pan on the stove, put some oil in it, and started to cook chops and eggs.

Harry and Bert hoed into the meal. 'Skinny chops, I'm afraid.'

'Nah, it's better than our stew. This one didn't turn out too good.'

Harry and Bert were famous for their four-day stews, They usually had everything in them. The meat was cut up with a blunt meat cleaver, so there was a large amount of bone splinters as an extra barrier to anyone foolish enough to try one. The four days entailed. Day one, the stew was barely cooked; day two, the vegies were just getting soft; day three, there was a green mould starting to grow around the edge of the pot; and day four, the two mangy dogs usually got the rest.

'I reckon you would have a new strain of penicillin in that pot of stew if anyone was game to test it,' joked Helen as she served more chops and eggs.

The discussion became more serious as the night progressed. John told the men about his run-in with the Lizard. 'Why don't you come up to Coober Pedy with us? There's plenty of unpegged ground around where we are working.'

The Kellys had gone to Coober Pedy some ten years before when things on the farm were not too financial and had found around twenty thousand dollars then. 'The funny thing is that the place where we are working is next to the spot we got the opal before. All the miners reckon it's a dead area and there is no opal there. There's heaps of room if you and Tony want to have a go.' Bert and Harry had gone up the previous time with a home-made windlass and an assortment of picks and shovels off the farm. They had dug a few shafts by hand down to around twenty-five feet. They were about ready to come home as they had not found anything, when they had bottomed out on to a seam of opal. They had sold the opal and returned home to Kimba. There had been stories a few years ago around town as to how they had found a half a million dollars. These stories always seemed to abound when someone tried something new.

Helen was the one to suggest that the men give mining a try. The prospects of anyone getting any other income seemed almost impossible at the present time.

'We're going back to have another go at the mining in two weeks' time,' said Harry. 'You'll be very welcome to come up with us and have a look.' Tony and John decided to give the opals a try and agreed to go with them to have a look.

The Kellys had one advantage over John and Tony. They had sold all of their sheep the year before. 'Don't worry about them,' Helen reassured them. 'I can look after the sheep for about ten days. It would do you both good to get out of the farm for a while.'

The two weeks seemed to take a long time to pass. Both John and Tony were getting quite excited at the prospect of the new adventure.

The number of crows had diminished considerably. They had caught over two hundred in the last two weeks. Occasionally, a new dead sheep was substituted for the previous one. Occasionally, a couple of the hapless crows were hung on the fence of the chicken run to frighten off their mates. Crows were notorious egg stealers.

The morning after the Kellys had left was quite a fiasco where the crows were concerned. John had the bright idea as to get the crows out of the trap. 'All we will need is a long piece of eight-gauge wire with a hook on the end. The same as we use to catch a chicken when we want to eat one.'

There were about thirty crows flopping around in the trap when the men arrived. They got very agitated when the men walked up. John put the heavy wire into the trap from under the edge of the wire netting, which he had lifted slightly. 'I told you it would be easy,' he boasted as he hooked the first struggling crow out. Tony took the crow and hit it on the head with a short piece of wood. The other crows watched this happen. John hooked another and then another. The crows were studying the method of capture. Suddenly they seemed to work out that to be near the thin piece of wire was bad news.

As soon as the wire was poked into the trap, most of the crows would climb up the sides of the netting, making it almost impossible to catch them. Finally, the men honed their skills and emptied the trap. The dead crows were put into a bag ready for the trip to the cemetery, as the hole where the dead sheep were put was called.

There had been a few light showers of rain. It was certainly not enough to get excited about, but it did make the crops green up a bit. 'God, I hope we get a bit more in the next few days,' said John at breakfast as he emptied the rain gauge into the measure. 'Twenty-two points.' He walked over and wrote the figure on to the rainfall chart with the pencil hanging on a piece of string from the nail which held the sheaf of yearly rainfall charts on the back of the kitchen door. These charts also contained information as to when shearing and seeding were completed and what the harvest and wool clips yielded.

'Hell, there's a lot of gaps between each lot of rain on the bloody chart. No wonder things are so dry.'

John sat down at the table to a bowl of cereal. He poured the fresh farm milk on to the breakfast cereal. 'Four days to go. I saw Bert yesterday when you were out checking the sheep, and I was down at the main road, fixing the hole in the fence, which the kangaroos had made. He stopped for a bit of a yarn mainly to see if we had not changed our mind about the trip up north. I reckon they must have given the pub a bit of a go lately. He sure looked skinny.'

Chapter 2

The ute had been packed the previous day. There were spare drums of diesel, a plastic jerrycan of water, a large toolbox, blankets, and a large icebox full of food.

The trio walked out of the house to see the sun just coming up over the horizon.

After a teary farewell from Helen and lots of cuddles for both men, John and Tony got into the ute and slammed the rattly doors; the old ute finally drove off, leaving Helen alone. Helen watched as the ute drove the full length of the drive and then turned on to the Kimba road.

When the plume of dust was no longer visible in the early morning sun, Helen walked back into the house. She suddenly felt very lonely. Helen tried to shake the loneliness off by trying to think of the good things which might come from the men's adventure. Her thoughts then centred on the fact that the farm was getting very hard for the men to bear over the last few weeks and the change would do the men good.

Bert and Harry were not waiting at their gate. The gate was typical of the rest of the farm. It had been hit on numerous occasions on the way home from the hotel after the two had over imbibed. The middle of the gate had a large bend in it.

Tony unhooked the gate, which nearly fell over as the top hinge was broken. He carried the gate to an opened position. As there were no livestock on the farm, Tony left the rickety gate open whilst they drove up the driveway to the Kelly's mansion.

The shack in which they lived was not much better than the rickety gate. It was a lean-to on the side of the large implement and shearing shed. One large shed partitioned off into three; a small galvanized iron ablution block stood five metres from the shed.

The dogs usually had free range inside the dwelling unless they were covered with fleas or some other unmentionable affliction.

The inside of the shack was furnished with cast-off furniture, which Bert and Harry had bought cheaply at farm clearing sales throughout the district. There was hardly room to move between the boxes which had been bought at the farm auctions and carried inside but had never been unpacked. These boxes were heaped one on top of the other against the walls. There was a strong dog smell in the air.

The two dogs were chained in the back of the ute and could be heard barking as the Nickolses drew near. 'Shut up, you mangy buggers,' growled Harry as John pulled in next to them. The dogs wagged their tails. This was usual. When the dogs were growled at, they usually wagged their tails, but when they were spoken to kindly, they cowered off with their tails between their legs. Nice talking and coaxing usually meant that they were being caught for some unpleasant reason—a wash—down with some concoction to kill their fleas or a belting for some wrong doing.

After a couple of minutes of talking, Bert said, 'Follow us. We'll lead the way.' They headed off down the driveway. Bert drove through. Harry got out to shut the gate and then waved John through. The two utes then headed towards Buckleboo, a small town with not much more than a hall, an oval, and a few old houses. Tony knew this area well as he often visited the town to compete in football and cricket matches.

All of the paddocks were brown with only a few tufts of grey green showing on the lighter soil types. Things were worse here. At least, most of their crops were still alive, albeit struggling to do so. There was an air of desolation about the place—so different from four years ago, when record crops were reaped in the district. Dust blew across the red paddocks in the light breeze. Some of the fences along the roadside were already half buried with the red sand, which had blown off the bare paddocks in the strong winds of the last few weeks.

Past Buckleboo, the farming country started to get less. It was a patchwork of cleared farming ground amongst the mallee scrub. Finally, the farming country with its cleared paddocks ended. Then the narrow road went, winding through the large mallee trees, with open-range land between them. This was the start of the station country. The open areas between the trees were covered mainly with salt bush, but, because of the drought, even this hardy plant looked stressed and nearly dead. The few sheep that were seen did look in better condition than the poor ones in the farming country because they had the saltbush and other natural herbage to graze on.

The road was no more than a track graded through the red dirt of the plain. This road was notorious for being un-passable in the rain because the red mud would stick under a car and nearly block the mudguards with it. There was sure no problem with wet weather this year.

They followed Bert and Harry at a safe distance to keep out of the red dust, which billowed out from behind their ute.

After about forty kilometres, the mallee finally gave way to the traditional vegetation of the station country, myall, mulga, and saltbush.

Every few kilometres, there was a gate to be opened and then shut behind them. They were lucky as a lot of the gates now had stock grids replacing them. These were built up on to a mound because the traditional grid with a pit under it would fill up with dirt in times of dust storms and flood. Up and over the old utes clattered.

On and on the road wound, occasionally, a small side road led off from the large mailbox—sometimes an old kero fridge but mostly an old oil drum bolted to posts. They had the names of the sheep stations painted on them. John had been up into this country some years before, shooting kangaroos for their meat, which was sold as pet food. Even the few kangaroos seen were too skinny for this at present. Also most of the kangaroos had departed, chasing better pasture elsewhere.

John had to fall back further behind the Kellys because of the fine dust which floated in the air for a long way behind them. This was getting through the ute and into their eyes, nose, and throat. 'I know now why the old coots were in such a hurry to go first,' said Tony as he blew his nose to clear the dust out of it.

Occasionally, there was a windmill and tank to have water for the sheep. There were also two large galvanized iron roofs which covered some steel next to water tanks. These were to catch the rain water where there was no underground water.

Finally, just before lunch, the small town of Kingoonya came into view. Kingoonya was almost a ghost town now as the Adelaide to Alice Springs road had been re-routed when it was bituminised. There were only the remains of the timber and iron service station, an old pub, a hall, and a few other derelict buildings. Most of the houses had been sold and carried away.

The old service station was very interesting as it was surrounded by the carcases of the unfortunate cars which had broken down on the rough road over the years. It was like a trip back through time to see the old Austins, Vanguards, Dodges, Chevs, Fords, and Holdens lying derelict in heaps. They then crossed the main east-west railway line, which led to Perth, and then turned towards the new, sealed highway.

Just before turning on to the main road, Bert had stopped and was waiting for them. They pulled in next to them. 'How was the dust?' Laughed

Bert, and John spat out of the window on to the ground. 'You can have some of it back if you like.'

'We'll shout you blokes to a steak for lunch,' yelled Harry. 'Follow us into Glendambo to the pub.' John hesitated.

'No, it's all right. Helen packed some sandwiches. They are in the Esky.' John felt guilty about bludging on someone else for a meal.

'Don't be so bloody stupid. What about all the times that we have eaten at your house?'

'That's different,' said John. 'Ah, bullsdust! You're the only people in the district who feed us old buggers. No one else wants to know us. Follow us.' Bert drove off, and John followed as they turned right, back down the new road to Glendambo, which was only about a kilometre away.

Glendambo consisted of two service stations and a few houses, some of which had been moved from Kingoonya some years before when it was bypassed by the new road.

The large hotel was a copy of a bush-shearing shed. There were a few accommodation units along the side of the main building.

The two utes pulled in to the parking area in front of the hotel. All four men got out and stretched their legs. Bert let the two dogs go for a run to stretch their legs and relieve themselves, which they did on most of the car tyres outside the hotel. Where they got the extra fluid from for the job was a mystery. The dogs were told to get up in the bus, and they quickly did so. 'Don't you move,' warned Bert. The dogs made themselves comfortable in amongst the bags of clothes on the ute tray.

Bert and Harry walked through the large doors into the bar. They were followed by John and Tony. A few people sat at tables in the large bar, some jackaroos from one of the nearby sheep stations, which was evident from their cowboy hats.

John caught up with Bert at the bar just as he was ordering. 'Righto, matey, we'll have four steaks and eggs and four schooners of beer,' Bert told the waiter.

'Cummin roit up,' said the waiter.

'A bloody pom! What the hell is a pom doing all the way up here?' said Bert in an undertone, as the waiter walked away.

After two more schooners of beer each, the steaks arrived. The men moved from the bar to a table and sat. Bert started to chew. 'Shit! I wish I had my bottom teeth in. This steak is like bloody leather.' They all agreed. They picked at the pieces which were chewable and piled the gristle up on the edge of the plates. At least, the eggs were edible. They mopped the plates with a piece of bread. The waiter walked past.

'What's your meal like?' he asked.

'Do you get your own meat up here from a station?' asked Bert.

'No, mate, it all cums oop from Adelaide. Why?'

'I thought that this one might have been driven up from down south in a bullock team. I reckon he might have mated a few cows on the way. This is some of the toughest meat I have ever tried to eat.'

'Suit yourself, mate,' the barman said and walked off. 'Bloody old coots!' He could be heard to mutter as he walked back into the kitchen.

'Right, we had better leave. There's not much chance of us being served any more beers. Thanks to Bert,' joked Harry. They all departed. The waiter looked out of the door of the kitchen and was talking to someone as they walked through the door.

What a change to be driving on a sealed road! They were able to drive a lot closer without dust. A few kilometres past Glendambo, a little blush of green grass started to show up on the side of the road. The further the men drove, the greener the surrounding country became. There were beautiful wildflowers, brilliant scarlet Sturt peas, Blue Desert roses, and a carpet of purple and yellow succulents. Dead, road-kill kangaroos, emus, and the occasional sheep lay on or near the side of the road—mostly victims of the large road trains, which travelled the highway at night.

After a few more kilometres, the country reverted to its normal brown. The green had evidently been the result of a thunderstorm a few weeks before.

Nature was strange. Kangaroos, many from a long way off, congregated on the new green feed. 'How did they know it had rained so far away?' asked Tony. John had no answer for this as a lot of unusual things like this occurred in the bush. Some of the dead kangaroos were really smelly. The odour took some time to be blown out of the ute. Most road kill had some crows and a few wedge-tailed eagles feeding on them. This was fairly dangerous as some of the greedier eagles waited until the cars were nearly on them before they took to the air. A bird of this weight and size could easily bust a windscreen if it was hit at speed. A half-dead, wedge-tailed eagle in the front of the ute would not be a very exciting experience. The eagles had extremely sharp beaks and claws.

John was deep in thought. *I wish we could fluke a thunderstorm like that back on the farm at the present time. Just think of the change it would make to our poor wilted crops.*

The road seemed to go on and on. There was not much change in the landscape other than the dry water courses and the low hills, which they climbed and descended. A few small mobs of sheep were seen, as well as some emus and a few kangaroos.

Occasionally, there was a signpost on a dirt track, leading off the main road with the name of the distant sheep station and the distance from the road. Most of the station names were well known by hearsay to the West Coast population.

Finally, there were old car bonnets propped up with fence droppers every few kilometres. Each one had messages like 'Best Opal At The Big Winch', 'Cheap Meals At The Acropolis', which had long since ceased to exist after it had been blown up by some disgruntled miner, and 'Cheap Fuel At Bulls'. All of these signs were hand-painted; some displayed a bit of artistic licence, but most looked as if they had been painted in the dark by a blind man with a stick dipped in tar.

In the distance, a cross-shaped structure appeared over the low hills. John could not work out what this might have been. Finally, the cross started to turn. They worked out it was a large wind generator. Further along, there were some small mounds of earth which looked as if they had been pushed up out of the ground by giant ants. Behind these, there was a seemingly endless line of white mounds. The town finally came into view on the right of the main road as they turned around the next corner.

What a dry dusty barren-looking place, thought John as they drove off the main Alice Springs road in towards the town. There was a flat area, leading from the main road to the town. This was covered with a stunted, shrub-type vegetation. Every second shrub seemed to have at least one plastic shopping bag caught on it which was blowing like pennants in the wind.

The roadside signs were closer together but of a more orderly nature, and most, at least, had been painted by some sort of a sign writer.

On the right side of the road, about fifty metres from the road, were some houses. Nearly all these had some sort of machinery outside—tractors, backhoes, old drilling rigs, and an assortment of wrecked cars. Most machinery looked as if it had not been used for many years.

There were some clubrooms flying a foreign flag. On the other side of the road was a large, almost new, petrol station. Past this was an imposing building consisting of large, two-storeyed motel units and then the hotel. John was not surprised to see the Kellys' turn in to the front of the hotel. John pulled in next to them. 'Christ! I think it's beer time,' croaked Harry.

'Let's go in and see if the beer's still all right. It was the other week.'

Harry got a plastic drum of water and filled a cut-off, four-gallon drum with water for the dogs to have a drink. The dogs were pleased to see the water as the last walk and drink had been at Glendambo.

The four walked towards the bar. This was so different than any pub which John or Tony had ever been into before. They passed a small group people at the door. Their hair was matted together, and their clothes torn and dirty. They had obviously been drinking. The men made sure that they did not step into the group. One of the people asked for some money for a drink. 'I can be pretty friendly when someone buys me a beer,' she slurred. The party skirted the group, not answering the request.

A long bar ran along the rear wall of the room. There was a mob of people inside, some at the bar, some standing at a servery window, betting on the races and others sitting at tables, checking their betting tickets. All were speaking loudly in one or another language.

The people in the bar were an odd-looking lot, a mixture of most of the races on the planet. Bert described them. 'There's meant to be people of fifty different nationalities living here,' Bert said.

'Here, wash the dust out of your throat.' Harry handed out four beers and sat them on the table. 'Bottoms up!' It didn't take long to down the first round of beers.

'I think we should see about getting somewhere to sleep. Some kind of shack or house,' said John.

'Leave it to me,' said Bert.

Bert walked over to the bar and spoke to the barman, 'Do you know of anyone who wants to rent a house around here for a few weeks?' Bert and Harry had rented an old caravan the last time they were in town. The barman thought for a while.

'Go and ask that slippery-looking little guy over.' He pointed to a man sitting with a motley-looking group at a table by the betting window. 'He usually knows if there's any vacant shacks. Silvio is his name.' Bert walked over to the small, stringy, mean-looking man.

'Excuse me, but the barman said that you might know where we could rent a bit of a shack for a few weeks.' The little man looked up from his betting tickets.

'Nah, sorry, mate, I don't know of nothing for rent in town.'

Bert walked back to the table. 'Looks as if we might have to get a room at the pub for the night and have a look around for a shack tomorrow. We should have kept the caravan we had a few weeks ago.' They enjoyed another beer.

Silvio walked over to their table. 'Excuse please, but I don't have the house. But my mate over there do.' He beckoned another mean-looking, grey-headed man with a lopsided mouth over to the table. 'This is Tom. A friend of his has a dugout over by the waterworks reserve for rent. You want to have a look?' The men introduced themselves and then bought a round of beers for the four men at the table.

After some small talk, they followed Tom and Silvio out of the hotel. Tom got into an old Ford utility, which had a winch mounted to its tray. 'You follow us,' yelled Silvio as he got in.

The old ute roared out of the car park, nearly collecting another ute which was driving down the main road at just as dangerous a manner. The ute then tore off down through the town at breakneck speed. When through the main shopping area, it veered to the right around a corner and drove off towards a low range of hills, smoke billowed from its exhaust.

It was hard for the men to keep up. After that, it then wound its way through some old mine workings. There was an old concrete mixer barrel by the side of the road. They turned right again and then wound up through a small lane way and stopped outside a doorway which led into the side of a hill.

There was a verandah outside the hill, which had been cut away with a bulldozer, leaving a flattened area for a car park. There was a small shed at one end of the verandah, evidently a toilet and a shower. The men climbed out of their utes.

'Here you come inside. Bloody good dugout.' The dust was still settling from the rapid stop. The four men followed them into the dugout. The dogs barked to be let go to no avail.

Tom unlocked the flimsy door. This led to a tunnel of around three metres, leading to the first room, the kitchen. The room was surprisingly large. It had rough walls, still showing the pick marks from when it was hand dug many years ago. The ceiling was domed above their heads. The floor was just the virgin sandstone with a few squares of old carpet scattered around the most used areas.

Silvio turned on an old fridge which started with a jump and whined away in one corner of the room. There were various dressers, a gas stove, and a sink with one tap above it. The old table had an assortment of mismatched chairs. Two other tunnels led from the room. 'This first bedroom.' Tom turned on the light to show two old, piping-framed beds. A niche had been dug into one of the walls and was covered by a dirty curtain. This was evidently the wardrobe.

The other room was slightly larger with almost the same layout, except for the large safe, which dominated one corner of the room. 'Bloody good safe that one if you find any opals, only one set of keys, we give them to you if you want.'

A deal was stuck at hundred dollars a week. Harry dealt the twenty-dollar bills out on to the table for two weeks' rent. Tom and Silvio took a long-neck bottle of beer, which they were offered, with them and left, driving in the same manner as they had come.

'Cripes, what a shifty-looking twosome they are! I reckon they would slit your throat for twenty dollars.'

'Well, at least, we have got somewhere for a base. Let's have a look at the bathing facilities.'

Harry walked over to their ute and let the dogs go. The first thing they did was to pee on John's ute tyres. Then they departed for a good empty out, away from their sight, thank goodness. John really did not want to have to step over dog poop around the door of the dugout.

The bathroom consisted of a toilet, which was, at least, not a long drop, and a shower. In the far end of the shed was an old Simpson wringer-type washing machine. There was also a cement wash trough with the drain leading out of the shed wall. The walls of the room were full of nail holes from when the iron had been used on other covering jobs. Sunbeams from the setting sun shone through these, illuminated by the dust in the air, not exactly private. The shower was heated by an old chip heater, which was bolted to the wall. The heater had a drip feed of diesel for its fuel. A can hung from the rafters by a bent piece of wire. This old gallon can had a tap soldered to the bottom of it. This led to a spout of thin copper pipe, which poked through a hole, which had been drilled into the door of the heater. John and Helen had used a similar heater on the farm when they had first bought it.

The shower was lit with a wad of newspaper, and then the water was turned on. The drip feed of the diesel was adjusted back so the diesel dripped slowly into the cylinder. Smoke rings shot out of the hole in the door as the heater roared.

The men went back inside the dugout. They then carried all the provisions and clothes inside. 'You can have a shower,' said Bert. 'I don't think too much water on your skin does you any good.' Tony walked past the twosome with his towel draped over his shoulder. 'You can please your self, but I reckon I stink.' Bert and Harry offered to go and get a pizza for tea whilst they had their shower.

John had not noticed the closed-in feeling when they had first walked into the dugout, but as they were waiting for the men to come back, he felt as if he wanted to go out into the fresh air outside. The musty smell of the earth certainly did not help. He commented on this to Tony, who did not have the same feeling.

When the men returned with pizza, the feeling seemed to go, and after a few more beers, he forgot about it altogether.

John woke about 3 a.m. He felt really clammy. The roof of the dugout seemed to be closing in on him. It was pitch-dark in the dugout, similar to being deep in a cave. John lay for quite some time, unable to sleep, until, finally, he dozed off again.

God, this old bed is uncomfortable. It must have rocks in the mattress. I'm glad I brought my own pillow, thought John.

John decided to keep his feelings of being closed in to himself as he knew that the others would only make fun of him.

'Hey, are you two awake?' John woke with a start. The room was as dark as doom.

'What time is it?'

'Nearly eight o'clock,' upon checking a small shaft of light weakly struggled through the small air shaft in the corner of the ceiling. The men had not thought of the lack of windows.

'I think we had better get a small clock radio to wake us in the morning,' said Tony as he sleepily rose from the old bed. They both dressed and walked out into the kitchen, yawning in unison as they walked.

'Hell, that old flock mattress was full of rocks. I had a job to get to sleep, even though I was dog-tired.'

'You young blokes don't know what it is to rough it. When we were young, we only had a chaff bag half filled with chaff to sleep on.' John and Tony had been told this story over and over before.

'Anyone for bacon and eggs for breakfast?' They all agreed. John lit the gas burners on the stove and proceeded to cook the home-cured bacon and farm eggs, whilst Tony watched the toast on top of the gauze toaster on the other gas burner of the stove.

'Hell, that farm-cured bacon tastes good. What do you think?' Harry agreed.

They all walked out of the door. Harry locked the flimsy old door after them.

Harry yelled out for the dogs. They came around the hill and walked up to him with a sheepish look on their faces. Both were covered in a smelly green slime. They had found something smelly whilst on patrol at night. 'Ooh, you dirty buggers. Get up in the back.' The dogs effortlessly cleared the side of the ute and wedged their way as far from Harry as they could. Harry could not reach their chains, so he left them loose.

John and Tony got into the ute and followed the men out through the town. They then turned on to the main road towards their claim. First, they travelled out of town on the bitumen road towards Alice Springs for about fifteen kilometres. All along the roadside, there was worked ground, mainly the mounds left by blowers. Occasionally, there was a larger mound which had been pushed up by a bulldozer. Old trucks with unusual-looking blower machines on their trays were in small groups next to white mounds of worked sandstone.

They turned off the main road on to a good dirt road, then followed the Breakaways road for about two kilometres, and then turned left towards a large worked area of ground. Both John and Tony had marvelled at the amount of machinery which was visible from the road. There were drills, bulldozers, excavators, and another unusual-looking machine, which were built on to the back of an old truck and looked like a giant bird squatting on the plain. Quite a few of these bird-looking machines were working, spewing a huge amount of white dust up into the still morning air.

Bert wound his way through old workings, bulldozer cuts, and conical heaps, which were seen under the blowers, the bird machines.

Bert stopped in a large non-worked area about the size of four football ovals. This was surrounded by the high dumps of old bulldozer cuts. There were two small heaps of dirt, one of which had a motorised winch next to it. On the outskirts of the workings were four posts with little pointers on each one.

'Pretty low-tech, our mining operation. Hardly anyone uses these hoists any more, but we've found a few bucks, and it's reasonably cheap to run.' Harry was busy unloading tools and electrical cable from the ute. 'There's all of this ground around us which has never been worked. No one has even bothered to drill it to look for trace. We could never understand why. I suppose it's like fishing. Someone found some opal elsewhere so everyone shot through to the new area and left this area non-drilled and non-worked.'

Tony and John gave the men a hand to unload the ute and then helped them to lower the threemetre-long sections of ladder down the shaft. Each one of these was hooked together. The top ladder was hooked on to a stout length of water pipe, which crossed an edge of the round hole. Bert turned the petrol on, then pulled the rope, and started the alternator which was on the ute. The tools on the back of the ute rattled with the vibrations of the motor. The dogs jumped off and started to bark at the engine noise. 'Shut up, you mongrels,' yelled Bert over the noise of the motor. The dogs walked of and dug a shallow hole and then lay together on the ground.

Bert then plugged a lead with a trouble lamplight into the extension cord, making sure, as he did, to tie a knot at the plug so the joint would not come apart. He lowered the lamp carefully down the shaft.

Tony followed Bert down the ladder into the round mineshaft. John also reluctantly followed. The shaft was only around seven metres deep by one point two metres wide. John had a very uneasy feeling as he descended below the level of the ground. The hole, which was just over a metre wide, felt very constricting. He could hear Bert and Tony talking as he wobbled down the ladder. Bert was explaining the different colours of the level which they were following. 'If it's OK by you guys I would rather go back up to the top again,' quavered John nervously.

'Don't be so bloody silly,' retorted Bert with a laugh. 'You'll soon get used to it.'

Tony followed Bert along the narrow drive. Bert was showing him where they had found a bit of opal trace, which was still shining in the wall.

Bert shone the light further in front of them 'The stinking rotten mongrel bastards. Look what they have done.' He shone the light on a large pile of dirt, which almost blocked the drive. Even John, who was nervously waiting under the shaft, edged forward to investigate.

'Some rotten cow has been down our shaft when we were down south and has put some shots in the wall and blown some opal out. There were some thick traces here. We were going to work them next.' Bert shone the light on the heap of dirt and then started to dig into it with his hands. There were small chips of potch and opal gleaming in the light of the electric lamp.

'Cripes, you can't trust anyone. I would like to catch the bugger who has moonlighted our claim and pinched our opal.'

The men turned, then walked back towards the ladders, and then climbed out of the shaft. John hurried to be first as he did not want to be left until last as the claustrophobia had really got to him.

'Some rotten mongrel has moonlighted our claim whilst we were away,' yelled Bert over the noise of the alternator. 'I have just noticed a few car tracks around here whilst you were underground. I thought it must have been some aborigines noodling our dump.'

'Well, I don't suppose that there's much we can do about it except dig the dirt out and start again. It's no use going to the cops. This evidently happened a few weeks ago. It's bloody hard to prove who has been around here. There's always someone checking out your claim when you're not here.'

Before they started back down the shaft again, Bert showed John and Tony around, explaining as to where the run of opal was thought to go. He gestured with his hands to the expanse of good, non-worked ground in front of them. 'I reckon there's plenty of opal just in front of us if you want to peg a claim and give it a try. Opal usually goes in what they call a run. It follows a line, making and breaking opal, then nothing, and then opal again.'

Harry walked back to their ute and rummaged around in the tray for a while. He came over with two thick bronze welding rods, which had been bent at right angles near the ends, and started to walk across the ground with these poked straight out in front of him. Tony and John stood fascinated by this odd display. 'What the hell is he doing?' asked Tony as he watched the rods swing out at right angles to Harry's body as he walked ahead.

'He's divining the slips and slides under the ground, just like divining for water. All of the slips and slides are cracks in the sub-surface and usually are damp,' said Bert.

'Here have a go.' Harry handed the rods to Tony. 'Hold the rods as hard as you like, if it's going to work for you. You won't be able to stop them swinging.' Tony took the two welding rods and started to walk.

This is all bullshit. I must look like a real dork walking around with these wires, he thought. As he slowly walked, he could feel the wires pulling in his hands. He could not stop them from pulling out at right angles to his body.

'I'll tell you a good test. When you find a slip, go a couple of metres further down and cross it again. Try to find the line in which it is running, and then go well back and walk towards it with your eyes closed. Tony did this and was amazed that every time he crossed the line drawn on the ground, the wires swung out.

'Here you have a try, Dad.' He handed the wires to John who walked back and forward to no avail.

'All a lot of crap if you ask me,' he said after some time without any results.

'It does not work for everyone,' said Harry.

Bert and Harry went back to work, emptying out the moonlighters' mess. They had shown John how to use the Yorke hoist so he could pull the large buckets filled with dirt up from out of the shaft. Tony went on divining the large area which was not inside the pegs and not worked ground.

The Yorke-hoist way of mining entailed a lot of hard work, something which Bert and Harry were accustomed to. Bert filled the buckets, which were sixty-litre oil drums, which had an eight-millimetre steel rod handle added. These were pushed into the rocks and sand, and then the dirt was scratched into it with a short-handled, round mouth shovel. Harry pushed each bucket along the floor of the drive on a custom-built, low barrow to the shaft where John had the emptied bucket sitting on the floor of the drive waiting for a full one to be attached to the cable ready to be winched out. Under the shaft was an opened-out area, so there was room to manoeuvre the buckets on and off the winch cable.

The winch was driven by a small petrol motor, which spluttered away noisily. A steel piping pole held the winch. This was guyed with some heavy fencing wire to three substantial pegs. The winch was positioned so the pulley end of its long arm was directly over the shaft. When the bucket was pulled up, it could be swung in an arc so the bucket could be emptied some distance from the shaft, a far cry from, and safer than, the old-hand windlass idea.

The winch itself was controlled by a lever. In the down position, the brake was on. As the lever was lifted, the drum of cable would freewheel, and then as it was lifted higher, the outer part of the drum would come into contact with a small fibre wheel driven by the motor. This would wind the cable up with the drum. It was difficult at first to get the controls into the right position for a start, but John soon got used to it.

After an hour and a half, Harry yelled out for John to turn the motor off. There had been a lot of buckets of dirt pulled out of the shaft. Harry poked

---

his head out of the shaft first. 'The bloody swine have had a field day. They dug in about three metres. You can see the opal trace on the walls where they have been.' He climbed out of the shaft, quickly followed by Bert.

'Shit! I wish I knew who the pricks were who moonlighted us. I'd ring their bloody necks.' Both men were covered in the sandy dirt from the walls of the drive. Both had been sweating profusely. The sweat was still running out of their pores. The smell of bo prevailed.

'A bit of booze coming out,' joked John.

'Probably is, but everyone sweats like this when you work underground. There's a lot of humidity down there. Go down again and find out.'

'Bugger you, that's the first and last time I go underground. I nearly crapped myself.' Bert went over to the ute and turned the alternator off. The globe in the trouble light on the ground slowly lost its light and faded to nothing as the motor slowed down.

Tony walked over. 'Find anything interesting?' asked Bert.

'I wouldn't have a clue. I have drawn out on the ground a heap of lines where things seem to cross each other, but I don't know what it all means.'

'If we knew that, we would all be millionaires. This wiring a claim is only a guide. There's no rules when it comes to opal. Sometimes you can have everything right—beautiful sandstone, plenty of good slips, and no opal. Other times, it shows up where you would least think it would be. It's easy to put a shot in and blast next to a pocket of opal and ruin it.' They sat down in the dirt and had lunch off Helen's sandwiches she had made for the previous day.

Bert and Harry asked if John and Tony wanted to go to the pub for a meal. The men declined the offer as they felt tired from the trip up the previous day. They knew what a trip to the pub meant to Bert. When he got started on the grog, he was a real pest to try to get to go home. He usually became belligerent and argued when he had too much to drink.

John cooked some bacon and eggs again, and soon after, they both went to bed.

Around 3 a.m., the Kellys came into the dugout, banging and crashing around and talking loudly. 'Shit! I wish they would shut up. I'm bloody tired.'

'Don't let them hear you, or they will be in here with us. We'll never get back to sleep.' After a while, the noise subsided, and the men got back to sleep.

'We got lost, coming home from the pub last night. You should try and find your way around this place in the dark. We must have done miles, looking for some sign of how to get home. At one occasion, we were driving around in the small settlement just out of town. A couple of men told us to tick off. If it hadn't been for the old concrete mixer barrel down at the corner, we would have had to sleep in the ute. It was really cold.'

After a couple of strong black coffees, Bert and Harry started to look a bit more human. 'Want some eggs and bacon?' asked Tony. 'You can stick your food.' Both the men agreed.

'You should go to the Department of Mines and order your tags so you can peg a claim each, if you want to, of course.' Bert poured another coffee.

'Black and strong, just like my women,' he said.

Chapter 3

Bert and Harry had driven out to the claim to start working. John and Tony had decided that they had no alternative than to give the opal mining a go to try and relieve their financial dilemma. They had talked about this well into the night. There did not seem any other way to make enough money to get out of the finance problems they were having on the farm. Tony was prepared to spend the few hundred dollars he had been saving to buy a second-hand utility. He had earned this money from his sheep shearing in the previous years. 'If I lose it, so what? We'll also lose the farm,' he said with a final resignation.

Bert explained what to do about getting a precious stones prospecting permit each. This allowed them to peg a claim each. The size of the claim was either fifty metres square or fifty by one hundred metres for a large claim. The claim was only leased from the Mines Dept for a twelve-month period, and of course, a large claim was dearer to lease.

Bert and Harry had gone off to work. They had explained the way to get the tags needed for the men to peg a claim, before they had left.

John and Tony drove through the town towards the Mines Dept office, which was next to the new police station. They took their time, as this was the first occasion they had driven through the town at a normal speed, although everyone else seemed to still be in a hurry.

The town seemed very busy. A combination of the obvious mining vehicles and the tourists in their four-wheel drives with caravans moved around the streets. Number plates from all over Australia were displayed on the visiting vehicles. The men turned right before the new service station, left the main street, and then pulled in to the car park in the front of the mines office building. There were two other vehicles in the park. These were the typical Coober Pedy miners' vehicles—rough, old, four-wheel drives, complete with the winch on the back and a tray filled with tools of all kinds.

The Mines Dept building was a large transportable structure surrounded by a high-chain wire fence with barbed wire on top. The men walked through a small gate and entered the building. Two groups of people stood at the counter, each speaking in a foreign language. One of each group was trying to act as interpreter for the rest of the group. They were not doing a very good job. Both the groups and the counter staff were getting agitated, gesticulating wildly with their hands as they tried to make the woman at the counter understand them. Finally, one group left, and the large blonde woman behind the counter asked what they wanted. John explained that they wanted to apply for the prospecting permits. 'Thank god, you can speak English. That mob is the fourth lot that we have had this morning. The trouble is most of them are trying to do something dodgy, and the translation does not ever seem to fit what they are wanting to do.'

The woman reached under the counter and got the appropriate forms and handed the men the forms to be filled out. The woman explained what they had to do. They filled the forms out and then had to hand their drivers licences over for identification. Tony took out his wallet and counted out the money and paid for the permits. 'The tags for the claim pegs take three days to come up from Adelaide,' said the pleasant, friendly woman. So this meant the men had three days to spare before they could put the posts in and officially peg the claims.

'We should go for a drive and have a look around the field to try and get an idea of how most other miners were working,' said Tony as they left the Mines Office and walked over to the Toyota ute.

They left the Mines Department. First, they drove west from the town, after crossing the main road, driving between bulldozer dumps on each side of the road. Occasionally, they would stop, get out, and walk down one of the old bulldozer cuts and look at the walls for signs of opal traces. Tony picked up a few pieces of potch from one of the dumps they had stopped at. One piece even had a bar of red colour in it, their first opal.

There was a billowing cloud of dust coming from one of the old dozer dumps. It blew across the road in the light breeze, obscuring the source. After driving slowly through the dust, they could see a large rubber-tyred, four-wheel-drive loader loading an unusual-looking machine. The machine seemed to be screening the dirt from the dump, after the dirt was screened. It passed through a small shed, finally coming out the other end and then being carried away by a long conveyor belt.

John and Tony spent some time watching the four-wheeled drive loader dig into the dozer dump, reverse back, turn, and then tip the dirt into a hopper on the end of the machine. The hopper had a heavy screen on top of it, which rolled the large rocks off on to the ground. They had never seen anything like this before and were both intrigued as to what this machine was really doing.

The loader stopped, and the operator got out and walked across towards the men. John had a feeling that they may have been on the man's claim, although they had made sure they were outside of any mining pegs. Harry had warned them about going on to someone's claim without asking.

'G'day, mate, ow're you going? I'm just gunna have a cuppa. Do you want to come over and have a look at the machine?'

The loader driver was a farmer from the Ceduna area. He was working with his son, trying to keep the bank off his back as well, for things had not been any good seasonally at Ceduna for some years as well. His name was Charlie.

Charlie banged on the door of the noodling machine. The belts and the rotating screen stopped turning, and the door opened. A lad of about Tony's age poked his head out. 'This is me, boy, Josh.' They all introduced each other, then squatted down in the dirt, and had a talk. A diesel motor thumped a short distance away. It drove the alternator which ran the machine.

Greedy banks and droughts were one of the main subjects of discourse. Charlie and Josh were making around two thousand dollars a week. Some weeks, it was a lot more. The best that they had done was to find a pocket which had been missed by the bulldozer checkers. This had been fifteen thousand dollars in one day.

'Do you want to have a look whilst we are working? The more eyes, the better.' The men were interested in finding out what this weird machine was doing. John and Tony followed Josh up the short ladder into the small shed. There was a long conveyor belt running the full length of the shed. Above this was a series of fluorescent lights. These lights had a black tube in each one. Josh asked Tony to climb over the belt so there was more room. He explained where to put the opal when it was picked off the belt. A small bucket was hooked conveniently next to each chair.

Josh pushed the starter buttons for the electric motors and then shut the shed door. The shed was pitch-dark inside. Josh then turned the ultraviolet light on. This cast an eerie dark purple light down on to the belt.

Rocks started to run along the belt. They ranged in size from a baseball down. The rocks glowed a dark purple colour. 'Occasionally, one would shine a dull yellow. Alunite,' Josh explained. Dispersed with and in the rocks were pieces of material which shone a brilliant white as if they had a light inside of them. This was potch or opal. This had to be picked off and went into the bucket. Occasionally, a large piece of shining material would travel down the belt to be picked up.

John and Tony became engrossed with picking the opal out of the rocks. Suddenly after around half an hour, John had the funny feeling that the belt had stopped moving and the chair was travelling next to the belt. It made him feel a little giddy. The feeling finally went away.

After another hour, there was a loud bang on the side of the shed. John nearly jumped through the roof. It gave him such a fright. Josh stopped the belt, turned on a light, and then opened the door. At first, the men could not see from the bright light, but after a short while, their eyes became accustomed to the light.

'Let's see what we have got,' said Charlie. Josh reached into the machine and got the three buckets out. He tipped the contents out into a large flat plastic bowl. Josh then pulled a large plastic drum from under the machine and then poured a small amount of water from it in the bowl. This helped to wash the dirt off the opal. The men then started to sort through the material in the bowl in the bright sunlight.

A large portion of the material was discarded and tossed into another bucket. About a third of the material was opal. Every now and then, Josh would lick a special piece which he had found and then hand it to Charlie, who, in turn, would show it to John and Tony. There were a few very nice pieces of opal. These were placed in another bucket. 'We keep the potch and check it again under a large magnifying lamp, just in case there is a bar of colour in it.'

'It's easy to miss some opal when you are doing a dozer cut. Either the checkers don't see it, or the dozer blade skims it off the floor before it is ripped. Sometimes the loss can be around 30 per cent, and seeing some of these claims has produced a few hundred thousand dollars worth of opal. It's worth looking for.'

'Well, we had better get back to work,' said Charlie as he put the opal back into a small bucket and then stowed it inside their ute cabin.

John thanked Charlie for showing them the machine. Charlie suggested that they meet at the Italian Club for a cheap meal and a couple of beers that night. John agreed.

They walked back to their ute. 'How did you feel in the machine when it was going?' asked John.

'I felt as if the belt was stopped and I was moving along the floor on my chair. The feeling went away after a while, but I felt really giddy at the time.' John was pleased that Tony had felt the same. He felt as if it might have been only him who had felt this way.

They had come to the end of the mine dumps, so they turned around and headed back towards town, past the working noodler. Just before town, John turned left along another track and headed for a huge area of blower dumps. They worked their way through the dumps, amazed at the amount of work which had been done over the years. There were still the occasional blowers standing like a big bird. The odd one was working, blowing the fine white dust from the pipe above the fan.

Occasionally, there were the remains of an old campsite, consisting of a concrete floor, one or two old kerosene refrigerators pulled to pieces, a few old car bodies, and the usual large bottle heap. There were usually a large assortment of different types of bottles in each heap, mainly the brown beer bottles, but with an assortment of clear whisky and green wine flagons.

Finally, they drove out on to a well-graded dirt road. Ahead of them in between the dozer dumps, they could see the remains of a small cluster of wind-blown shacks.

The remains of an old service station with all the 1940 and 1950 car bodies heaped around. There were also the remains of, it seemed, anything which would dig a hole—dozers, old drills, and loaders. Some of the camps looked lived-in, most having some sort of wind generator, the blades twirling and whistling in the wind.

The remains of a sign announced, 'Eight Mile Garage'.

There were a lot of bulldozer cuts around the Eight Mile area. The Eight Mile field had been a very rich field when it was first found. Lumps of good quality opal as big as house bricks were found in some of the claims, making the lucky claim holders wealthy men, wealthy beyond their wildest dreams in some cases.

The worked ground then stopped, only to start to appear again about a kilometre away on their left.

From there, they travelled back towards the main road through blower dumps back to the main bitumen road and then headed towards the Fifteen Mile field where Bert and Harry were working.

Bert and Harry were out of the shaft and sorting through a bucket when they arrived. 'Have a good look around?' asked Harry. 'So did we.' He tipped the contents of the bucket on to an old wheat bag which had been spread out on the ground. The material looked like liquid fire running out of the bucket. Both John and Tony gasped and sighed when they saw the opal. 'Not bad for a couple of old codgers. A bit better than farming at the present time.'

'What would this lot be worth?' asked Tony as he studied some of the opalised shells.

'I reckon about fifteen grand,' said Bert. 'A nice morning's work.' He was feeling pleased with himself. 'Here, look at this one.' He picked a solid perfect opal shell out of the pile on the ground. Half of the shell was still covered with dirt, but the part which wasn't shone as he turned it in the sunlight. The red, green, orange, and purple colours danced over the stone. 'Looks as if dinner is on us tonight. At least, the bloody moonlighters didn't get all of our opal.'

John told them about the morning in the noodling machine with Charlie and Josh and how they were going to meet at the Italian Club for a few beers. 'They serve a good steak up there on a Friday night, so that's where we'll go. I've met the bloke and his son from Ceduna a few times before. Nice people.'

Bert and Harry had to be cajoled into the dreaded shower but finally gave up their protesting and had a short shower each. 'We don't even drink water unless we have to,' protested Bert as he entered the wash room. 'People have been known to drown and die in the water, plus fishes crap in water.'

The Italian Cub commanded a prime position high on a hill, overlooking the town and the surrounding area. It was a long, low building with a car park along each side. An assortment of trucks, utes, and cars was parked outside. The building was also low inside as well and also full of cigarette smoke, which seemed to billow from the bar area, trying to find some means of exit.

A group of around fifty people stood around the bar, talking. 'Four beers, OK?' asked Bert as he walked up to the bar. As with the hotel, there seemed to be a lot of different languages being spoken.

Charlie and Josh came in just as they were finishing the first beers. They already knew the Kellys, so introductions were not needed.

Charlie and Josh joined them all for the meal. 'I told you the meals were all right up here. A bit better than the old dry boot we had for a steak on the way up, eh?' Bert recounted the tale of the tough steak to Charlie and Josh, embellishing the tale a bit as he went.

Following the meal, Josh asked Tony if he would like to come down to the local pub for a disco. Tony and Josh left to check the local girls scene out.

The night's conversation centred around the prices and where most of the opal was coming from. A new find had produced some opal which had been sold for over thirty thousand dollars an ounce. 'Imagine one piece as big as your hand. Probably ten to fifteen ounces. Three hundred thousand or more.'

This conversation made John all the more determined to have a try for some opal. All other prospects to make some money legally to save the farm seemed to have been thought of and discarded.

That night when he went to sleep, John had vivid dreams of the colours of opal moving back and forth in front of his eyes. He woke a few times, but every time he went back to sleep, the dream returned.

John told Tony about the dreams of opal. Tony had experienced the same.

'Ha, you're hooked. That's the first sign of opal fever. The gold miners get a similar thing happen to them when they see a lot of gold for the first time. We had it. We still dream of the colours occasionally. The experts say if you dream of opal in the night, you will find it the next day. Keep on dreaming.'

There was a lot of superstition surrounding the opal fields. Everyone, it seemed, had a different theory.

Tony walked out into the kitchen. John had let him sleep in because he had arrived home in the wee hours of the morning. 'Have a good time last night?'

'Yes, I met some of the locals. Gee, there's some different-looking chicks up here. There were a lot of Greeks at the disco. A lot of the men had jewellery on, opal pendants and flashy rings so forth. Shit, I wouldn't be seen dead wearing some of the gear they had on. Met a couple of nice birds too. I was talking to one nice-looking Greek bird, and her brother came over and told me to shoot through. She wasn't allowed to hang around with Aussies. I nearly got into a fight with this arrogant prick.' Evidently, Tony had enjoyed himself. It was a long time since he had a night out at Kimba because of the lack of money situation.

'We thought we might get a late start and go and pull a bit more dirt out of the hole. What are you blokes going to do?'

John thought for a while. 'I think we might do the tourist bit and have a look at the opal shops around town.'

The traffic was even worse. Cars and old bombs roared up and down the main street, swerving around each other instead of showing a bit of caution and slowing down a bit. The cars seemed to rev up. Small groups of people sat in the dust by the edges of the road. A police van was stopped by one group. Two police were interviewing the rowdy mob. One of the women was swinging wildly at a man with a stick, trying to hit him. They parked the ute. They both got out and walked down the street. They walked into the first opal store. A small dark man hurried out of the back and turned on the display lights above the opal display cases. 'You want to see special opal, very cheap price?'

'No, we're just looking, thank you.' The man looked disappointed and turned the lights off and went back inside.

The treatment in most stores was of a similar off-hand nature until they came to a store selling not only opals but cutting machines and art supplies. This was run by a happy plump Irishman. He had a lot of stories of yester year—some of the cons and crooked partners of best friends turning to enemies as soon as there was money involved. In between the interesting stories, the man served customers, asking the men not to go as he had more stories to tell.

They walked back to the ute and drove around the bottom of the Italian Club hill to an old mine which had been opened up for tourists. The Irish man had recommended this as one of the best tourist stops in town.

The men walked into the shop and paid for a permit to go into the mine to look. The pretty blonde assistant gave them a hard hat to wear before they went down into the old mine. 'Wow, did you get a good look at the young bird?'

'You should be ashamed of yourself. I'll tell mum when we get home. She had a wedding ring on.' Tony had evidently noticed the pretty girl also.

John and Tony clambered through the narrow drives, marvelling at the hardships which had been endured by the early miners. One main one was the lack of water in the town before the desalination plant was installed. 'Bert and Harry would have had an excuse for not washing a few years ago,' said Tony. John didn't' feel the claustrophobia that he felt when he had gone down the shaft out. In the field, it was possible because the drives were well lit and the air was not stale and clammy. There was still opal in the walls of this mine, covered in glass, of course, to keep the tourists from digging it out.

The Kellys were back at the camp when they arrived. They had put some shots in, had blasted the face of the drive, and then, after the fumes had settled, had bucketed out the dirt. A vacuum cleaner was rigged up with a long hose to blow fresh air into the drive after blasting. It was plugged into the alternator. The hose of the vacuum was nailed to the wall of the drive a suitable distance from the blast area. As soon as the shots were fired, they started the machine to blow fresh air into the drive. This was Bert's idea.

Going into a drive too soon after blasting could prove fatal if too many of the fumes from the gelignite were present. Men had died from this, whilst others who had survived had been sick for a long time.

John had bought some meat and fresh vegies and had offered to cook some tea for them. He certainly didn't want to go out for a meal again as it was too expensive on their limited budget.

Chapter 4

John and Tony drove through town and then turned right past the hotel and, after a short distance, called at the Mines Dept office to see if the tags had arrived. The woman walked over to another counter and sorted through a pile of mail in a low cardboard container. 'Nickols, you said your name was?' she asked. John assured her that was right. She pulled two plastic bags from the pile and turned back to the main counter. As she walked over, she informed them that they had arrived. The men had to sign for their tags, after which the woman handed each of them a small plastic packet with the plastic tags in it.

The men left the Mines office, started the ute, and then turned back towards the main street. Then they drove to the hardware store behind the supermarket, where they bought eight wooden pegs. These were square pine posts about a metre long with one end sharpened to a point. John thought they were pretty dear, but as they had to have them, he paid the money. 'Hell, we've got hundreds of posts the same as these at home,' he remonstrated as he got into the ute.

They felt a sense of anticipation now, as all the red tape had been dealt with. They talked about what they would do if they were lucky enough to have a find like Bert and Harry as they drove out to where Bert and Harry were working. The thought of paying off the bank as Bert had done was foremost in their conversation. They knew this was pure fantasy, but at least, there was now some sort of hope of getting out of their financial quagmire.

When they arrived at the claim, Bert showed them how to put the pointers on to the corners of the pegs. These were pieces of steel packing tape from around boxes. They had been told to pick this up from the hardware store. Tony cut the thin steel for the pointers into eight pieces with a pair of tin snips. The pointers were nailed on to the top of the pegs to show the direction of the claim boundaries. The small plastic tags with their precious stones permit number were then nailed on under the pointers. John hit his finger with the hammer as he tried to hold and hit the small nails through the thin steel. He cursed the hammer roundly.

Bert and Harry helped them to measure out the claims with the fifty-metre-long tape. Each claim was a hundred metres long, making an area two hundred metres by fifty metres along the line in which the Kelly's were getting their opal.

Harry had an old compass, which he had taken out of the ute glove compartment. They then walked around the boundaries of the claims and took the compass bearings from each corner and wrote these down on a piece of paper with a plan of the claims drawn on it. A compass bearing then had to be taken from a mines department survey peg, which was an iron dropper with a brass tag bolted to it. It was some distance away. A measurement had to be taken from the closest peg of each claim to the department peg, which also had a number on the tag. The number had to be recorded on the plan.

They helped pull some more dirt for the men and then headed back to town to register the claims before the Mines Dept closed.

'What would you suggest our next move should be?' John asked Harry when they arrived home later that night. Harry thought for a while as he sipped on his beer.

'Well, there's two ways to go about that. You could drill a big shaft with a Caldwell drill like we have, or you could get a bloke with an investigator drill to sink a heap of smaller test holes to see if you can find any trace of opal. You will get a lot more holes done over your claims with the smaller drill. The big drill costs about ten times as much to drill a hole and also takes a heck of a lot longer to drill, plus it is a bloody dangerous machine.'

This was dangerous as it either entailed a trip to the pub or to the Italian Club to see if they could find a driller willing to do some cash holes.

John had a brilliant idea. He drove into town and called at the Irishman's opal shop and asked him where he could hire a driller for a day. 'Go up to the Italian Club any time after six o'clock. Ask for Luigi,' he was told. There was no getting away from the Italian Club or the pub. It seemed that most of the town's business was done in either. The man also told him to be careful of some of the drillers, as they would tell their mates if they cut any opal traces. The next thing was, the whole area would be pegged around them. This had happened to some people who had found that the blowers and tunnelling machines working on their boundary had worked well into the neighbour's claim. This Luigi bloke was meant to be OK and kept his mouth shut about what he had drilled for other people.

John drove up to the Italian Club and asked for Luigi at the bar. A small man sitting at the bar a short distance away turned and asked, 'What you want with Luigi?' John explained about the drilling. 'Hey, that's OK. I think you might be from my ex-wife to look for more bloody money. She always chases me. Money, money, money. That is all she knows, how to say. Here, have a beer. What kind you drink? West End? Fosters?'

'Make it a West End Draught.' Luigi ordered a can of beer from the barman and handed it to John.

Luigi was a small, wizened-looking man with skin like dried-up leather, very similar to Bert and Harry's—a legacy of many hours' work in the sun. John explained what he wanted to do and arranged to meet Luigi at the start of the Fourteen Mile field road at nine the next morning. They had another beer each, and John excused himself. 'Hey, don't go yet. The night, she be young yet. Stop and have a few more of the beers. I like to have someone to talk to.' John was not going to let himself fall into that trap again, so he insisted that he had to go and help back at the camp. John walked out into the cool night air and drove back to the camp. He nearly got lost this time himself.

Luigi's drill could be seen driving down the Breakaways road and then turning left towards the men waiting in the ute. The drill slowed to nearly stop, next to John's ute. John waved out of the window. 'Follow me,' yelled John. The big drill followed behind them through the field to the freshly pegged claim.

Luigi gingerly climbed out of the six-wheel-drive yellow international army truck, nearly falling as his foot slipped off the step. 'Shit! I should have gone home when you did. A couple of mates they come in. We got bloody pissed. Oh, the bloody head she hurt. I think my eyes are going to drop out. Mama mia! Phew!' Luigi stood next to the drill. It towered over his small frame. 'What you think of my drill?' he motioned proudly towards the drill with his hand. 'She pretty good, hey.'

The drill consisted of a nine-metre auger, which was turned by a hydraulic motor on the top of a tower and was pulled down by strong steel cables. There were three, four-metre extension augers which could be joined on, which gave the unit a drilling depth, if needed of around twenty-five metres. The main auger was in a boom, which was laid down on top of the rig and protruded past the truck cab. All of the rig was driven by its own diesel motor coupled to a series of hydraulic pumps—a very impressive looking machine.

Luigi looked around. 'Why you come here? I don't think you do much good around here. Everyone piss off from here years ago. They say this is dead ground. I work over there with some mates ten years ago. We didn't do no bloody good.' John assured him that they would try the claims any way. 'OK, please yourself. It's your money. Where you want to try first?' asked

Luigi sickly. Tony pointed to a small pile of rocks which Tony had built on the junction of one of the crossings he had wired with the divining rods. 'You guide me back so the back of the truck is about a half a metre from the rocks. That's where the drill points when she is lifted up in the air.' Luigi climbed back into the truck and started the motor. Tony guided him back to the rocks and waved for him to stop about a half metre from the rear of the truck.

The truck stopped, and Luigi slid out of the cab. The cab was so high and Luigi so short. It looked as if he would need a ladder to climb aboard.

Luigi walked around the truck to the rear of the rig and started the diesel motor from a control panel situated in the left-hand corner of the drilling rig frame. He adjusted the throttle so the motor was revving at a fast idle. He then lowered the four hydraulic feet and levelled the drilling rig by looking at a level which was built into the rig near to where he stood, and then he raised the mast and auger. Watching the long tower and auger being lifted was an unusual experience. The tower looked as if it were going to fall as the clouds raced past it. The auger was then lowered down the short distance through the mast so it was resting on the ground, and then the hydraulic motor was started, turning the auger in the dry red dirt.

For a start, the auger pushed out dark red dirt, and then it started to grind as it hit a layer of hard stones at around the two-metre depth. There was a small, circular screen located at the rear of the auger. Luigi pulled a lever and started this turning. This screened the fine sand and dirt out of the material which the drill bored out of the ground, making it easier to see any of the traces of opal, if there were any.

Slowly, the drill bored its way down into the ground until it was to the full depth of the first long auger. 'Do you want to go any deeper?' asked Luigi.

'No, Bert and Harry are only working at around seven metres.' Both John and Tony were disappointed at not finding any traces. Luigi slowly lifted the auger out of the hole, cleaning the dirt off it with his gloved hand as it rose so the dirt was funnelled through the screen to be checked.

He then lowered the ten-metre mast. 'Where do you want to try next?' Tony showed him a new pile of stones nearby. The procedure was repeated. Still no traces of opal. The next four holes were the same—no opal. John was starting to count the dollars as each hole was costing thirty dollars. 'I tell you the opal, she not too easy to find, especially around here,' said Luigi as he noted the disappointment on the men's faces. Five holes and not a bit of trace—150 dollars.

There was a small hollow in the ground in which some green grass grew. 'Try there,' Tony asked. He was running out of piles of stones. He had been so convinced that the opal would be easy to find. The depression in the soil was a departure from the divined areas as there was not even a trace of anything to keep them interested.

This hole was different. Right from the start, the dirt was wet. When the drill was about three quarters the way down, the auger crunched and shuddered slightly. Tony took no notice of this, but Luigi cocked his head slightly; he had heard this sound before. A half minute later, something glistened as it dropped out of the screen.

Both Tony and John had lost most of their enthusiasm by this time and had started to think they were wasting their time and money. Some more pieces dropped out.

Suddenly, Tony stopped daydreaming. 'Stop the drill,' he yelled to Luigi. Luigi had already seen some small pieces of trace in the sand being sieved out of the screen. He smiled as he stopped the auger and screen turning. John and Tony were sieving the material in the pile and building a small heap of opal in John's hat on the ground. Luigi put some of the small pieces he had picked out of the sieved fines into the hat. He reached in and took one of the brighter pieces out and licked it. 'By shit, you lucky buggers. I drill five hundred holes the last few weeks for myself and not find a bit of opal, only bloody potch (opal without colour). This bloody top red material. Look at the red rolling flash over it. About fifteen hundred dollars an ounce.'

The drill auger was started turning again, and a bit more opal came out and then only sandstone. The auger was nearly right in when it shuddered again. Luigi let the auger turn for a while and bring more material to the surface. He was just going to start to raise it when more opal started to come. This was shell material, mainly green.

'Shit, you lucky bastards! You got two bloody levels here, one seam, the other shells.' John turned to face Luigi.

'You think we're lucky? You should ask our prick of a bank manager. He was going to sell our farm and kick us out. He'll tell you otherwise,' said John.

Four more holes were drilled, each around two metres away from the first one, set out like the five pattern on a dice with the first hole in the centre of the pattern. Each hole produced opal.

Bert and Harry had just come out of the shaft. 'What do you look so happy for?' asked Harry with a wry smile. 'Find some bloody opal, did you?' Bert and Harry inspected the different piles of opal, some in cut-down drink cans and a couple in handkerchiefs. 'Good luck to you. This looks as if you have got a pretty big pocket of good opal here.'

'What would you suggest we do now?' John asked Bert.

'Well, you could get a bloke with a Caldwell drill to dig a shaft for you, or you could bring the old dozer up from the farm and put a cut in. Personally, I would put a bulldozer cut in seeing you have got the dozer. With a dozer cut, you see all the ground from the top down, whereas we only see what is in front of us in the drive.' Both John and Tony had the feeling that maybe their trials of the last few years might be about to resolve themselves. Hope at last.

Tony and John talked excitedly about the drilling to Bert and Harry. Luigi was paid for his work. He climbed back into the drilling rig. 'Good luck to you,' he shouted. He waved and then drove off towards town.

'Looks as if dinner's on us tonight. That's a bit of a turnaround.'

When they got arrived back in town, John stopped the ute at the phone box by the supermarket and rang Helen to tell her the good news. John and Tony took it in turns to tell her of their good fortune. Helen was thrilled to hear about the opal find but had some bad news from home.

Two days ago, Helen had gone out to feed the chickens and to collect the eggs from the 'girls' and had found a hole had been dug under the fowl yard gate. There were feathers everywhere; some of the 'girls' lay dead on the ground with their heads bitten off whilst the rest were standing hunched together in the far corner of the fowl run. They looked a sorry lot, far different from the usually beautiful Sussex hens they had been the day before.

Helen was furious, how could anything do such a thing to these lovely birds. They were her friends. She used to talk about her problems to them as she collected the eggs and fed them. She had walked into the fowl run and looked into the hen house, only to see the fat fox asleep inside. She had stormed out and looked around for something to block the hole under the gate. She found a small sheet of roofing iron, which she pushed into the hole under the gate. She had then hurried back to the house and got the double-barrelled, twelve-gauge shotgun and some shells.

By the time she had returned to the fowl run, the fox was running back and forth, trying to find a way out. The poor fowls, which were still alive, were also running, trying to keep out of its way. Helen loaded both barrels of the gun and sighted along the barrel, pointing it at the fox, who was in the far corner of the yard, cowering. She pulled the trigger. There had been a loud bang and a cloud of smoke. Her last recollection before she had been pushed back to sit on the backside was of the fox disintegrating before her eyes. Helen had never shot out of a shotgun before and had pulled both triggers at once. Revenge may have been sweet, but she had a very sore shoulder and backside to remember this one by.

John recounted the sad story when he returned to the camp. 'By God, I would like to have seen that. You want to watch out when you get home. A woman with a shotgun can be a dangerous creature,' said Harry with a laugh. 'I think we will head back home tomorrow morning and get the dozer ready and bring it up to Coober Pedy.' The excitement of the opal find was the main thing on their minds.

CHAPTER 5

The road rolled on and on in front of them. Travelling on the tarred road was not too bad, but when they turned off on to the Kingoonya to Wirulla road, dodging the dusty holes and rocks, it made a long trip home. Both Tony and John felt tired from the excitement of the last few days' working and could hardly wait to get the dozer up to Coober Pedy and start working on the claim. They were in a hurry to get home.

As they neared the farm, some of the country started to look a little bit greener than when they had left. There was a slight tinge of green on the pasture paddocks, and the wheat crops had changed from the sickly blue colour. They had been to a slightly darker shade of green.

Helen had spent the afternoon anxiously watching for the ute to drive off the Kimba road into the lane way. She was waiting at the gate in the house yard when they finally arrived. 'Have a good trip?' she asked as she gave both of the men a big hug. Helen recoiled back. 'Phew, watch out for my shoulder. It really hurts still. Here, look at the bruise.' Helen pulled back the sleeve of her jumper to show them the large bruise the shotgun butt had made on the shoulder. The outline of the gun's butt had left a dark blue outer bruise, grading to an orange angry-looking centre. 'Revenge may be sweet, but I'll sure remember this lot.'

Helen recounted the fox story. John gave her an extra careful hug. 'I'm very proud of the way you defended the castle whilst we were away at our crusades.' They all laughed.

Tony helped carry the dirty clothes into the outside laundry. 'Gee, it's good to have you back home.' She cuddled up to John, and then she went back into the house and made three coffees.

The men recounted the story of drilling the opal up and how they had pattern-drilled to prove the size of the area. The excitement was carried through the conversation to Helen. John had the traces in a bag. He tipped each lot of opal into a dinner plate with a small amount of water in it on the kitchen table. 'Get the desk lamp from the office,' asked John. Tony hurried in and got the lamp and then plugged it in and put it on the table so the light shone down on the small pieces of opal. Helen marvelled at the beauty of the coloured stones and the way the light changed the flashing colours.

The thought of having some way to get out of the financial mess was at least something to hope for. The whole mood in the house had changed from one of doom and gloom to one of hope.

Helen put a frying pan on the stove and dropped some chops into it for tea. She then peeled and diced some spuds and carrots and put these on to boil.

The animated conversation centred around the chances of finding a big seam of opal in the claim. They all fantasized as to what they would do with their money. After the meal, John rang Tom Morgan, who lived at Kyancutta, and asked if he still owned the old low loader he had used when he had a dozer. Bert had said about the low loader. He was sure that Tom still had the machine. Tom assured them that he still had it on his farm but it would need a bit of work before it could be used on the road. He did not want to sell it but would hire it if they thought they could use it. John and Tony arranged to have a look at the loader in two days.

The next morning was spent feeding and checking the sheep and crops. The crops and the feed situation had improved slightly. At least, there were no more dead sheep to contend with. The crow trap's side had been lifted when they went away so any hapless crow who dared to go into it would not have had to stay in the trap and finally die. Even crows needed a little bit of compassion.

The next morning, they drove off in the utility. It was around forty kilometres to the Morgan farm. As they travelled, they noticed that the country was quite a bit greener as they neared Kyancutta. Evidently, they had received some rain lately.

They were not quite sure where Tom's farm was, as it was on one of the back roads which led from the small town. John was sure they were on the right road, but as most of the farmers had not painted their names on their mailboxes, it was hard to know which farm it was. Tom had described how to get to the farm, but as most things, it was different from the phone description when driving down a strange road. Finally, John drove into one of the unmarked gate ways and drove the short distance down the lane way to the house and shed complex and then pulled in to a shed near the house where they could see two men working. John climbed out of the ute, walked over, and asked the men for directions. They were close. Tom's farm was the next property.

The sheds and the house on the farm were almost new. Evidently, the Morgan's had been able to put some of the income from the farm back into improvements. The old timber and galvanized iron house stood forlornly some distance from the new one. It was very small and looked as if it would have been very hot in the extreme heat that this area was noted for. John turned into the circular driveway in front of the reasonably new house. Tom Morgan walked out of the house to greet them. 'G'day! We've just come up from the shed for some smoko. Come inside, and have a cuppa before we go back down to the sheds,' invited Tom as they got out of the ute. They walked through a neat lawn and garden and then entered the large modern kitchen, which smelt of freshly baked cake. 'You've met Mary before, haven't you?' The plump, grey-haired woman turned, smiled, and then walked across the neat kitchen and shook their hands.

'Take a seat at the table.' She motioned towards the table with her hands.

The usual country commentary followed as was the normal manner—who was related to whom and where they had come from before moving to the district.

The men finished their tea, left the house, and walked over to the sheds to look at the old low loader. John noted that the machinery in Tom's implement sheds was of a pretty high standard and was reasonably new. A far cry from their old worn-out plant. John felt very envious of the shiny tractors and headers.

The loader trailer was used to keep the bulk grain bins off the semi-trailer on, in the winter. It was parked under a lean-to next to the main implement shed. The tyres were fairly flat. John and Tony had a quick look around and under the loader. A couple of tyres would need replacing if it was to make the trip to Coober Pedy. 'We sold the dozer a few years ago. The bloke who bought it made us an offer on the loader, but it was so low that we decided to keep it. As you can see, it needs a fair bit of work. The tail lights have been broken. The bloody kids had some mates staying with them on the farm a few years ago, my sister's kids from the city. Real little *s hoons they were. Got into everything. I reckon you should be able to get a few second-hand tyres from the* local council. They usually take them off when there's still plenty of tread on them.' Tom agreed to let them have the low loader for the trip up to Coober Pedy for two hundred dollars' hire as long as they fixed the few problems. 'There's one other problem. I think you may have problems registering the low loader as it hasn't been registered for years. You know what a mob of mongrels the registration mob are to deal with.' John thought for a few seconds.

What if we change the rego and plates from our semi-trailer? If we don't have a prang, we should at least look registered. We don't want to hang around for another six months, going broken whilst some shiny-bottomed twerp in an office in the city finally makes his mind up if we can use the low loader or not.

'We'll be back tomorrow to pick it up, as long as this is OK with you.' Tom nodded. They shook hands on the deal. 'I'll take the bins off this afternoon ready for when you come to pick it up.'

They headed back home along the dry dusty roads. 'Well, that's the first problem over with. Now we had better do some work to the dozer and truck. Maybe our luck has finally changed for the better.'

John left the kitchen and walked across to join Tony who had just opened the door of the truck.

The sheepdogs were very keen to see the truck started as they were the dozer a few weeks before. It was another of their favourite machines for sport, catching the rats as they ran out from under the truck.

The rats had been particularly bad the last few months, even though they had tried to keep them down with rat poison. Tony had got an unpleasant surprise when he opened the door of the truck. The dirty rats had eaten the rubber grommet from around the steering column and got inside the cab. *What a mess!* Tony pulled out the nests from under the seats and threw them out on to the ground. The nests were made from old baling twine and some of the inner-seat cushion material. There was rats manure everywhere throughout the truck cabin.

The dogs made short work of the baby rats in the nest, one quick nip on the back of the neck to each one, whilst Tony accounted for a couple of the parents with his boot as they tried to escape out of the hole by the steering column. He tossed them out of the cab, where upon the dogs made doubly sure that they were dead.

Suddenly, Tony was out of the truck, clutching at his trousers and madly trying to take his trousers down at the same time. He was hopping around on one leg like a Scotsman doing a reel. John was worried that Tony had hurt himself in the truck cabin. Tony finally got his trousers off, whilst still holding the leg firmly. He ran out of the shed in his undies and then called loudly to the dogs. Laddie came over with an amused look on his face. John was still wondering what the trouble was. Tony shook his trousers wildly until finally a huge rat ran out of the trouser leg. Laddie true to his form ran in and dispatched the rat with one bite. John by this time had realised what the trouble had been and was by now crouched down, laughing uncontrollably. Tony was not amused. 'That's all right by you, you old coot. If that bloody rat had latched on, you might never have been a grandfather to my kids.'

Finally, they tried to start the diesel motor. John was still chuckling from the recent pantomime. Nothing happened. Tony turned the key over and over, and the starter would not turn.

John got a piece of fencing wire and quickly shorted the battery terminals. 'There's plenty of juice in the batteries. Check under the dashboard.' Tony looked under the dash. The rats had eaten the insulation off the wiring loom and chewed some of the wires through.

'Would you get me some pliers, some insulation tape, and some wire joiners? The blooming rats have had a party under here.' Finally, the wires were re-joined. Tony turned the key again. The truck started, whereupon more rats ran out from under the motor. The dogs yelped with excitement as they chased their quarry.

Tony slid out of the cab, walked over to the house, and mixed some disinfectant with hot water in a bucket. He walked back to the shed and splashed this through the cab and over the truck's motor.

'We'll draw straws to see who drives the truck over to the Morgan's.' John pulled a matchbox out of his pocket, then took two matches out of the box, and broke one in half. He held them out in front of himself, having them firmly held between two fingers. Tony pulled a match out. It was the short one.

'Bad luck, it looks like you can drive the truck,' offered John as he quickly put the other short match into his trouser pocket. Unbeknown to Tony, John had broken two matches in half. He knew from past experience what the cab would smell like when the motor heated up.

John and Tony wound the jacks on the semi-trailer down and uncoupled the trailer. The trailer still had the bulk grain bins on it from earlier in the year when it had been used to cart the superphosphate for their crops. This was the truck's only use—carting grain into the silos and bringing superphosphate up to the farm from Port Lincoln. An old, seven-ton petrol engine Bedford truck did all the other work on the farm.

It took almost an hour to get to Kyancutta. Tony had all the windows open and had driven the first few K's with his head half out of the window. The disinfectant smell had not worked. It had only made the rat smell more sickly. John chuckled to himself as he watched from behind. He had been in this position himself many times before.

The truck bounced through the potholes in the dirt road. It had never been a very comfortable truck to ride in. It was even worse without the weight of the trailer behind it.

Tony was pleased when he finally drove in to the Morgan's farm and reversed the truck back to the low loader. The loader trailer had been unloaded and pulled out of the shed ready. The tyres were pumped up ready. Tony reversed the old truck back and hooked the two rigs together. They drove the truck to Tom's house for a cuppa, whilst Tony paid the two hundred dollars. 'When do you want the rig back?' asked Tony.

'Keep it as long as you like. But I do want it back home one day.'

'How about driving the rig home?' pleaded Tony. 'I nearly spewed when the engine got hot and the rat poop started to cook. That bloody disinfectant I put in the cab made it smell worse. It's a lot better now,' John agreed. It was only fair to drive the truck on the trip home.

The truck cabin still smelt strongly of rats. John also drove with the windows down. He would rather bear the cold air than the rat smell. It was a long trip home. He was pleased when the truck finally drove up the drive to the sheds.

John parked the truck close to the workshop end of the implement shed so they were near to the welder and tools.

The rear of the trailer was jacked up. John set about trying to take the wheels with the worn-out tyres off. Finally, they had to get the oxy welder and heat the wheel nuts before they could finally undo them.

They were hot and dirty. They went across to the house for a cuppa. John rose from the table and walked over to the phone, which was mounted on the wall, and then rang the local council workshop. The mechanic assured him that they had plenty of quite good tyres for the job.

After they had finished the cup of tea and jam scones, John drove off into Kimba with the wheels in the back of the ute to have the tyres changed, whilst Tony tried to get the tail and blinker lights working.

John arrived back home around dusk. The tyres had been just as hard to get off as the wheel nuts were. They had been rusted on to the rims. John was filthy and also had lost quite a bit of skin off his knuckles as he had helped to change the tyres at the local tyre repairer who was also not impressed having the job of helping change these tyres as it was a very hard work. John had also picked through the council scrap heap and had selected ten partially worn ripper boots to fit the dozer. The council also had a Cat D7 dozer. It was a lot later model.

Tony had changed his clothes and had a long shower but thought he could still smell the rats' poo on himself even through the strong aftershave he had doused himself with.

The truck was greased and the oil changed as was the dozer. John cut up some worn-down grader blades with the oxy and re-tipped the ripper boots with these pieces of grader blade by welding them on to the worn ripper boots, which, with a lot of effort, had been knocked off the ripper tines. Then he was hard-surfacing them with special rods, leaving them to cool down before replacing them on to the tines. The council scrap heap boots were brought from the ute. These were re-tipped and hard-faced as well.

Tony had the compressor and paint sprayer out and sprayed the low loader trailer frame with the leftover paint from the last truck spray job. At least, it would look registered. They were prepared to take a chance on the low-loader-looking part of the truck. Tony took the number plate off the semi-trailer, which was usually towed behind the truck, and screwed it to the freshly painted trailer. It looked legal even if it wasn't.

The truck cabin was washed out and the motor squirted down again to try to get the rat smell out. 'Right, Father, this is your big chance. You can drive the truck.'

Everything was filled with fuel, and a spare two-hundred-litre drum was filled with diesel on the back of the ute, plus all the heavy tools and a couple of jacks. The dozer pilot motor was started, and then the large diesel was started. Finally, the dozer blade and rippers were lifted, and the machine was slowly driven up on to the steep ramp at the rear of the loader trailer. The dozer pivoted in the centre then tipped forward and then flattened out to follow the tray of the low loader.

John carefully lowered the blade and the rippers. Tony threw a heavy chain over the blade, whilst John secured the back. They pulled the chains tight with some chain dogs and then clipped them shut. The final thought was to paint two wide load signs on some flat iron, as the blade of the dozer was wider than the truck tray. These were attached to the front and rear of the truck. The procession was ready for the next morning.

As the men had their evening meal, they both talked of things they might have forgotten, but everything which they could think of was packed ready. Helen could feel the sense of the loss of her two men starting to creep up on her again, but she could also sense the glimmer of hope in their speech, which was something which had been lacking for quite a while on the farm. The excitement and enthusiasm the men felt was carried over to her.

The sun was just rising over the horizon. The sky was filled with the streaky red clouds of sunrise when they left the next morning. Helen felt quite alone again when the truck and ute finally disappeared from view.

After the men had left Buckleboo and had entered the real station country, Tony would have to drive ahead and open the gate next to the cattle grids and then drive through and wait for John, as there was no way the truck and dozer could cross the risen-up grids. It would have bottomed out and got the low loader stuck. Tony would then let the truck pass through and then close the gate behind the truck. He would then pass the truck and drive well ahead to stop the dust from being a problem, ready for the next gate.

It was a slow trip. The old truck was flat out at eighty kilometres an hour on good roads. The speed had to be cut back to between forty and fifty kilometre on these rough tracks.

Just before the procession drove out on to the bitumen highway, they stopped and had lunch. John jumped down from the truck and brushed the dust off his clothes. He blew his nose loudly. 'You must have had a good trip the other day. That bloody rats' shit on the motor still stinks even with the new deodorant blocks we put in it and all the dust which has come into the cab.' Tony agreed to drive the truck the rest of the way.

After lunch, Tony pumped diesel into the ute and truck's fuel tanks from the drum on the ute, whilst John checked the oil in the old Mercedes truck. 'Not bad, the old dear hasn't used much oil so far.'

Late afternoon, just as they got to the turn-off to the Coober Pedy township off the main highway, John put his indicator on and turned left in towards the Black Flag field on the old dirt main road, which had been bypassed by the new bitumen highway. Tony followed for a short distance. John then drove off the road on to a track and parked the truck. 'I don't want to drive this through the town. It would just be our luck to have one of the maniac drivers run into us. Then the cops would find out the trailer isn't registered.'

Bert and Harry were nearly pickled when they arrived. 'We had a bit of fun whilst you were away. We found another twenty thousand bucks worth of opal. There's a nice pile of cash in the old safe now.' The cold beers were really appreciated first to wash the rotten rat smell away and then just for no reason at all.

'What's that smell in here?' asked Harry. 'It smells just like rat poop.'

'You don't smell too good either,' answered John.

Harry cackled. 'That's the smell of money, my boy.'

At half past eight in the morning, they drove out to the truck. John climbed into the cabin and started the old truck and then headed out north to the Fourteen Mile. Tony followed in the ute. So far, everything was going OK. Getting the dozer and the truck up to Coober Pedy without any large problems was a real bonus.

The truck and the dozer were parked on the Kellys' claim. John climbed out of the cab and then up on to the tray of the trailer. He put his foot on the blade arm, climbed on to the platform, and then sat in the seat. The dozer was started and left to idle, whilst the chains were removed by Tony. The blade and then the rippers were lifted, and then the tractor was reversed carefully back and unloaded. 'What do you think we should do with the truck?' asked Tony.

'I reckon you should leave it out here. There's less chance of anyone fiddling with it here than back in town,' said Bert.

John and Tony walked over the claim and talked about where the bulldozer cut would be situated. They finally agreed on a spot. Tony fetched some rocks and marked out a rectangle, which had the five holes from which they had drilled the opal in the middle. 'OK, by you,' asked John. Tony then got some more rocks and made a line of rocks which pointed across the rectangle, which lined up with the area from which they had drilled the opal. Harry had told them to do this so they would be able to see where the area the opal traces were drilled from when they were getting close to the level with the dozer.

'Right then. Let's make a start.' John climbed up on to the old D7, which had been idling, revved the motor up, turned the machine, and drove it over until it was in line with the long edge of the rectangle they had marked out. He then pushed the full length of the marked area, pushing the rich red dirt as he went.

This manoeuvre was repeated over and over until around a half a metre of dirt was shifted off the marked area. By now, the ground was slightly moist and considerably harder, so John had to drop the rippers and rip back and forth. All of this time, Tony followed the tractor, carrying his miner's pick, checking the ground as it was ripped, or pushing dirt. Harry had told Tony to keep his eyes peeled as the Fifteen Mile area was known to have alluvial opal in the red dirt in some places.

Back and forth ripping, then pushing the dirt, the dirt changed to very hard round stones, which made the old dozer's tracks squeal in protest. These were the stones which had made the drill protest when they were drilling the test holes. The hard round jasper rocks were in a level of about a half-metre thick. Then after the jasper, the ground started to change to a lighter-coloured subsoil type with some areas slightly crunchy.

Tony followed the dozer, every rip and push, back and forth. *What a boring thing to do*, thought Tony as he walked.

Around four o'clock, the ground started to change from the subsoil dirt to a more biscuit-like, crunchy light brown material. Tony's feet were beginning to get sore from all the walking on the uneven ground. The dozer was pushing a blade full of dirt in front of it and was making hard work of the job, spinning its tracks slightly. One track spat out a piece of rock which had been broken in half by the weight of the machine's tracks. It fell on to its side, and as it did so, the dying rays of sunlight caught it, causing it to flash. Suddenly, Tony's thoughts came back to reality, the reason why they were there. He reached down and picked up the piece of rock, and as he did so, he noticed the beautiful flashes of the opal fire dancing over the broken surface. He turned the piece of opal transfixed by the colours, almost forgetting the dozer. By this time, John was reversing the dozer back. 'Stop! Stop!' yelled Tony. John was evidently thinking of other things also, as he was nearly back to where Tony had found the opal. Tony bent down, picked up a handful of dirt, and threw it over the fuel tank of the dozer. As the small stones hit John, he decelerated the motor and then stopped the machine moving. He turned around, puzzled.

'What's up?' Tony waved the piece of opal around, too excited to talk. John throttled the big motor back, then climbed down off the machine, and walked back to where Tony was squatting, busily scratching at the ground.

'Here's some opal,' croaked Tony as he handed him the piece of opal which was about the size of a cigarette packet but half as thick.

'Bloody hell, look at that,' said John reverently. He was amazed to see the first piece of opal that they had found themselves with the dozer.

Tony walked back out of the shallow bulldozer cut to the ute and got the sieve, a shovel, and a small bucket. They then sieved the dirt from where the piece of opal had come from, being careful to remove and check any stones that were nearby. They found some other pieces of opal, and when the pieces were placed together, they could almost be arranged like a jigsaw to form one piece. The lump of opal, when roughly joined together, was about the size of a saucer, the thickest being over a centimetre thick. The outside of the stone was covered with a rusty iron-stone-coloured coating, so if it had not been cracked, Tony would not have noticed it. Only some small chips were missing from making the piece of opal back into one piece again.

Bert and Harry climbed out of the shaft. Harry walked over and shut the alternator motor down. Bert walked over to where John and Tony were still digging and sieving where they had found the opal. 'Found a bit of opal?' asked Bert nonchalantly.

'Yeah, have a look in the bucket.'

'Wow, this is nice opal. Shit, I reckon it would be worth around three thousand an ounce.' Bert put all the pieces into his hand and guessed the weight. 'Around five ounces. What do you think, Harry?' Harry, who had just walked over, had a good look at the stones and then weighed them in his hand.

'More like six ounces.' He did not want to agree with his brother. Harry licked the side of some of the stones. Tony noticed this and thought of how many people evidently licked the opal to see the colour highlighted by the moisture. Licking something after Harry had licked it was not on his menu. 'I reckon you might be right. Bloody nice colour.' They put the stones back into the bucket. 'I've heard the alluvial opal here was pretty good, but we had never seen any before. We've been working too deep. Found any more?' John and Tony both stood up.

'No, it looks like we've got the lot.'

'That will sure help with the fuel. Looks like tea and beers are on us tonight.'

'How do we go about selling this opal? We sure need the money for fuel, plus I would like to send some home to Helen so she has some spare cash for a change. I'll make a call to her when we go to the pub.'

'There's a pommy guy we have had classed ours. I can get him to have a look at it,' said Bert.

After they had showered, even Bert and Harry made the effort, they all went up to the pub for a few beers and a meal. The opal was secured in the old safe.

Bert rang the opal classer from the phone box outside the pub as soon as they arrived. 'Well, it looks like you had better go and get the opal. He will have a look at it now. He's not a bad sort of a bloke. For a pom, that is,' added Bert. This was the usual Aussie banter about people from the mother country. No animosity was meant by it.

John took the safe keys offered by Bert, then left the men at the bar, and drove back to the dugout. He opened the old flimsy door, then went inside, and got the opal from the safe. The old safe door squealed in protest when it was opened and then shut again. John came back to the pub.

Bert drove in front of John to show the way to the classer's dugout. They all walked through the gate. John knocked on the door. The yard around the front of the dugout had the usual machinery and tools lying around. A large Rottweiler dog was locked in a cage at the back of the car shed, which was in front of the dugout. The dog barked loudly as they walked through the gate. It ran to the end of the cage and banged on the front mesh wall close to the men walking into the yard. Barking, baring its teeth, and growling as it did so. The dog was very intimidating. A very good watchdog. By the look of the dog tracks and chewed-up bones in the yard, the dog was usually let free to roam at night.

The bloke was evidently married and had kids, for a lot of toys were arranged on dirty and dusty roads which had been pushed by the children with their toy graders and bulldozers.

A skinny man with ginger hair opened the door. 'Are you the guys with the opal?' he asked. They nodded. 'Right, follow me.' They followed the man to another door way leading into a separate dugout. The man turned back towards them. 'The name's Leon,' he said. John and Tony introduced themselves. The classer shook hands all around 'Come in. Let's have a look at the opal then.'

They followed Leon into the dugout. Leon reached past John and switched on the light. There was a large table and an assortment of chairs in the room. The top of the table was covered in black plastic, which had some large desk lamps, an assortment of containers, and numerous sets of different scales on top of it. Leon turned one of the table lights on.

The men sat down. John passed the ice cream container with the bag of opal in it. Leon opened the plastic shopping bag and tipped the contents under one of the bright lamps. He picked the first piece of opal up and studied it. 'This is pretty good opal, alluvial. From the Fifteen Mile. Am I right?' They nodded. Leon turned the stones back and forth under the light and then weighed them. 'Just under five ounces, I reckon you should get twelve thousand for this lot.' He wrote the price down on to a piece of paper. One price was the top price they could expect; the other price was the lowest they should take. 'I'll ring one of the Chinese buyers if you like. There's one guy who likes this type of opal.' The men agreed as it saved them the trouble of chasing a buyer. Leon rang the buyer from a cordless phone which was on a shelf. He spoke to the buyer for a couple of minutes. 'He will see you at the dugout. You had better give me some instructions as to how to find it.' Tony explained where the dugout was. 'Will a quarter of an hour's time be OK.' Leon hung the phone back into its cradle.

'I charge 2 per cent to class opal, so if you sell the opal, just bring the cash around in the next few days.' The men thanked Leon and walked out to their utes and drove back to the dugout. John and Tony had no idea of what to expect with the Chinese buyer. It was just before dark when the Chinese buyer arrived. He drove an old brown Holden car. The small man got out of the car, locked the door, and then lit a cigarette. Tony was waiting outside the dugout in case the man could not find them. He waddled up to Tony. 'You have opals for sale?' he asked in broken English. 'That's us,' said John. The man walked back to his car and opened the door with the key. He then reached into the car, got a battered bag, and then re-locked the car door. The man then rudely pushed past Tony and walked into the dugout.

The Chinaman sat himself down at the table. He put the battered bag out of the way of the light but within easy reach. 'Opals, I look.' Bert turned the desk lamp on. This was the first time they really took notice of the small man. He turned towards them, took the cigarette out of his mouth, and then smiled. The man had extremely rotten teeth, which were also brown with tobacco stains. Whilst john handed the opal over to him. The man puffed on the cigarette. The smoke filled the room with a horrible smell. He butted the stub of the cigarette out on to a dirty plate on the table and then lit another straight away. The man puffed the cigarette, drawing deeply and exhaling the acrid-smelling smoke towards the men. He had an unusual way of holding the cigarette. He held it backwards into his hand as if to keep the wind off it.

The buyer then tipped the opal out on to the black plastic sheet. He turned the stones over and over under the light, picking pieces up and studying them close to the light to see if there were any imperfections in them.

'How much you want for this opal?' he asked.

'Thirteen thousand dollars,' said John. The Chinaman sat back and laughed.

'Ho ho, I not pay that much. Much too, dear. How much this classed for? What is real price?' The little man drew back on his cigarette and blew the smoke over towards the men. 'I give you nine, that top dollar for this opal. Some of the stones are clacky (cracked). See this one this have cotton in it (small filaments of gypsum).

'No, thirteen thousand,' said John. The bargaining went on and on. John was getting really angry.

'If we can't get twelve thousand, you had better piss off.' This tirade did not seem to faze the man at all. Finally, after three more rotten cigarettes, they agreed on eleven and a half thousand dollars. The little man reached forward and pulled the bag towards him, opened it up, withdrew a wad of cash, and then started to count the money out. John and Tony watched intently as the piles of cash grew. The little man stopped counting, then lit another cigarette, and blew acrid smoke over the men again. He looked up at John.

'You count again.' He motioned at John. John counted the money and agreed the figure was right. The man got up from the table and picked up the opal.

'If you have more opal, you ring me. I give you top dollar.' He then arose and handed a dirty printed card. 'See, Johnnie, That me. That my mobile number.' He turned and walked out of the door. When he got into his car, John let out a sigh.

'What a crook!' said Tony. Neither of the men was used to the bartering that the Chinese buyers were noted for.

'How do you like dealing with the Chinese?' asked Bert with a wry smile.

'I feel exhausted. That was as hard a work as pulling teeth,' said John.

'Well, at least I know what they make their Chinese cigarettes out of. It smells like burning horse poop in here,' said Bert. 'Right, put the money away. Let's go. I can't stand the smell in here.'

After the first few beers, John went outside to the phone box and rang Helen with the good news. Helen also had some good news. It was raining steadily. The first proper rain for the year.

Whilst John was away, phoning Helen, the Greek lad, who had warned Tony off his sister, walked over to the table with another older man. The lad had a grim look on his face. Tony was worried because both looked serious. *I hope they don't want to fight*, thought Tony as they stopped at the table.

'G'day, mate,' said Bert. 'What can we do you for?'

The older Greek man turned to Tony and spoke, 'Ay, boy, my son he has an apology to make to you.' The young man looked down at the floor. He then slowly held his hand out to Tony and took his hand.

'Hey, man, I'm sorry about the other night, man.'

'That's OK, I'm prepared to forget it,' said Tony. The older man, evidently the lad's father, cut in.

———

'Bloody, boy, he came home and boasted about how he chased you away from his sister and was going to thump you. Stupid bugger, we in Australia now. We bloody Aussies like everyone else. If she want to talk to an Aussie, that's OK by me. Just to talk though is all right. You do anything else, I help my son to thump you.' The man turned and then walked off, followed by his son, back to the bar, where they rejoined their friends.

'Thought you were in trouble there. It might pay to keep your mind off some of the New Australian sheilas up here. Some of the Italian or Greeks might be OK, but don't go chasing any of the Serb or Muslim women. You might have some trouble walking behind the dozer for quite a while and a change in your voice to a soprano.' Laughed Harry.

John walked back into the bar. 'Looks like a double celebration tonight. Helen says it's raining. We've had a half an inch of rain already, and it's still raining.'

The beer flowed freely, a lot freer than John was used to, but the first opal sales had buoyed his confidence. The main level which they had drilled still beckoned to them.

'God, what time did we get home last night? My bloody head hurts,' said Tony as he pulled a chair out and sat at the table. The smell of the buyer's horrible cigarettes still wafted in the air. It was hard to get any ventilation down into the dugout.

'That's the trouble with you young blokes, no staying power. When I was your age . . .' Bert was interrupted by John.

'It's all right for you. I don't feel too good either. I've heard a lot of stories about your younger days. Most shouldn't be told with a young man like Tony's presence.' They all laughed.

The strong black coffees had helped a bit. By the time the dozer started, both the men were feeling a bit more like work. The excitement of the previous day was still in their minds.

Tony was full of enthusiasm at first, but as the day crawled on, he reverted to plodding behind the dozer, turning the stones over with his miners' pick and breaking the odd one with the side of the pick head.

Towards the end of the day, they started to find hard rock. This material seemed to be a mixture of gypsum and jasper. It was a very tough material, if it had been the hard red-and-white banded jasper, the rippers would have shattered it, making it relatively easy to get through. The rippers on the dozer would chatter and would not penetrate. Smoke was coming off the ripper boots. Every now and then, John was able to hook under one of the rocks and make a hole he could work from. He would have to drop the rippers into this hole and drag a few stones out and then come in from a different angle to get some more. It was a slow and tedious job as well as being hard on the old dozer.

John was worried that the old dozer might not have held together in the rough ground.

'I thought you might have a bit of fun with that rock. The guy with the Caldwell drill who dug the shaft for us doesn't like drilling out here very much because of this rock. This field is noted for the hard rock on top. It is probably why this spot was left years ago. You guys are lucky you can prise the rocks out. Sometimes you have to use explosives. We have been told this crap hard to drill.'

'We had to dig three metres through this rock,' said Harry.

Bert had found a small pocket of skin shell material. It had a beautiful colour but was a very thin material.

Skin shell was formed when the cockle shell, which was turned to opal, was opened at the time. If the cockle was tightly shut, this would form a solid shell, all solid opal. Some of the best of these commanded a lot of money—fifteen or twenty thousand dollars for one really good shell.

John was still worried about the dozer. It might not stand up to the rough work much longer. There were bolts coming loose and a lot more squealing from the tracks.

John went to the opal miners store to get a new packet of hard-facing welding rods to face the boots as the tips were wearing off very quickly, and as soon as the cutting edge was rounded off, the boot just slid along the top of the tough rock. Whilst he was walking through the aisles, he noticed some tungsten-tipped cutting tools which were used in the large Caldwell drill buckets. The buckets were modified to take these tools by having the old tool holders removed and then new blocks welded on to take these tungsten-tipped picks. On a whim, John bought four of the picks and two blocks. 'Where can I get some welding and cutting done?' he asked the man at the counter. He was directed to a small street about three hundred metres behind the shop. John got out of the utility and walked into the yard. There was a huge pile of scrap steel at one end of the large block of land and a dugout and large workshop on the other end. Near the workshop, there were a man and a woman working on a large blower. John walked over and stood watching the two working. The woman was working just as hard as the man, hammering a bent piece of steel with a sledge hammer. They stopped working, and the man introduced himself. He was Ivan; his wife was Anne.

'This is Anne's blower. She works it by herself when I am working in the workshop,' explained Ivan. 'What can I do for you?' John explained that they were working a dozer at the Fifteen Mile and were in the hard jasper. Ivan had worked this area and knew all about the tough material.

'What I want to do is to cut the ends off two worn ripper boots and weld these two blocks on the nose of the boot to take these picks.'

Ivan thought for a while and said, 'I think you should cut the boots down enough to just be showing the end of the pocket where the boot fits over the ripper tine. This would allow you to remove the old pick with a hammer and long drift.' The design was worked out, and Ivan agreed to do the job the next day.

'That's a really good idea you have thought of. I have never seen this before. If it works, you should patent it.' A rough price was agreed on, and John left for the dugout.

John told the men about his new invention to try to stop the dozer from falling to pieces. He was also getting knocked around by all the severe jerking and twisting. He could not keep the dozer going in a straight-line as one of the rippers would hook in and pull the dozer off line all the time. This was extremely hard on the brakes and other parts on the dozer.

Tony's feet were getting really sore from all the walking over the rough stones. He still checked under these stones because there was a little bit of the brown opal-bearing level stuck to the bottom of some of these rocks. There was no opal to be found though. The only thing he found was a thin line of potch stuck to the bottom of one of these stones. He nearly gave himself a hernia, trying to turn this stone over, and was disappointed when he had finally achieved shifting it to find it barren. He was really interested to see if John's new idea would work.

Friday night was pub night. The men cleaned themselves up and departed to the hotel.

They had just had their second beer when Silvio, the ferrety mate of the dugout owner, walked past their table. 'Oi, good doy, mite. You finda the big opals yet.' He laughed.

'Nah, mate, we haven't found anything but potch yet,' lied Bert. Silvio had evidently been in the pub all the afternoon. He could hardly stand up.

'If you find the opals, you got no worries with the safe. She's a gooda one. You got the only keys.' Silvio staggered off to the table with his mates, a most unsavoury-looking mob of crooks.

'Who is that little prick?' asked Tony.

'Don't you remember? He's our landlord's best mate. That other crook with the grey beard is the landlord. It makes you wonder about the safe, doesn't it? Every one of them has probably got a key.'

'They look like a mob of bloody pirates to me. That other crook has even got a big gold earing,' said John. 'I wouldn't like to do business with any of them.'

'That's why I didn't tell them about the opal. The less you say, the better.'

'What are you mob of bastards doing up here?' John turned around. It was a farmer neighbour Peter Murphy. Peter had his son, Joe, with him. Peter and Joe sat down at the table. 'Here, Joe, get a round of drinks. Make yourself useful.' Peter handed Joe a fifty-dollar bill.

Peter was having the same problems as the rest of them. 'Bloody greedy banks', was his answer. Peter and Joe had built a small noodling machine to noodle the missed opal out of the old dumps and had brought it up behind the farm front-end loader. They were finding around a thousand dollars a week on an average. 'A lot better than the farming game,' he stated.

'Hey, did you hear about the rain?' asked Peter.

'Yes, I rang Helen the other night, and she said it was raining then. I don't know how much we finally got.'

'I rang Joan yesterday. We had just under an inch. Hell, that will sure help the crops along.'

Tony had teamed up with Joe. 'You old bludgers can talk about old times if you like. Joe has asked me to go around to one of his mate's places. There's a bit of a party. I just thought I would like to check out some of the local talent.'

'Well, don't talk to any Greek girls,' said Harry. 'If you find an extra one, bring her back for me,' said Bert, laughing.

'How do you think I should describe you?' asked Tony.

'Tall, young, and handsome,' added Bert.

'Piss off, and don't do anything I wouldn't do.'

'A couple of rough diamonds those two,' said Joe as they walked through the pub door.

The party was pretty rowdy as the two boys arrived. Joe had an Esky with some beer in it. He carried it inside the gate. There was loud music coming from inside the timber-framed house. The boys walked inside and were greeted by an Italian lad. It was his birthday party. Joe introduced Tony to most of the people he knew. The topic of the conversation was opal-based as most of the guys were mining or noodling. Tony did not let on to anyone about the opal that they were finding. Tony had a few dances with some of the girls, in between talking and drinking beer. Joe suggested that they leave. Tony asked why.

'Some of the guys here have got some grass and have started to smoke it. I don't want to get mixed up with the marijuana scene. My young brother got on to that shit and lost his marbles.' Tony agreed. There was too much relying on the mining venture to get tied up with the dope scene and shoot one's mouth off about the opal find.

Peter had asked John and Tony to come out and have a look at their noodling machine the next morning.

The sun was well up when John drove out into the Olympic Field. They had called into Ivan's workshop and picked up the finished tools. Tony was very impressed with the look of the tools as was Ivan. 'Let me know if they work OK. I can't see why these pointy tools should not in the Tough jasper.' John agreed to let him know.

He tried to follow the directions he had been given the previous night, but they ended up getting lost. After driving around for about a half an hour and backtracking their tracks, they could see a cloud of dust blowing off a machine in the distance. Tracks led everywhere. A lot of them ended in dead ends. They had to reverse out from between the white mounds of sandstone which had been left by the blowers quite a few times, being careful when they did so, not to drive down one of the many shafts which accompanied most of the mounds. Finally, they arrived at the machine.

The machine looked like something out of the *Mad Max* movie. It was built out of lots of things which came from the farm. The chassis was an old truck which had the motor, tray, and cab removed; only the chassis springs and wheels remained. On one end was a small bin with a coarse screen on top to remove the large stones. This was lifted occasionally with the loader bucket to tip off the accumulated large rocks. Under the bin was a conveyor belt. The belt led to a rotary trammel screen, which dropped the screened material on to another small conveyor, which, in turn, led through a small darkroom. The darkroom was made from an old van body. On the other side of the van, the material from the conveyor dropped on to another elevator which carried it up and away. The men could recognize most of the parts in this machine as coming from old farming plant, similar to what they had in the scrap heap on their farm.

There was a cone-shaped pile under the elevator, which Peter would pick up with the front-end loader and carry away to a dump.

All of the machine was driven by a diesel-powered alternator, which was situated some distance away to keep it out of the dust.

Peter dropped the bucket full of material into the hopper and then stopped the tractor. 'You're late! Did you sleep in?' John explained how they had got lost. 'Bloody easy to do around here. I was talking to one of the miners one day who owned a drill. He went out drilling one day in this area and drilled up some opal. He got pretty excited. He put the mast of the drill down and went back to town in his ute. The next day, he could not find the drill amongst all the dumps. He had spent nearly all day looking and was almost going to the cops because he thought some crook had pinched it when he finally found it.'

Peter banged on the door of the darkroom. Joe shut the electric motors off, which drove the machine, and then opened the door. 'Come in and have a look.' There was only room for Tony and Joe in the confined area. 'Shut the door behind you. I'll show you how it works.' Tony pulled the sliding door shut. It was pitch-dark inside. Joe turned on the ultraviolet florescent lights, which shone an eerie purple. Tony looked down at his sneakers, which shone a bright yellow in the UV light.

'Wow, just like the lights at some discos,' said Tony. He had not noticed this in the noodling machine the other day.

Joe started the conveyor belt moving. The small rocks were carried by. They shone as a dark purple colour. Occasionally, there were some which shone orange. 'Alunite,' explained Joe. The small pieces of opal shone a brilliant white, similar to Tony's shoes. The men picked these up and put them into the small buckets which were next to the belt. Occasionally, a feather or a piece of greasy dirt would fluoresce. There was a brilliant green piece coming along the belt. Joe yelled as Tony was going to pick it up—a scorpion. Tony pulled his hand back. Joe shut the belt off and turned the bright light on. It took Tony a while to be accustomed to the light. Joe speared the large scorpion, put it aside, and then carried on noodling in the purple darkness.

Suddenly, Tony got the funny feeling again that the belt had stopped moving and that the stool he was sitting on was moving instead, as it had done in the noodling machine before. After a while, he got used to the machine, and it all settled down again.

Joe stopped the machine. 'Well, that's enough for today. It's about two o'clock.' He turned the light on inside the room and then shut the electric motors down in sequence. First, the bin, then the screen, then the conveyor through the room, and, finally, the elevator outside. The men walked out into the sunlight, squinting at its brightness as they did. Joe carried the small buckets filled with material out with him and the skewered scorpion.

'When we first came up here, we saw a noodling machine working. The bloke asked us if we wanted to have a look. They were from Ceduna. Cockies like us,' said John.

'That would have been Charlie and Josh. I know them,' said Joe. They all looked at the very large scorpion. 'I have been told that they are not deadly poisonous, but they hurt like hell if they get you.'

Joe poured some water into a tray and then tipped the contents of the buckets in. The material was mostly worthless potch, but hiding amongst this were a few good pieces of opal. The potch was discarded and the opal put back into one of the buckets. 'A lot of the opal they found in the fifties and the sixties was considered unsaleable, so it was tossed into the dumps. Now some of these are worth around four or five hundred bucks an ounce.' The days opal was probably worth around three hundred dollars. 'Not a bad pick up, considering the farming game at present. We get this nearly every day. Every now and then, we find a good piece which someone has missed. We got three thousand for a good shell one day.' The men agreed it was far better than any way of making money in the Kimba district at the present time.

Joe and Tony went for a drive around the field the next day. John was left with the washing. Even Bert and Harry had a washing session. Their clothes were so full of sweat and dirt that they would hardly bend.

Monday morning, working again. The dozer had to be filled with fuel from the two-hundred-litre drum every two days. Tony usually did this, whilst John checked the oil and greased the dozer.

John had picked up the new ripping tools he had got from from Ivan's workshop. Ivan had still insisted that John should patent the idea if it were to work. 'This tool could save a lot of people a lot of money,' he had said.

The new tools were fitted to the ripper tines. Ivan had done an excellent job welding the tools together. The pointy tools looked a lot more aggressive than the normal, spade-type ripping tools.

John drove the dozer into the cut and lined up along one wall for the first test of the tool. He lowered the tools into the tough rock and gunned the dozer motor. These new tools penetrated the rock and started to rip. The dozer was not pulled off line, and instead of skipping along the top of the tough rock, the tools ripped it up. John got off the dozer and walked back to Tony, Bert, and Harry. 'What do you think of this?' Tony was amazed at the difference these tools made to the job. The tough rock seemed to explode in front of the tools, throwing up the pieces from hard rock with a puff of smoke. Bert and Harry were also impressed.

'You should have done this in the start. Just think of all the hard work you would have saved.' John agreed. It was farmers' thinking which had designed the tool. John had modified a lot of machinery when they were developing the farm. A lot of the machinery did not like crashing over stumps and stones.

Tony's feet and legs felt a lot better, thanks to the weekend break from walking. Back and forth he walked, carrying the pick and turning the stones over as the rippers pulled them from the solid tough rock.

At the end of the day, the rippers started to break through the hard rock. The bottom of the cut was starting to settle down now, and the solid rough stones were almost gone. The old dozer now made light work of ripping the soft sandstone around thirty-centimetre deep.

Where the level of hard stone had been, the walls of the cut had started to slope in. If they lost some of the width of the cut from crooked walls, they were also losing a lot of the floor area. John set to work with the corner of the dozer blade at an angle to the wall and peeled as much of this rock off as he could. This was extremely hard work on the old dozer.

When work was finished, John got the camera out of the utility and took a lot of photos of the new tools from different angles. He called in and told

Ivan all about the new experience on the way home. Ivan still insisted about the patent.

Some brown lines were beginning to appear in the floor of the cut. Bert told Tony to pay particular attention to the junctions where these lines met and also any changes in the colour of the sandstone, especially to a mustard colour as this usually meant that a level was not too far away.

The only things which Tony had seen in the last few days were a couple of thin pieces of potch. He did notice that when some of the sandstone were ripped, the shapes of shells were present, but only sandstone. 'Mud shells,' Bert had called them when Tony had shown some of them to him. *Bloody boring*, Tony thought to himself as he walked. He had convinced himself that the events of the first day when they found the opal would have continued every day.

The sandstone had appeared to be getting harder during the last couple of rips. Tony had noticed this but did not know what it meant. He was following the dozer closely when he noticed that the ground being ripped changed colour to a dark mustard brown. This must be the level which Bert had told him about. The cut was around four metres deep by now.

Tony had renewed his efforts in turning the stones over now and was following the dozer closely when he heard a sound like glass being cracked by the ripper tine as it was dragged through the solid rock. He looked hard at the place where this happened and noticed a very small reflection of the sunlight shining on the side of one of the larger rocks. Tony got his pick, and with an effort, he turned the large rock on to its back. The whole bottom of the rock was covered in opal. The fiery colours reflected off the opal as if the bottom of the rock was alight. John had just started to reverse the dozer back. Tony ran to the side of the tractor and waved for him to stop. John slowed the motor and then pushed the tractor's gears to neutral. He climbed down. 'Opal,' Tony croaked, not feeling the need for any other words.

The two men scratched at the rocks with their bare hands to turn as much of the opal-bearing rock over as they could, marvelling at each stone they turned.

John walked out of the cut, got the tools and sieves out of the ute, and then walked back down, carrying the awkward load. Tony was squatting next to a large stone, picking the smaller stones out from around it and inspecting each one carefully. He had two piles of rocks next to him: one, the barren sandstone, and the other, the rock with the opal stuck to it.

John looked around for a comfortable spot to work. Finally, he sat on a large rock, whilst he chipped the opal off the stone with the chisel point of his pick on to an old piece of canvas which Tony had handed him. Tony used a hammer and screwdriver to chip the material from the sandstone. The opals went into the bucket whilst the stone was rechecked and then discarded on to the barren pile. They were working quite a large hole out from where the opal had first appeared.

Bert and Harry had come up from the shaft and had walked down into the cut. 'I think your bank problems are over, my boy,' he told John as he looked into the bucket.

'Where were the holes you found the opal in when you drilled?'

'Not here,' Tony said, 'I reckon it was more towards the front of the cut. In fact, I'm sure it was I who lined the holes up with those stones. I placed next to the cut so I would have some idea of where to look. They are further towards the dump.' The men all went to work, getting the opal off the sandstone and into the bucket, ready to be carried out of the cut.

The seam of opal still continued into the sandstone where the ground had not been ripped, so John got back on to the dozer and revved the motor. He reversed back and then ripped the area slowly and very carefully. It was quite late when they had finally cleaned the pocket of opal right out. There were close to two twenty-litre drums full of rough opal.

'You realise that this is not all good saleable opal,' said Bert as they loaded the drums into the ute. 'There's still a lot of sandstone stuck to the opal, plus there's a certain amount of potch, but there's a hell of a lot of money in these buckets. A couple of hundred thousand dollars, I reckon.'

'That much?' John croaked with amazement. 'I think you should go to the Opal Miners Co op and buy a concrete mixer to tumble all of our opal. We will pay half.'

John and Tony called into the Opal Miners Co op to see about the concrete mixer. The miners Coop store had a concrete mixer for three hundred dollars. John bought it and also bought a nest of sieves to grade the opal into different sizes. The mixer was lifted with Tony's help, and he loaded it on to the ute tray amongst the tools.

John and Tony talked about what they would do to the farm with the money from the opal. The Lizard would be the first visit. They joked of all the different ways they would try to fix the Lizard when they paid the money.

When they got home to the dugout, the rough opal was tipped into the concrete mixer with some water and left to run to wear all the sandstone and grime off the opal. After running for an hour, the opal was tipped out through the nest of sieves. The sieves full of opal were then washed in a half two-hundred-litre drum full of water to get the grime off. The sieves were shaken and taken inside where the opal was sorted out from the potch. About a quarter of the opal was either potch or potch with a bar of opal in it. The opal was then put into plastic bags and stored in the safe.

The next morning, an hour after they had started, two car loads of aborigines turned up. The occupants walked up and settled down on the dump and then started to noodle by hand. There were about ten adults and ten kids. *They must have been stacked into the cars well*, John thought as he watched them scratch at the sandstone with steel rods shaped like spears. The women seemed to do most of the work. The men would do a bit of sieving now and then. When they thought that one of the women had found something good, they would confront them and usually take it from them, under protest.

When John started to push the dirt from where they found the opal the previous day, the aborigines quickly settled on to the fresh piles of worked dirt which were pushed up on to the dump. John could see them putting pieces into small shopping bags which they carried.

More opal came out of the next rip. A few others had turned up to noodle, including Silvio, Tom, and the part aborigine, Wombat, who seemed to be with them always.

How the hell did they find out, John wondered as they sat behind the dozer and dug the opal out.

'I thought I saw some aborigines watching us from over on the far dump yesterday. It doesn't seem as if you can keep too many secrets around here,' said Tony as he put some opal into the bucket. Bert and Harry came down to help them to gather up the opal. 'You blokes must be lucky. This is only the top level. You don't usually get too much opal in this level.'

Everything was cleaned up, so John reversed the dozer out of the cut and shut the motor off.

The aborigines had gone for quite some time, but Silvio and his mates had persisted, digging and watching intently. Finally, they walked over to their old ute and climbed in. The motor would not start; the battery was flat. The men tried to push the ute, but it was in the loosened, soft rough dirt the dozer had been driven over. Silvio walked over. 'Hey, boss, could you give us a push? The bloody basta she no go.' He tried to look into the bucket on the tray of the ute. Luckily, it had an old towel on top of it. 'You find some good opals today, hey.'

'Nah, only a bit of potch and colour. Get in to your ute. I'll give you a push with the bull bar on ours.' Tony had no intention of showing them the opal that they had just dug up. He got into the ute, started the motor, and drove around so he was lined up with Silvio's ute. He then pushed the bull bar up against their tray and gunned the motor, pushing the ute in front of him. Their old ute coughed into life and drove off. 'I don't like that little bastard,' he said to himself as he drove back to pick John up.

There was getting quite a pile of opal in the safe now. The bags were stacked one on top of the other.

The next morning, Tony filled the dozer with fuel, whilst John checked the oil and water. John climbed up on to the seat and turned the key to start the pilot motor. Nothing happened. *Bloody flat battery. It must have shorted out*, he thought. He lifted the battery cover to check the terminals. The battery was gone. Someone had stolen the battery after they had gone for the night.

John looked at the ground and noticed where someone had dragged something to get rid of any tracks. John was angry. He was sure he knew who the culprits were. But on thinking it over, people like these were known to have their revenge if they were dobbed in. 'Those crooks have pinched the battery out of the dozer. Get the ute close so we can use the jumper leads to start the pilot motor.' Tony got the ute and drove it next to the dozer.

'The bloody mongrels! I'll bloody have a piece out of them if they show up today,' growled Tony.

'No, we'll shut up about this. If we cause trouble, those types of men would just as likely fill the sump of the dozer up with sand or something else like wrecking the truck motor.'

The aborigines were back just after they started to work, not long after Silvio and his rotten mates showed up.

The day produced another small pocket of opal, not of a very good quality this time.

When John had shut the dozer off for the day, he noticed that when Silvio and the pirates got into the ute, the motor started with no trouble at all. *There's some real thieves around here. They're probably the mongrels who moonlighted our claim when we were away*, was Bert's thoughts on the day's activities.

That night when they filled the fuel drum up with diesel at the Opal Miners Co'op, John had to buy another battery for the dozer. He bought some latches and a padlock as well.

The next morning, John put the new battery into the dozer and then fitted the latches with pop rivets. He locked the battery box with a new padlock he had bought. 'Padlocks only keep out honest people,' warned Harry.

Tony noticed that during the next rip, they did not find any opal. The sandstone had mostly changed back to what it had been like before they had found the opal. A different type of material started to show. It was a soft moist, dirt-like grey ashes.

John pushed the dirt and then started to rip again. When he ripped through the ashy ground, Tony noticed the shape of shells on the edges of the soft sandstone. No flashes of colour could be seen. John looked around as he started to back up. Tony motioned for him to back nearly right back to where he was, out of sight of the noodlers.

Tony carefully picked out one of the shells and tapped it on the pick head. A brown skin fell off to reveal the beautiful colours of opal. All of the shells were covered in a brown coating of iron stone.

Tony showed the shell to John. John turned the shell so it caught the sunlight. 'Wow, this is pretty good opal. We'll try to get it out in large lumps, and then we'll clean it up at the dugout when we get home. The dozer hid them from the prying eyes of Silvio and the pirates, as they had become referred to by the men.

It did not take long to extricate the opalised shells from their nest, as the ashy ground was very soft. John took the bucket back to the side of the cut where they had been keeping it. By this time, Silvio had crept around from the rest of the noodlers to try and see what they were up to. He walked back when he saw that they had taken the bucket back to the side of the cut. Tony sat his hat on the top of the bucket and then put a stone on top of it to stop any prying eyes.

John got back on the dozer and continued ripping the floor of the cut.

Bert and Harry came down into the cut when they finished work. They had also found some opal. Harry had put the bucket inside their ute and locked the door.

'We found some really good shells today, but don't look in the bucket whilst the pirates are watching. I don't think they know. We picked them up pretty quickly and tossed them into the bucket whilst we were behind the dozer, I don't think we missed any. They were really easy to get out of the soft ground. That bloody Silvio crept down and tried to see what we were up to.'

John drove the dozer out of the cut past the noodlers and then turned back to the ute. 'Let's get back to town and have a couple of beers to wash the dust out of my throat.'

Whilst the first batch of opal was being tumbled in the concrete mixer, they had a good look at some of the shells which John and Tony had found. Bert scratched the outer coating off, some with his pocket knife. 'Look at this one, Harry.' The outer shell was only a cheap grey type of opal. There was a small piece chipped off the end of the shell, which revealed a totally different quality of opal underneath. 'Shit, I would not have known this. I thought the shell was only rubbish,' he said in awe as he passed it over to his brother. John took this shell from Harry. He got his pocket knife out of his pocket and prised the cracked end of the shell. One complete side of the solid shell came off, to reveal a completely different quality of opal underneath. The new opal shell was worth nearly ten times much as the poor one which they had seen for a start.

The others had separated the shells by this time. There were eighty-five full colour shells in the pile, plus a small amount of skin shell as well. 'This is a real top find, you lucky buggers. Beats the shit out of farming, don't it?'

Each lot of opal was left turning slowly in the tumbler for about an hour. John was amazed to see the difference when it was finally pulled out and then tipped on to a black polythene sheet on the kitchen table. The colours danced in the bright light as if they had a life of their own. It looked as if someone had poured metho on the stones and had set it on fire. The flames were dancing over the top of them. There were two mixers full of opals to clean, so it was a late night by the time they had finished. They had a job to concentrate from looking at the vivid colours. 'I think we'll have a day off from the field tomorrow and try to get this opal graded,' said Bert as he yawned. The opal must have had an effect on both Bert and Harry as they had forgotten to have their usual dozen cans of beer each that night.

The next day was spent cleaning the dead pieces of potch from the good opal. This was done with a pair of tile cutters. The pieces of opal were studied, and the dead pieces were cut off. Some of these pieces still had a small amount of colour. These were to be sold as potch and colour for a lesser amount. The shell material, which John and Tony had found the previous day, did not need much cleaning at all. The tumbler had cleaned all the rubbish off them, taking the coated grey opal as well. They were top crystal opal shells.

Bert looked at the shells and the other seam opal that John and Tony had dug up in the last two weeks. 'I reckon, there's about five or six hundred thousand dollars sitting just here. And you still haven't got to the main level where you dug the material up with the drill.'

Bert and Harry had over one hundred thousand dollars worth in their stash. 'I think we should see about selling some of this opal soon. I am getting a bit paranoid about this safe and how many people who might have keys for it,' said John.

Both John and Tony were surprised at how much the opal, which had filled all the buckets, had shrunk in volume by about a half when it was cleaned.

Bert went down to the town and phoned the opal classer to have a look at the opal, class it, and put a final price on the material. Then an opal buyer with enough resources to be able to pay what it was worth had to be found. This amount of opal was usually out of the small-time Chinese buyers league. They would sometimes buy a large parcel, only if they could con the owners.

Two o'clock up at north-west ridge. 'We'll see the pommy guy who classed our last lot of opal. He doesn't seem to be as big a crook as some we have tried before. There was a Greek, John, who looked at and classed our last lot and offered to buy it for fifteen thousand. We got fifty.'

They loaded the opal into the ute after lunch and headed out to the opal classer's house. Leon met them at the door of his house. 'Come on down to my classing room. The men entered the dugout room, which had the long table covered in black plastic and the assortment of chairs around the side. 'Take a pew,' offered Leon, the classer.

'Would you mind getting a round of beers out of the fridge?' he asked Tony. Tony obliged.

'Now let's see what you have got in the bags.'

'You guys have been busy.' Leon opened each bag of John and Tony and carefully tipped it out on to the tabletop. 'This is Fifteen Mile opal again, am I right?' They agreed. 'You've got some bloody good material here. Cripes, those shells are good.' Leon started to build little piles out of the opal, sometimes shifting a piece from one to another. It took a couple of hours to finish. He then weighed each pile, then put it into a new, clear plastic bag, and wrote the weight and a number on each bag. So many ounces and so many penny weights. Leon then studied each bag over and over, finally writing a price per ounce and then a price for each bag number on to a sheet of paper.

'If my reckoning is right, the grand total should be six hundred and twenty five thousand dollars. You're lucky. There's a guy in town at the present time who would be very interested in this parcel. His name is Achmed Farrah. I'll give you his mobile number if you like, or would you like me to try and phone him.' Leon wrote the number down on to the piece of paper with the prices on it.

'It might be easier if you would phone him,' added John.

Leon then proceeded to class the Kellys' opal. This came to one hundred and forty thousand dollars. 'OK, I'll ring this guy for you, if you like, and tell him about the opal.' The men sat, whilst Leon rang the buyer and described the parcel of opal to him. He then asked again how to get to the dugout they were renting. Leon told the buyer the relayed directions and then hung the phone back on to its hook. 'He reckons he knows where you are. He'll see you in an hour's time.'

The men left with the opal, all bagged up into its new bags ready for the buyer. To John, this seemed like a dream. It was only a few weeks ago that the bank was going to foreclose on them and they were going to be kicked off their farm. Now if all of this came off, there would be no more worries.

The hour wait seemed to take a hell of a long time. Finally, there was a knock on the door. Harry opened it up. Then ushered a plump, very well-dressed man with a short dark beard and dark olive skin. He carried a large briefcase into the room. Achmed politely introduced himself, then sat at the table, and talked of the opal business for a few minutes. 'Now I understand you have got some special opals to show me.'

Harry turned on the large desk lamp, whilst John passed the large bag with the opal in it. Achmed opened each bag and studied each lot. 'Hmm . . . ah . . . hmm,' Achmed said as he turned some of the better opals over in his hand. John and Tony were feeling a bit ill at the time from the tension. They had heard of the stories how the Chinese buyers wanted to get everything for half its value. Achmed put the opal back in the bags. *Oh shit*, John thought, *he's not interested.* Achmed smiled, showing a large gold tooth. 'What price have you got on your opal?' asked Achmed.

'Six hundred and twenty five thousand. That's what the classer classed it at.' John answered in a croaky voice. Achmed sat back in his chair.

'I see no point in beating around the bush, gentlemen. I will agree to that. Now there was another parcel, I understand.' Bert showed him their opal, which he agreed to buy also.

Achmed took the large briefcase he had brought with him. He opened it up on the table. On the top was a very large handgun. A Colt 45 automatic. Under this, the case was full of money. There were packs after packs of hundred-dollar bills pulled out. 'Now, gentlemen, I would like you to count and check all of this money. I have a reputation for fair dealing in the opal business, and I do not want anyone to say that I short-changed them.'

By the time both lots of money were counted out, the bag was nearly empty.

Achmed picked up the opal in the shopping bags and bid them farewell. 'If you ever find anything special again, I will be very interested. Have you got a piece of paper and a pen? I'll write down my Adelaide phone number.' Bert found a sheet of paper and a biro. Achmed wrote the number and his name on to it. He shook all of their hands. He then walked out the door. The men followed and watched as he got into the large Mercedes and drove off.

'Holy shit, I thought I was going to faint,' said John as he walked in through the door.

'Now what will we do with all of that money. I don't really feel like leaving it in this old safe. I don't trust that mob of pirates who watch us every day.' John agreed with Tony. The size of the bundle of cash was a problem. It was about two large shoe boxes in volume.

'What if I go and get the small toolbox out of the ute? I'll put the tools in the other toolbox.' Tony went out and got the toolbox. John and Tony jammed the money into the box and then shut its lid. John and Tony then went outside and dug a hole at the back of the old laundry and buried the cash. They kept out one of the bundles of notes for fuel and expenses. It was dark, so no one could have seen the twosome secreting the cash. They rolled an old drum back over the hole and flattened the dirt out.

'We'll just jam ours up under the dash of our ute. Ours isn't as big a stash as yours.'

John had a job to sleep that night. Every time he shut his eyes, he could see the flashing colours of the opal that they had been working with all day. In the morning, he grizzled to Tony about the bad sleep he had. Tony had experienced the same problem.

When they left for work, John walked past the drum which they had shifted the night before. It looked no different from the day before. There were no signs of the hole being dug.

The noodlers were still at the claim when they arrived. They had slept in; even Bert and Harry had not risen until nine o'clock.

John started the dozer, drove into the cut, and started the first rip for the day. Tony followed. The cut was about six metres deep by now. John spent a long time trying to square the walls of the cut-up again. He had a devil of a job, trying to keep the walls square when they were still in the hard material higher up. Now they were in the softer sandstone material, it was a lot easier.

Back and forth again with the dozer. The cash was on Tony's mind all day to think. Their problems with the bank were finally over. Tony's one thought was to see the look on the manager's face when they went in and paid the mortgage off. The day was fairly uneventful with only a small amount of potch being found.

The next day, the noodlers' numbers had dwindled; the aborigines had evidently found somewhere else more profitable to noodle. Silvio and the pirates still remained, though. John was hoping that they would have left too. John drove the dozer down the steep ramp into the cut. Tony followed with the bucket and tools.

During the first rip, Tony noticed that the ashy ground was starting to appear again. He scratched at it with his pick, but there was no sign of any shells.

John had finished pushing the dirt and was ripping through the ashy ground for the second rip, when Tony noticed a large, round piece of material roll out of the ash. John was looking over the back of the dozer. Tony motioned for him to stop.

John climbed down off the dozer and walked back. Tony was on the ground, carefully scratching the ripped ashy ground. He had two oval objects, each nearly as big as an emu egg, lying on the ground next to him. He was just carefully prising another out of its nest of the last hundred million years.

John picked up the egg, got his pocket knife out, and scratched at the coating on the egg. Finally, he made a small hole in the coating. He then turned the knife and prised the coating. A quarter of the coating came off in one piece, to reveal beautiful black opal underneath.

John was taken aback. He nearly dropped the opal. 'Holy Christ, these must be dinosaur eggs. And black opal. What would they be worth?' John handed the egg to Tony. Tony thought that no one could have seen them behind the dozer. He held the egg up to the light to get a better look at the colours. All the colours of the rainbow flashed back and forth across the dark curved surface. Tony carefully laid the egg into the bucket.

Both men worked carefully, extricating the eggs from the nest. John looked up and noticed that Silvio had walked along the top of the cut again and was watching them with great interest. There were four eggs. All had been heavily coated so the colour could not be seen. Tony took the bucket back to the wall of the cut. He put a couple of pieces of the ashy stone on top of the eggs so Silvio could not see into the bucket.

They finished the rip and then pushed the dirt out. It was home time by now.

'We think we may have got something pretty special today,' John told Bert as they loaded the ute.

'We'll have a look when we get back home.' He motioned with his thumb to the band of pirates who were still watching. 'I reckon that the crooked little bugger saw the opal when you held it up to the sunlight.'

John carried the bucket into the dugout. He sat at the table and carefully took the first egg out of the bucket. He took a kitchen knife from near him on the table-top and scratched the rough coating on another egg. It resisted his efforts for a while until John was able to make a crack in its surface. He got the point of the knife under it and twisted the blade. About a quarter of the coating fell off in one piece, the same as the first egg had done. All of the men were dumbfounded by what they saw. 'Christ, it's solid black opal. The same as the last one,' croaked Harry. 'If the others are the same, these are worth millions.' John repeated the exercise with the other two eggs with the same result.

Chapter 6

The men sat around the table, admiring the opalised eggs. They turned them over and over under the desk lamp. They were almost hypnotised by the array of changing colours, which flashed brilliantly across the surfaces of the eggs. There were scattered beer bottles on the table from the celebratory drinks which had accompanied their meal. John was deep in thought. 'I've got a funny feeling about that old safe. I don't trust those bloody pirates who have been watching us every day. I reckon that we should head off out of town back to the farm with the opal and money. I would feel a lot happier if I was at home with all of this opal. We can easily come back later and finish the cut.'

'We will still keep our cash up under the dash of our ute. No one would know,' said Bert.

'I wouldn't worry about the bags of potch and colour.' These had not been sold to Achmed with the parcel of opal. He was not interested in buying potch and colour. 'Anyway half of that is yours,' said John.

Tony went outside and looked around to see if there was anyone nearby. The coast was clear. He shifted the drum and then dug the cash out of its hiding place. Tony then dusted the toolbox off and brought it inside to the table.

It was just getting dark when John and Tony had finally loaded the ute. The two-hundred litre drum on the back was still half full. This would mean that they could get home without having to fill at a service station in the middle of the night.

Tony put the toolbox full of money on the seat of the ute next to where he sat. The bag of opal eggs was put under the passenger seat. They both shook hands and thanked Bert and Harry for their change of fortune, then slid into the ute, and drove off. 'Well, good luck. We'll see you when you have your millions,' chuckled Harry as they left the dugout. The men waved goodbye.

The ute was filled with fuel at the new service centre. 'Hell, look at the price of their fuel. It's nearly ten cents dearer than we are paying. It must be good to be a tourist not knowing the difference.' The ute was finally filled and the fuel paid for. The men drove off out of town into the dusk. It was hard driving at night because of the kangaroo problem on the roadside. The large driving light mounted in the middle of the bull bar made it a lot easier to see off the side of the road. There were a few newly run-down kangaroos on and next to the road. Occasionally, John had to swerve to miss one of the hapless animals which had been recently run over. The occasional road train with its ultra-bright lights was the only traffic on the road.

The longer that John drove, the more the shrubby bushes on the roadside looked like kangaroos. Tony had drifted off to sleep by this time. It was very tiring, trying to concentrate by now. So many things were on John's mind at the present time. The thought of seeing Helen, the farm, and especially the opal they had to sell. This did help to keep him awake.

The men reached the Kingoonya turn-off. John drove down the dirt road for a couple of kilometres and stopped. 'Right, sleepy head, your turn to drive.' Tony woke groggily, got out of the ute, and walked a short distance off the road to have a pee. The desert air was like ice, which helped to wake him properly. 'How about starting to fill the diesel tank whilst you are out there? It will wake you up.' Tony started to fill the ute from the drum, pushing the pump handle back and forth.

Driving on the dirt road was worse than the bitumen. The shadows cast by the lights were really tiring. Even with the large spotlight on, the shadows still seemed to move as the ute neared. Tony had to concentrate when he came to a cross road so he did not get lost. The road looked completely different in the dark. John had long since gone to sleep. Tony was close to sleep as he drove on. He had two frightening experiences: one with a few sheep which had camped on the road, and the next was a kangaroo which had hopped across in front of him, but thankfully, they had not stopped or turned back and had kept going.

Tony was trying to keep himself awake by thinking of the opal and the farm. His mind kept wandering off. Suddenly, the whole of the road in front of the ute seemed to be filled with a huge roo. The roo had come from behind a small bush and was hopping across the road and had stopped, evidently dazzled by the bright lights of the ute. It squatted down and turned to face the bright lights coming towards it. Tony hit the brakes and swerved, trying to miss the kangaroo, but it was too late. The kangaroo hopped the same way as Tony swerved. The ute slammed into the huge kangaroo. By this time, Tony was well off the dirt track and into the small shrubby bushes. The ute bounced wildly as it careered across the grader ridge left on the side of the dirt track. The ute then swerved madly, leaning sickeningly, almost tipping over. John sat bolt upright. 'What the hell has happened? Where the hell are we?' He slurred sleepily. The ute finally stopped.

'We've hit a bloody huge roo,' Tony informed him. He put the ute in reverse and reversed slowly back on to the road. The ute was making a grinding noise in the front as it went backwards to the road.

'Well, that's great. I think we must have busted something. Cripes, what a place to be marooned. We're a hundred kilometres from nowhere.'

John and Tony both got out to inspect the damage with the torch, which lived under the seat of the ute for emergencies. John got down on his haunches and shone the torch under the ute. 'Well, thank god for that. We've still got our lights, and the radiator seems OK. No water dripping. There's no oil dripping out either. Just drive on slowly, whilst I see if I can pinpoint the noise.' John shone the torch towards where the noise was coming from and found that the front mudguard had been bent against the tyre. He was able to pull it off by hand. 'Bloody hell, that was lucky. If the diesel tank had been full, I reckon I may have rolled the ute.' The heavy farm-built bull bar had taken the brunt of the impact on the passenger side of the vehicle. Even the driving light was still in place. The impact with the roo had bent back the bull bar almost to the bonnet. One side indicator light had been torn off in the collision.

Tony reversed back to check the roo. It was very dead. John got out of the ute and pulled it off the road so no one else would run over it and smash their vehicle.

'Hell, that was a big roo. I had a job to pull it off the road. Oh shit, smell my hands.' John was covered with the musty smell, which only a buck kangaroo can smell like. 'The old bastard must have been chasing the does around lately.' Roos, like a lot of other animals, always smelt a lot worse when they were in season. 'Oh shit!' John started to scratch and squirm.

'That old buck must have had kangaroo ticks. I can feel them running around under my clothes.' Tony looked over at John. 'Just make sure you stay over your side of the seat. I got those on me one night when I was out spotlighting with a couple of mates. They nearly drove me mad.'

Tony took a lot more care, watching for the rest of the journey. Having a bad accident on these barely used roads could be very dangerous, as there may not be any cars along for a long time.

John still wriggled and scratched. *It'll keep him alert at least*, Tony thought.

The sun was just showing the first streaks of red on the horizon as he drove up the drive to the house. They could hear the dogs barking as they pulled into the rear of the house. Helen opened the door and walked out through the back gate in her nightie and dressing gown just as the men got out of the utility. Helen yawned. 'What are you doing home?' she asked sleepily. 'I knew it was you from the way the dogs barked.'

The morning air was very crisp. A light frost lay on the ground. After the warmer climate of Coober Pedy, the men felt frozen. They hurried into the house. Helen stoked the fire back into life, tossed some more sawn wood through the grate door, and then filled the old blackened cast-iron kettle with water. Tony had brought the old toolbox into the kitchen. 'Have a look in there, Mum.' Helen lifted the lid and then carefully tipped the contents of the box out on to the table. She gasped.

'How much money is there? There must be hundreds of thousands of dollars!' John sat the other bag on the table next to the money.

'That's not all. Look at these.' He carefully lifted one of the eggs which was wrapped in layers of newspaper out of the bag and undid the wrapping, leaving the egg sitting in the middle of the newsprint nest. The colours rolled over the dark base of the egg. It was spectacular even in the dull light of the kitchen. Helen's eyes widened as she looked at the black opal. Helen, as a lot of people, had never seen any really good opal before. She was fascinated with its dancing colours over the egg.

'What would that be worth?' she asked incredulously.

'Somewhere around a million dollars, we think. There are three others.'

John had warned Helen not to touch him because of the kangaroo tick problem. He went outside and stripped down to his undies, tossing his clothes into the wash trough. John turned the hot tap on and then rummaged in the laundry cupboard for a bottle of dog shampoo which was used when the dogs had fleas. *Drastic measures for drastic problems*, he thought. No wonder the roo was not worried about being run over. John poured a liberal amount of shampoo on the infected clothes. Then after turning the tap off, he adjourned to the shower in the laundry, with the bottle of dog shampoo. John threw his undies in the shower cubicle and then proceeded to soap himself down with the shampoo, starting with his hair, which felt as if it was the local tick race track. He pushed his feet up and down, making sure the undies got a fair coating of the shampoo.

Tony went on to explain to Helen about the doubts they had in the old safe and also the men whom they rented the dugout from.

John had another shower when he finally woke just after midday. 'I know why those bloody dogs go so crazy after we give them the flea treatment. Hell, the shampoo gets bloody hot on your skin.'

John and Tony went for an inspection of the farm after lunch. Things had changed dramatically since they had left. The crops no longer looked grey; they were now a dark shade of green and had started to stool out well. Even the pasture paddocks had changed to green; the sheep now sat contentedly in the corner of the paddock, feeding every now and then. There had not been much rain but just enough to change the farm's fortune.

John rummaged through his case and found the piece of paper which Achmed had written his Adelaide phone number down on. John phoned Achmed that evening and told him of the eggs. Achmed was amazed. He had never heard of any eggs ever being found before. There had been the occasional opal bones of some sea creatures, plus, very rarely, a few turtles had been found. He sounded amazed by the description and weight. They had been weighed on the kitchen scales. He was very interested in purchasing such rarities. John arranged to meet him in Adelaide in two days' time at his home, where he had his office.

Helen rang the bank and made an appointment to see the manager. It was made for the next day after lunch. John was eagerly looking forward to this meeting.

The trip to town was a more joyous occasion than the last visit to the bank. How different they felt! Even the old car didn't seem to rattle as much. No more having to grovel to unpleasant people.

They entered the small bank building and told the teller that they were present. She buzzed the manager and informed him that they were waiting.

The manager evidently had another farmer in his office. The sounds of a heated argument emanated from behind the door. Finally, a red-faced man emerged from the office. 'I hope you have more luck in there,' he said, pointing his thumb in an obscene gesture towards the manager's office, knowing that the manager could still hear him. He stormed out of the door.

The manager met them with his superior smile, more like a smirk—*the look of a lizard as it was about to pounce on a small beetle and gobble it up*, Tony thought. He ushered them into his office and bade for them to sit down. The Lizard sat down at his desk and shuffled the wad of papers with their name on them in front of him. He leaned back in his chair and then looked up at them, over the top of his steel-rimmed glasses; the smirk seemed more obvious. The Lizard knew what John's opinion of him was. 'We still seem to have this major problem of your overdraft. You have not made any attempt to change this situation in the last four weeks. You had better start to make arrangements to sell some of your farm to recover some moneys to rectify this problem in the next week, or the bank will have no option but to place you in receivership and sell it ourselves to try to recoup the moneys you owe us.' He looked up at them with his superior sneer.

John reached over to the folder of papers in front of the Lizard and pulled them towards him. The Lizard jumped up and tried to get the papers back. 'These are the property of the bank,' he squeaked.

John started to tear the papers up. There were too many papers in this sheaf to rip through them in one go. 'I'll get the police on to you. You'll go to jail,' squeaked the Lizard once again. John reached down to the floor and picked all the papers which had dropped. He then put the torn papers back on to the desk. He stood and then leaned towards the Lizard, towering over his small frame.

'You know that things have not been any good on the farm for the last few years. We have been trying our hardest to get the money. We do not appreciate being bullied by a sanctimonious little arsehole like you. You should be ashamed of yourself for treating all the good people in this area the way you have. It's small wonder that someone has not thumped you for your insulting remarks that you have been making to everyone.'

The manager had not had this treatment before. The smirk disappeared from his face, to be replaced by a vicious sneer. 'I see that I cannot reason with you,' he said icily. 'The only recourse the bank has is to put your farm on the market forthwith.'

'I don't think you will do that,' said John in a matter-of-fact voice. 'How much do we owe you?' John already knew this to the cent but wanted the Lizard to still think he had the upper hand. The Lizard shuffled through the torn papers.

'The sum is 74,522 dollars.' He smirked again.

John pushed the torn papers aside on the desk and then lifted the bulging shopping bag on to the desktop. The Lizard cowered back in fright, evidently thinking that there must have been a gun or something else very unpleasant in the bag. John picked the bag up by one corner and tipped the contents on to the desktop. The Lizard's mouth fell open in surprise at the sight of the money. His prominent Adam's apple poked further out of his scrawny neck and moved up and down as he gulped. John had left three hundred thousand in the bag just for the effect. 'Now if you would count out what we owe you, we will get out of your office so you can have your nasty way with the next poor victim who has to see you.'

The Lizard's superior attitude vanished as he set about counting the money. He had to go out and get the change for the amount owing. 'I would like a receipt now. Thank you.' The Lizard fumbled in his desk and finally produced a receipt book and hand-wrote a receipt for the amount of the debt which had just been paid.

'I think that will be all.' John bundled the rest of the money back into the bag and then led the family out into the sunshine. 'What was that they said about revenge being sweet? I feel as if I have just had a sugar cube dipped in honey in my mouth. Wow, what a feeling!'

The rest of the day was spent paying some of the other outstanding accounts in the town. Finally, after paying another twenty-five thousand dollars, mainly to the stock firm for the stock mortgage, their slate was all square.

John took the camera into the chemist shop to have the digital photos put on a disk and had them printed off. Helen was very interested in the look of the new tools.

'I'll never forget the look on the Lizard's face when I dropped the bag on to his desk. He must have thought it was a bomb.'

'Well, I feel as if we have had a weight lifted from our shoulders,' said Helen as they drove back to the farm.

Tony got the cash and counted out fifty thousand dollars out of it. He then wrapped the remainder in plastic and then sealed it into a five-gallon paint drum, which had a tight-fitting lid. Tony picked up the drum by the steel handle and carried it over to the workshop where he found a posthole shovel. Tony then walked around to the machinery graveyard behind the shed and buried the drum under an old, wrecked header right behind the workshop. When he returned to the house, he explained exactly where he had buried the drum.

John rang a man he knew at Cleve who owned and chartered a light aircraft. John chartered him to fly them to Adelaide the next day.

They drove the old car from the farm to the Kimba airfield and sat in the car, waiting for the plane to appear. Soon after they arrived, the small plane could be seen circling ready to land. The pilot Peter Schubert got out and helped pack their luggage into the rear of the plane. 'I hear that you had a run-in with your friendly bank manager,' he said with a laugh. News travels fast in the bush. This news had travelled to the next town.

'Yes, revenge is sure sweet. We had a lucky find at Coober Pedy and were able to pay the little twirp what we owed the bank.' John put the bag of opal on the wing of the plane and opened it. 'Have a look at these.' Peter looked into the bag as John unwrapped one of the eggs. The colour flooded out of the bag as the egg caught the sunshine.

'Shit, what would that be worth?' asked Peter in a reverent voice.

'This is what we hope to find out in Adelaide. A bloke wants to buy them.'

The three got into the light aircraft with the pilot for the trip to Adelaide. The pilot got into his seat. John sat next to him. 'I wish you luck in the city with the opal,' he said just before he started the plane's motor. The opal had been wrapped up again in the tissue paper and then a newspaper and put back into the sports bag. Helen had packed a few clothes for the trip. 'Just think, girl, no more money worries. You can have a shopping day in the city for the next week.'

Helen was uncomfortable about flying in the small aircraft. She had never flown before. Both John and Tony had flown with Peter, who owned the plane, which they were travelling in now.

The plane taxied across the bumpy airstrip prior to take-off. Helen had a large lump in her throat. She was not happy about this flying racket at all. Finally, she settled down and even started to enjoy the trip, looking out of the window and marvelling at the scene which was passing underneath them.

The plane landed bumpily at the Parafield light aircraft airport. Even though she had started to enjoy the flight, Helen's knuckles were still white from having her hands clasped tightly around the edge of the seat all the way over.

This was only Helen's second time in the city. The last time was when she was a teenager with her parents. She had come over to see an eye specialist then, for treatment for a lazy eye. The trip then was only from the bus station to North Adelaide for the specialist visit and then straight back on to the bus for Kimba. Helen was amazed at the mansions they passed in the cab on the way out to Achmed's home. The leafy tree-lined streets were also different to what Helen had imagined the city to be like. Achmed's house really impressed her—the high wrought-iron fence and gates and then the beautiful bungalow-styled home inside them. The roses and lawn were neatly manicured.

Tony had told the cab driver to toot the horn three times to have the gate opened. These had been the instructions which Achmed had given them. The heavy gates opened slowly to allow them entry to the circular driveway, which led to the front of the home. The edge of the circular drive was bordered with lovely rose bushes; all the roses had beautiful pastel-coloured blooms.

When they had alighted from the cab, the back gates shut, whilst the ones in front of the cab opened. Achmed walked out of the house. 'Welcome, good people, to my home. Would you please follow me inside?' They walked on to the tiled verandah and then through the heavy oak doors in the doorway, which had multi-coloured lead light on each side. The lead light threw a scatter of colour through the inside of the large lounge room. This reminded John of the recent opal finds. They entered the room. Helen was amazed at the inside of the house. The expensive furnishings were only something that she had seen in magazines. Such opulence was beyond her wildest dreams.

Achmed's wife, a pretty small, olive-skinned woman walked out of the large kitchen. 'This is my wife, Fatima.' John introduced himself, Helen, and Tony. Fatima asked if they would like some coffee before they got down to business. They spent around twenty minutes making small talk, whilst Fatima served the coffee.

The coffee was served in tiny cups and was extremely strong, and the home-made sweet biscuits were so delicate in flavour. Helen was almost too afraid to sit on the furniture.

'Would you like to stay and talk to Fatima whilst we men look at the opal?' offered Achmed. Helen would have rather watched the opal being sold but felt that good manners dictated that she stay and talk to Achmed's wife.

The men followed Achmed through the house to the rear. They were confronted by a large steel door, which had a heavy lock on it. Achmed opened the door with the keys from a key chain, which was attached to his belt, and then entered the room. John and Tony followed. There were some opal-cutting machinery next to one wall, whilst almost all the other walls consisted of a huge safe. This safe was a far cry from the one in the old dugout at Coober Pedy. This one looked almost new. There was a huge desk. Achmed walked around the desk and sat in the heavily padded chair.

'I am so excited. I want to see this opal to see if it is as good as you say.' John put the bag on to the desk and opened the top. He carefully lifted one of the eggs out of the bag. John then proceeded to remove the wrapping. Achmed turned on the desk lamp. John placed the first egg in front of Achmed. Achmed's eyebrows arched. 'My god, this is even better than I thought it may be.' He turned the egg in the light, fascinated by the colour changes which took place. 'Are all the others the same?' he croaked, his voice full of emotion. John proceeded to undo the rest from their wrapping. Achmed was amazed.

Achmed pulled out a drawer on the desk, took out a set of opal scales, and then set them up on the desk. He put one of the four eggs into the dish of the scales and weighed it. Achmed repeated this gesture with the other three eggs and then added the total weight of the eggs together. 'Those kitchen scales are not too bad. The weights are almost the same.'

Achmed was deep in thought. He picked up each egg and turned it over and over. 'This is very unusual to have so much opal almost the same. They are almost identical.' Achmed leaned back in the chair, deep in thought. 'I am willing to offer you 800,000 each for these eggs. That is 3.2 million dollars for all of them. Are you interested?' John felt a little faint at the thought of all the money.

'Yes, we are definitely keen to sell,' he finally said when his wits had returned.

Achmed got up from his chair and walked around the desk to John and Tony. He shook them both by the hand. Achmed put the eggs back into the paper and then the bag and then walked over to the large safe. With his back to the men, he proceeded to punch the combination into the door. Achmed then turned the lock and opened the large safe door. It opened with a hiss of rushing air.

Achmed removed a large leather case from the safe. The large leather case was placed on to the desk. Then Achmed put the eggs into the safe, leaving its door open.

John had noticed that there had appeared to be drawers and more drawers full of material in the safe.

The case was opened, and the neatly packed money lifted out and counted by both parties. When the figure was finally reached, Achmed tipped the remaining money from the case and then replaced it with the counted notes. 'I think that completes our deal, gentlemen. I hope you are satisfied.'

'Would you like me to phone a cab for you?' John agreed. 'What about accommodation? Are you staying in the city?' John had not thought of this as his mind had only been on selling the opal.

Achmed rang the Sheraton Hotel and booked a room for Helen, John, and Tony. 'You must have a bit of luxury for you and your wife.' Then he called the cab.

During the trip back to the city, Helen recounted the tour of the garden that Fatima had taken her on. The beautiful roses, shrubs, and lawns had really impressed her. 'Well, darling, after all of your hard work and going without, it looks as if it's finally your turn to enjoy life. You will be able to have a proper garden too.'

The cab pulled into the hotel driveway, and as in the movies, a doorman opened the cab door for them. John felt as if the hotel staff would look down on the dilapidated luggage and their clothes.

Being waited on at the hotel in the elegant surrounds was a change from their normal frugal lifestyle.

The next morning, John gave Tony some cash from the bag of money they had brought from the farm. Tony was going off to buy himself a new utility, a thing he had only dreamt of a few weeks ago.

After a hearty breakfast in their room, John and Helen went down to the hotel office and retrieved the suitcase full of money and booked a cab to pick them up. They waited for the cab in the foyer of the hotel, worrying about the suitcase full of money at their feet. They told the cab driver to take them to the nearest large bank.

The cab pulled in, and John paid, as Helen alighted with the heavy suitcase. John walked over to information counter and asked the woman where they could see about leaving something in a safety deposit box. The only times they had seen this done before was in the movies on the television. The whole routine was similar to what they had seen. They had been directed to a teller who had them sign and pay for the box. Then they were ushered into the bowels of the bank through security doors to the deposit area. John had obtained some bags from the teller. They unlocked the large steel door of the box and withdrew the drawer. Helen opened the case and started to transfer the money from the case into the bags. John neatly stacked these into the drawer of the deposit box. Finally, he closed the heavy drawer and locked it with the key which had been provided. They walked from the bank with the now-empty case and hailed a cab to take them back to the hotel.

John looked through the phone book in the room and found a list of patent attorneys. He rang one of the numbers and spoke to the attorney for about ten minutes regarding the new tool they had designed. A time was made to visit the firm the next day.

The attorney's office was not far from the hotel. So they had a map drawn by one of the counter staff to show the way. They were ushered into a large office and met two men. They explained a lot about the patenting process, where to file patents, and what countries they should file in. The main point was a search to find if there was a similar type of tool already patented. Drago, the main attorney, looked at the photographs, sent them to be copied, and then started an account for the cost of the patent search. He commented that he had never seen a tool patent like this before. The meeting was over, and the pair walked back to the hotel.

CHAPTER 7

Silvio Tom and Wombat walked down on to the floor of the cut where Tony had found the opal eggs earlier in the day. Silvio had seen a brilliant flash of colour over a black background—the unmistakable colours of top black opal. The men had a scratch around but could not find any opal. 'Hey, look at this.' Wombat held up a piece of skin, the poor quality grey opal filled with sand, which Tony had prised off the first egg he had found.

'It looks as if it had an egg in it,' said Tom as he carefully turned the skin over in his hand. 'Have you ever heard of an opal egg? he asked the other two. They both shook their heads. 'Must have come off a big shell.' 'No, I haven't seen any shells this shape before. It looks more like a big eggshell,' said Silvio.

The men walked out of the cut and drove back to town from noodling. They drove along the main street through the town past the Council Depot and then stopped outside a small, corrugated iron house, which was set well back on a large fenced block, which was on the outskirts of the town. There was a sign 'Opal Buyer' nailed to the door by one nail; the sign swung in the wind. The house was surrounded by the usual old, wrecked mining machinery.

Silvio got out of the ute, walked up, and banged on the door. The door opened slightly, and a man peeped out through the crack.

The man who looked out would really have qualified for the title of a pirate. The thin man of part Asian and part Arabic appearance had a large scar on his left cheek, which caused his left eye to be permanently half closed. This was the result of a fight he had in his younger days. He did not fight his own fights now. He was too wise for that now. He had other people do his dirty work for him.

The man opened the door further and waved for them to enter. 'Come on, hurry up,' he said grumpily. The man scratched at the large scar on his face. He usually did this when he was annoyed at something or someone. It

———

92

was as if scratching the scar reminded him of the time he had acquired it. His skin was weather-beaten, and to top the pirate image off, he had a large gold earing dangling from one ear. He was known as the Dragon.

Over the years, the Dragon had been the mastermind behind a lot of the robberies and murders in the town. He was smart enough not to be directly involved in the crimes. He usually had other people do his dirty work whilst he always reaped the lion's share of the reward. The Dragon usually bought the opal which had been moonlighted or stolen by any other means.

Belying the image of the rough iron house, this man was extremely wealthy. He owned properties all over Australia and had a large factory in China cutting and setting opal jewellery.

'Hey, boss, you know those farmers we told you about the other day at the Fifteen Mile. I saw them dig a big bit of black opal out about an hour ago. There may have been more. They put a lot of stuff in the bucket. Here have a look at this.' Silvio handed the outer piece from the egg to the Dragon.

'Hmm, where did this come from?' Silvio explained about the opal again.

'I think this came off the opal they found.'

'What do you want me to do about it?' said the Dragon in a high, raspy voice. He scratched at the scar on his face again.

'We reckon they go out nearly every night to the pub with the old cockies they are staying with in your dugout. Let us have the keys to the safe. We'll pinch the opal and any money they have got tonight.'

The Dragon agreed to this simple plan. It sounded very easy. He left and went into the bedroom of the shack and came out with two keys joined together. 'Don't open the front door with this one. Kick the door in. It's not very strong. Then use the safe key and get the opal. Make it look like a proper robbery. I know of at least two other people in town who have got keys for the safe, so it would be hard to prove who broke in, unless you are stupid and leave your fingerprints all over the place or get caught in the act. Wear the gloves like I have told you before. Here take these.' The Dragon reached into one of the kitchen drawers and got some thin surgical gloves out of a packet. He handed these to Silvio.

The men drove off from the Dragon's shack and went to the hotel to wait until it was properly dark.

The trio drove the old ute from the pub and then the Italian Club looking for the farmers. Bert and Harry were at the Italian Club. Their ute was parked outside. John and Tony's ute was nowhere to be seen. 'Where's those other bastards? They always go to drink together. Bloody bastards.'

They then drove up through the old water reserve, then around the back of the hill above, and behind where the dugout was and, then with an effort in the half dark, climbed to the top and looked down on to the dugout's small yard, which was just visible in the moonlight. The top of the hill was very rocky, covered in round stones, which, if a person was not careful, would shoot out from under his feet. 'You see them fellers anywhere?' asked Wombat.

'No. You had better climb down and have a look,' said Silvio.

'Bugger you, it's bloody dark. I'll fall down the cliff and break my neck.'

'What about you, Tom?'

'Get stuffed.' Tom was no surer of making the descent unharmed as was Wombat.

Amongst the rocks, there were small shrubby plants, everyone having prickles, some were very nasty, having thin spines about a centimetre long, which, when got into the skin, usually broke off and took a lot of getting out.

'I can't see the ute there. Why don't we drive around to the front of the dugout?'

'What and leave our tracks, you dopey prick, and probably get caught if someone comes back?' The men walked back to the ute. 'All right, get the tyre levers out of the ute. We'll all go down and have a look.'

The first couple of steps over the side of the steep cliff face caused Tom to slip. He clutched madly for something to stop himself from sliding to the bottom. He managed to grab one of the shrubs. It was one of the worst prickly ones he could have chosen. 'Bugger,' he mumbled and then let go. Then he rolled into Wombat, knocking him over also. They both rolled to the bottom.

'Clumsy bastards. Have you still got the tyre levers?'

'Yes, of course, I have.'

Silvio had a hessian potato bag with him so they could carry the spoils. 'You two stay out of sight.' Tom and Wombat waited in the shadows cast by the half moonlight, whilst Silvio knocked lightly on the door. He knocked again. No one answered. The nearest dugout was around the corner of the cliff some fifty metres away, out of sight. 'Come on, down here, and give me a hand.' The men quietly sidled up next to him.

'These pricks must be out visiting someone. Here put these gloves on.' Tom and Silvio rolled the rubber gloves on to their hands. Tom had some extra trouble getting the gloves over the ends of the spines stuck into his fingers. 'Dopey bugger,' mumbled Silvio. 'Hurry up. If anyone had answered the door, I was going to tell that we had broken down. Right prise, the door opened. You stay out here and keep watch, Wombat. Let me know if you see any lights coming.'

The old door was easily prised open. The dry, rotten door jamb splintered easily, allowing the door to be opened. The two men slipped inside. Silvio handed a small torch to Tom. 'Don't shine it towards the door. One of the neighbours may see you. Everything OK out there?' he called softly to Wombat.

'No one coming yet,' called back Wombat.

Tom shone the torch, whilst Silvio opened the old safe. It squealed as it usually did as the door was opened. Tom had the thin surgical gloves on. 'Here shine the light on these bags. Let's have a look.'

'There's lights coming along the road,' called Wombat softly through the doorway. 'Bugger! Here, you hold the bag open, whilst I put all these bags into it.'

The job was soon finished. Silvio shut the safe again. They ran out of the door. The lights were getting closer. 'Quick, let's hurry up.' They ran around the side of the hill so the ute lights wouldn't pick them up. They then scrabbled up the side of the steep hill, losing a lot of skin as they went.

They watched the Kellys' old ute pull in front of the dugout. The two dogs, which seemed to live on the tray, barked as they stopped. Bert and Harry got out. Harry was just going to open the door, when he saw the broken door jamb. 'Hey, Bert, some prick's been here and broken in.' The two men rushed inside. The dogs followed behind them.

The three men stood puffing at the side of the ute. 'Jesus, that was close. We had better drive a way without the lights.' By this time, their eyes had become accustomed to the dark. They drove off slowly in the dark.

'Lucky the bloody moon was up a bit,' said Wombat as the ute crawled slowly along the road. 'Bloody lucky the old coots didn't catch us,' added Silvio.

The men drove back through the town and stopped outside the Dragon's house.

Silvio banged on the Dragon's door. 'Oi, open up. It's us.' The Dragon opened the door slowly and peered out through the crack.

'Don't make so much noise,' he hissed. 'I thought it might have been the cops looking for you,' he said as he opened the door fully to let them in. 'Hurry up. I don't want the neighbours seeing you here.'

The men entered the shack, blinking at the bright light. 'Those old bloody cockies came home early. We nearly got caught inside the dugout. We couldn't see the others anywhere.'

'Well, let's see what you have got,' hissed the Dragon. Silvio carefully took the bags out of the sugar bag and laid them on the table. The Dragon opened the first bag. 'Well, you didn't do any good with this bag, you useless turds. It's only potch and colour.' The rest of the bags were opened on to the table. 'Well, that was a good night's haul, you useless bludgers, about three thousand dollars worth. Not three million,' said the Dragon sarcastically. Silvio was angry.

'The rotten bastards, I have seen them take a lot of opal out of the claim in the last three weeks. That's right, isn't it, you blokes?' The other men nodded their heads in assent. 'There's not even any blasted money. We heard they sold some good opal to the Arab for a lot of money.'

'Useless pricks!' The Dragon shook his head. 'Those old buggers were even getting opal. We saw them sort through the bucket when they came out of the shaft.'

'Well, you had better tick off home and let me think about this. I just hope for your sakes the cops don't come around,' said the Dragon sarcastically.

'Those crooked bastards must have hidden the opals somewhere else. Christ, don't anyone trust anyone around here any more?' grumbled Silvio.

They drove home to the grotty dugout they shared. 'You may not have seen the opal they dug out yesterday, but you saw what they were getting on the other days. What about what we and the abos noodled in their dump? There were some pretty good opal there.'

The next morning, they went out to the claim to noodle again, mainly to check if John and Tony were working. The dozer was not working.

The men kept on noodling until finally Bert and Harry emerged from the shaft. Wombat sidled over to them. 'Where's the dozer driver and the boy, boss?' he asked.

'They had to go home to shear the sheep,' lied Harry.

'They get some pretty good opal?' angled Wombat.

'Nah, only a little bit,' said Bert. 'Why?' Wombat just shook his head and then walked back to the pirates.

'Them cunts have gone home. That's what them old buggers said.'

The pirates got into their ute and drove off. 'I reckon they're the arseholes who broke in last night. I'd bet my balls on it. I bet they were happy to find our potch and colour instead of the opal and cash.'

'Hey, boss, what you find out about the opal?' Silvio had told him about the farmers going back home.

'I ask around today. That Achmed, he was up here the other day. The rumour was that he bought a lot of opals from some broken-down farmers.'

'Hey, maybe you're not such a dumb cunt after all, Silvio. You heard the story right.' Silvio felt privileged. This was as close to a compliment that he had ever got from the Dragon.

'I told you we noodled some bloody good opal from the dump. That's the stuff we showed you the other day. The stuff you bought off us.'

The Dragon scratched at the large scar on his cheek and thought for a while. 'I reckon those pricks may have found something pretty good like you said. I have been thinking all day. There may be a way we get plenty of money if this is true.'

The Dragon sat down at the table. He motioned for the others to sit. The Dragon thought for a while. 'I want you guys to go down to Adelaide and pinch a car each. One of you is to keep watch on the Parafield airport, the one the little planes use out by Gawler. There are only two opal buyers who would be able to buy a big parcel if it is as big as you say, in Adelaide. All the others in South Australia wouldn't have enough money. The farmers have already dealt with Achmed. I think they would deal with him again. I want you to watch both houses. I'll find the addresses of both of them.' The Dragon rummaged around in a large roll-top desk, which sat next to the rusty safe. He finally found the address of both of the buyers. The Dragon took a small cash box out of the desk and put it on to the table. The Dragon then pulled the top of the desk down and locked it with one of the keys on a chain looped to his belt. He then got an old Adelaide street directory and found the right page for each address and circled each one with a marker pen. 'I give you each a mobile phone each so you can keep in touch with each other.' He then counted out five hundred dollars from the cash box and then handed the money to Silvio.

The Dragon went to the fridge and got three beers for the men. He was evidently planning as he did so. The Dragon did not drink. It was against his religion—the only thing he did keep sacred.

'If those farmers take the opal to the city as I think they will and sell it to the buyer, I bet he doesn't keep it long. If he sells it soon, he would probably double his money. That's the time to hit him. Pinch the opal and the buyer's money. That would be a lot more than the cockies get. It would be a lot better and easier than trying to rob those miserable farmers.'

The Dragon let the men have one of his cars to take to the city, a ten-year-old Holden Commodore station sedan. 'Park this one out of town. Hide it if possible, and pinch three others to do the work with. I don't want my car used in this robbery. Understand?' All three nodded in assent. 'I don't want the bloody cops chasing after me. Understand? If you involve me in any way in this, I will stitch you up. You won't want to chase the women any more. I'll have your nuts.' They each nodded their heads again.

The Dragon then had to teach the men how to use the mobile phones 'Don't forget to charge the batteries up every night. If one of the phones doesn't work, you will probably stuff the whole job up.'

As the men walked out the door of the house, the Dragon followed and handed Silvio the keys to the Commodore wagon. He then added, 'Take your old ute with you. I don't want it left around my place.'

The men took the Dragon's car back to their camp as well as their ute. The Dragon certainly didn't want the ute left at his place to incriminate him if the men were caught conducting the robbery.

Silvio felt very cocky as he drove the late-model station wagon down the road towards their dugout. 'Hey, what do you think of this car? She a bit better than the old ute, hey. If we do a good job on this one, we will all be able to have a good car. The boss said he would look after us if we did OK. Hey, and maybe we can get some mining gear of our own. Money would buy us anything, maybe even a woman each.' The three were not classified, even by Coober Pedy standards as very eligible bachelors. The only women who would have anything at all to do with them were a couple of the really down-and-out old women. This was usually paid for with a couple of casks of wine.

The men had been warned by the Dragon to keep off the booze. As they had left and the Dragon had handed them the five hundred dollars, he told them again, 'If you bastards stuff this job, or my car, I will have your nuts off and feed them to my dog.' The Dragon had given them three sets of number plates from wrecks around town. When they had stolen the cars, they would have to change the plates.

The men stopped at the local hotel and bought a carton of beer with some of the Dragon's money to see them out on the trip down south.

It was around dusk when the men neared Adelaide. They stopped at a small pub at Lower Light, a small hamlet just before Port Wakefield. There were only a half dozen houses scattered around the pub and very little street lighting.

Wombat was sent to check the cars over. There was a battered fifteen-year-old Holden parked in an inconspicuous spot, not far from the hotel. It had its keys left in the ignition with the window down. Wombat looked around carefully, then undid the door quietly and slid into the seat, started the motor, and drove off. No one noticed the car leaving.

It was dark by now with a half-moon just rising. Silvio stole another car at Port Wakefield, a Valiant ute. Now to hide the Dragon's car. Silvio remembered that closer to the city around Virginia, there was a lot of tall artichoke thistles growing on some of the side roads near the market gardening areas. They checked two roads out in the headlights before they finally found a good hiding place.

They drove about a kilometre from the main road and then turned down a disused track. The track was ideal as the artichoke thistles were taller than the car. The Dragon's car was left in the thistles. 'Why do I get all the shitty jobs?' moaned Wombat as he walked back to the stolen car from the Dragon's vehicle. 'I've got these bloody thistle spines stuck into my legs and hands.'

'Stop grizzling and get in. Just think how rich you'll be if this plan works,' growled Silvio.

The third car, another Holden was stolen from the car park of another hotel in the outskirts of the city. The men then found a deserted area near the Wingfield rubbish dump and changed the plates, using the headlights of one of the other cars to work by. They sure knew they were near to the dump because of the strong smell. They then drove off and found a cheap motel to stay the night.

They each booked a separate room at the run-down motel. They carried their clothes into their room and then went to Silvio's room for a conference.

The men studied the street directory maps the Dragon had given them with the homes of the two opal buyers clearly marked on the pages the Dragon had copied out of the street directory book. 'Walk down and get us a pizza.' Silvio tossed a fifty dollar bill from their stash to Tom. Tom walked out to walk the short distance down the street to the pizza parlour.

Next morning, they met again in Silvio's room. Wombat was given a map and sent out to Toorak Gardens to keep watch on the Aussie opal buyer's house, whilst Silvio went to Urrbrae to watch Achmed's home. Tom was to watch the terminal where the small planes land at the Parafield airport. Each man had the phone numbers of the other two written down on to a piece of paper.

The men had taken some food with them so they didn't have to leave their positions. The plan was to change cars every day so the people in the streets would not get suspicious.

Just after noon, Tom rang Silvio and Wombat with the news that John, Helen, and Tony had caught a taxi at the airport. He described the taxi. He was going to try and follow them.

The taxi roared off from the airport, heading for the city. Tom followed a couple of car lengths behind. The taxi was only halfway along Main North road, heading towards the city when Tom got caught behind a red light and sat and watched the taxi speed off. Tom rang Silvio with the news. Silvio realised that keeping up with a taxi in the city would have been almost impossible. Most taxi drivers drove like racing drivers.

Silvio was parked a few doors down the tree-lined street from Achmed's beautiful bungalow-styled home.

He took note. The house was set back from the road behind a manicured garden of roses and shrubs. There was a high fence along the roadway, which had a tall ornate wrought-iron gate at each end, which led on to the road from the half circular driveway, which led to the front verandah of the house. Silvio was very envious of the house.

The taxi pulled up in front of the gate and tooted its horn three times. The gate opened by remote control and let the taxi inside. Silvio noticed that the gate took around three minutes to finally close after the taxi had entered.

Achmed came out of the house and met the Nickolses as they alighted from the taxi. They followed him inside the house.

After the people had got out of the taxi and had just gone inside, the gate at the other end of the driveway opened so the taxi could leave. The taxi duly drove out.

After an hour and a half, another taxi tooted at the gate, which opened to admit it. The gate took a similar time to close. The Nickolses family emerged, carrying a small suitcase instead of the sport bag they had entered with. The taxi left through the other gate, which was evidently operated by a remote control in the house. Silvio rang the other two men and told them to meet him at the motel.

The Dragon was informed of the day's events. His only concern was to have thought the Nickolses had got away with all the money they had. To have tried anything with them would have jeopardised the rest of the operation. The Dragon did not like missing out on anything.

Silvio had noted the next day that Achmed's wife left in the morning with three children to evidently take them to school.

He was working on the fact that she also picked them up every evening, as she also went out around school leaving time and returned with three children.

'Right. Let's have a night out on the town. I would like to see if I can find a woman for a bit of company,' said Wombat. They all agreed as there was not much likelihood of the buyer turning up for a few days.

The men caught a taxi into the city and were dropped off in Hindley Street. They went into the first rough-looking night club they could see. The night club was filled with patrons of a similar ilk to the pirates. Also a group of bikies was at one end of the bar. A tired-looking stripper gyrated on a small stage near the bar, waggling her floppy boobs at the patrons.

Silvio was looking around and checking the women out. He liked the look of one of the bikies women sitting next to the bar. She would give him the eye every now and then. Silvio thought his luck had changed. He stood up and walked over, then sidled up to this woman, and made a lewd remark softly in her ear. The woman ran her hand up Silvio's leg. 'Come on, big boy,' she said, 'let's see what you have got.' Silvio stood up in front of the woman. The next thing he knew was that someone had reached from behind between his legs and had him by the balls. Silvio craned his neck around. A huge bearded man had him in his grip.

'I'll show you what he has got, Mavis.' The bikie squeezed harder. Silvio thought his testicles were going to burst. He tried to stand higher to get away from the man. All this he did made things hurt even more. 'Right, mate, I am going to let you go.' The bikie squeezed harder. 'If I look like I'm going to have any more trouble from you or your mates, my buddies and I will thump all three of you. We enjoy thumping people, especially arseholes like you.' Silvio felt the pressure on his testicles released. He dropped to the floor with pain.

The trio hurriedly left the club and walked further down the street to another strip joint. Silvio was treading very lightly and was not making any sudden movements.

This place was a real dive, tailored just right for the trio. They, finally, with the help of some of the Dragon's money, found three women who would talk to them. Silvio still sat very tenderly on his bar stool. He kept buying the women drinks. Finally, they caught three cabs to take them back to the motel.

Silvio held his head in his hands. 'Shit, my head hurts. You bloody rotten cows, why didn't you leave?' He sat down heavily. Then because of his sore testicles, he rose quickly and then adjusted himself carefully back on the chair. 'Shit, that woman you brought back, Wombat, I've never seen one uglier in my life.' Wombat scowled at Silvio through his bloodshot eyes.

'She was bloody good in bed. They say the ugly ones are always the best ones. They may not get another bloke for a long time, so it's worth trying harder with the one you have got.' Wombat sat down at the table and held his head in his hands. 'You weren't too bloody proud anyway, Silvio. The one you had was pretty ugly too.'

'She looked pretty good last night when I was pissed. I got a shock when I woke up and found her in my bed. I asked her where she had come from. She said I asked her to marry her last night. Shush, I must have been full of booze. Fancy waking up and finding her next to you for the rest of your life, yuk.' This was real boys talk as any of the women at the motel last night were better than the women the men were usually used to entertaining.

Tom wandered in from his room. 'Where's the girls?'

'They started to bay at the moon, so we sent them home.'

'It's funny how ugly women look good when you're pissed,' said Tom.

'What about the bikie bird. She looked pretty good, hey, Silvio.' The two men laughed.

'Not as good as her bloody man, though. I thought he was a big hairy gorilla from the zoo.' The recollection of the large bearded bikie made Silvio's problems seem to hurt even more.

They left the ute and one car at the motel, and all travelled out to Urbrae and watched Achmed's house. After a short while, they drove off and came into the street from the other end and parked the car so it didn't look so obvious. The car had dark tinted windows, which was an advantage, because unless you were to look closely, they were not easily seen sitting in the car.

They got used to the normal visitors and the children being delivered to and from school each day.

On the third day, a taxi pulled up outside the house and tooted three times. It was half past three in the afternoon. The gate opened, and the taxi pulled in front of the house. A fat, well-dressed man was met by Achmed. He was carrying a large suitcase. He ushered him inside. 'The woman has just left to pick the kids up. We'll follow her in when she comes back. Here put these ski masks and gloves on.' Silvio handed the masks to each of the men. The masks had been bought at a nearby supermarket two days before. They had bought the gloves with them.

After a half an hour, the large silver grey Mercedes drove up to the gate and waited until it opened. The car, driven by Fatima, slowly drove into the driveway.

Silvio started the car, roared the motor up on the old Holden, sped down the road, and then turned through the gateway just before the gates shut. Fatima was still in the Mercedes talking to the three children, when the old Holden swerved on the driveway, then drove over the rose bushes on to the lawn, and then slid to a stop next to the Mercedes. Silvio leapt out of the car, ran to the Mercedes, and pointed a revolver at Fatima through the glass of the closed window.

'Open the bloody door, or I'll shoot,' he said quietly but menacingly. He waved the revolver towards the children in the rear of the car. Fatima, fearing for her and the children's life, obliged. Silvio reached into the car and grabbed the keys from the dash. Then having second thoughts, he poked the key back in the ignition and broke it off in the off position. This would save being chased by the Mercedes. 'Right, you kids stay here or mum might get shot. Climb over the back with the kids.'

Fatima awkwardly climbed through the car and sat with the children, trying to be ladylike with her dress even in these circumstances. The children now were very scared and were whimpering. 'You,' Silvio pointed to Wombat, 'you sit in the front of the car and keep an eye on the woman and the kids. If the woman gives you any trouble, shoot one of the kids.' Wombat climbed into the front of the car and sat facing the rear. He waved the small automatic pistol menacingly at the family in the rear of the car. He did not say a word.

Silvio and Tom headed for the front door of the house and ran inside. They ran quietly down the hallway to the rear of the house, checking visually in each room with an open door for other people. The opal room door was different from the rest as it was heavily reinforced. Silvio could hear low voices coming from this room.

Silvio and Tom then burst through the partly opened door of the opal room.

The two men sitting at the desk were startled. Achmed made a move to reach under his desk. 'I wouldn't do that if I were you,' snarled Silvio. 'Shift your chair back from the desk, we have your wife and kids outside, and if anything happens to us, our mate will shoot them.' Achmed immediately put his hands up on the desk. The other man, a very plump man with a red florid face, was nearly having a heart attack. On the desk in front of them were the four eggs laying on a nest of newspaper and tissue. *Shit*, Silvio thought, *we've hit the jackpot*, as he saw what good opal the eggs were. 'Right put those back into the bag.' He waved the gun towards the four eggs. Achmed leaned forward and reluctantly replaced the eggs into the bag. Silvio handed the bag to Tom who held it in his other hand to the sawn-off shotgun he carried.

'Right, put the suitcase on the desk.' The florid man was trying to push the case under the desk slowly with his foot. 'Hurry up, or I'll blow your nuts off.' Silvio pointed the revolver down towards the man's crotch. This had the desired effect. The man reached down and lifted the heavy case with difficulty on to the desktop. 'Open it,' snarled Silvio. The man slowly reached into his pocket and produced some keys. He undid the case and opened the lid. The case was brim-full of hundred-dollar bills, all neat in their banded bundles. 'Right, shut the case.' The man shut the case and locked it again.

Silvio turned to Achmed. He pointed the revolver at his head. 'Right now, the bloody safe, Arab. Open it, or you will never see your wife and kids again.' Achmed was very shaken at this remark.

'I cannot open the safe unless I phone the security company,' he lied. 'Then I have to wait an hour before the lock will open. If there is a change from my regular habits, they send a security van around straight away to check.'

Silvio thought for a second. He did not know if this was true or not, but he did not want to waste time or take any extra chances. He pulled the phone cord from the wall. 'Right, your mobile phones.' He held his hand out and waved the gun menacingly at the two. Both men reached into their pockets and deposited their mobiles on to the desk. Silvio put the phones on the floor and stamped on them with the heel of his shoe. Finally, he was satisfied with the job.

Silvio and Tom backed out of the door with the opal and cash. As he shut the door, Silvio said loudly to Tom, 'You wait for ten minutes. If that door opens, blast whoever comes out with the twelve-gauge shotgun.'

'Right, let's get the hell out of here,' Silvio whispered to Tom as they crept down the hallway.

'How do you open the gate?' snarled Silvio to Fatima as she and the children cowered in the rear seat of the car.

'That button on top of the dash,' she said. She was so frightened that she had trouble speaking. Silvio pushed the button, and the large gate slid slowly open.

The bags were tossed into the old Holden, closely followed by the men. The car was started, and Silvio spun its wheels madly on the green lawn, burning a track into the green grass, and then swerved past the Mercedes, mowing down some more of Fatima's roses as it sped off the lawn and then spinning its wheels in the gravel of the driveway. It tossed loose stones back all over the Mercedes. The car then careered off through the gates and then on to the road.

Silvio slowed when they were around two hundred metres past the house, then turned, and merged with the traffic on the main road, heading back to the city.

Chapter 8

Silvio was carefully driving through the city. They had their seat belts on, trying to at least look legal. After driving in the bush for so long, driving in the city was a real chore. The Coober Pedy traffic was bad, but the two—and three-lane highways were totally different. The weaving impatient drivers were a real worry. Silvio was getting really rattled, driving through the city. There were at least four times they nearly sideswiped a car in the lane next to them. Silvio was yelling and making obscene gestures to the opposing drivers.

Finally, the heavy city traffic started to thin out as they neared the outskirts of the city The car was dumped in a side street in Gepps Cross, next to where the other Holden and Valiant ute had been left. The area where they dumped the cars was a pretty rough area with run-down houses, some with wrecked cars or rubbish in their yards. Silvio left the windows of the cars down and the keys in the ignition of the cars, hoping that they would soon disappear from the scene. The men transferred the bags and the case from the getaway vehicle. Then they searched to see if there was anything which could associate them to the car left inside.

The other Holden was exchanged for it. The whole robbery operation had only taken about ten minutes, but time had seemed to almost stand still and felt like hours in real terms.

'Did you see that red-faced old turd? I reckon he nearly crapped himself when we went into the office,' said Tom. Silvio laughed.

'The other Arab wasn't much better. I wonder if they are still waiting for us to leave the outside of his office.' They slowly drove off towards Virginia where the Dragon's car was hidden. 'How much do you think this lot is worth?' asked Wombat.

'That suitcase is full of hundred-dollar bills,' said Silvio. 'Must be millions. No doubt about the old Dragon. The old prick knows where to get a dollar.'

They turned off the main road and then drove off down the weed-infested road to where the Dragon's station wagon was hidden in the thistle patch.

Wombat again had the job of climbing through the tall thistles to reverse the Dragon's vehicle out of the road where it had been hidden. The Holden was then driven down the track by Tom to replace the Dragon's car. Tom also didn't like wading back through the tall thistles either. The men were now able to take their sweaty gloves off and drive away.

'What about getting some booze to celebrate?' said Wombat.

'Bloody good idea,' said Tom. They drove into the drive-in bottle shop at the Virginia hotel.

'What will it be, blokes?' asked the burly barman in the bottle shop.

'A couple of cartons of Vic Bitter stubbies and a bottle of brandy,' yelled Tom. 'I'll have a bottle of Bundaberg rum,' said Wombat.

'And a bottle of Scotch too, mate. Make it a good one,' added Silvio. They paid for the booze and drove to the petrol station and filled with petrol ready for the long trip home.

There was a phone box, not far from the petrol station. Silvio stopped the car and rang the Dragon with the news of the successful robbery. True to the intelligence of the trio, the mobile phones had been left on and not recharged. 'I think the old bastard even sounded a bit pleased with us. That's a bit of a change.'

The men headed back on to the main road towards Coober Pedy. 'Well, here's mud in yer eye.' Silvio opened the first stubby of beer and passed it on to Tom and then one to Wombat and then opened one for himself. They all joined him in a toast to the successful heist.

It was dark when they arrived at Port Augusta. The beer supply was fairly depleted by now. The car was refilled with petrol, which would be enough for the rest of the journey.

'Get another beer?' asked Tom as they sat waiting for the car to be filled with fuel. Wombat shuffled around, rattling through the empties.

'I think they have all gone.'

'Well, what do we want first, rum, brandy, or Scotch?'

'Let's start on the Scotch first. Here, Silvio, you have your first drink.' The bottle was passed over the back of the seat to the men in the front. The cork was dropped on to the floor of the car.

They started to drive out of the service station towards the bridge over the top of Spencer Gulf. 'Let's call into the pub over the bridge and get another couple of cartons of beer,' asked Wombat. They drove across the bridge, then turned left into the bottle shop of the hotel, and bought two more cartons of VB cans.

The beer and the odd Scotch were starting to take an effect on the men. They had just passed Pimba and were heading towards Glendambo. The men had made a lot of plans as to what they would do with their share of the loot.

'What the hell are we taking this back to the bloody Dragon for?' Tom said with a slurred bravado.

'Why don't we keep it all for ourselves?' Wombat chipped in. 'Yair, bugger, the Dragon.'

'You remember little Jimmy, the Greek, who was blown up last year. Everyone thought he had an accident. That wasn't an accident like everyone said. That was one of the Dragon's paybacks.'

'How do you know?'

Silvio answered, 'Well, who did you think set the charges down his mine? I did. You silly bugger.' A few minutes later, Silvio said, 'You remember that Serbian George who got shot up in Queensland. The one who pinched the opals off the Dragon. That was one of the Dragon's jobs too. He pinched some opal off the Dragon and got killed for his trouble. There's been quite a few. The old bugger is worse than the Mafia. He never does the jobs himself. I certainly wouldn't want to cross him. There's a lot of people who have been dropped down old mineshafts with a bit of dirt thrown on top of them at the Dragon's orders. We'll do all right out of this lot. Just take my word for it. The Dragon said he would give us 20 per cent.'

The car sped on through the night. They were past Glendambo. Both Tom and Wombat were fast asleep, snoring loudly. Silvio was having a real problem staying awake. The car was travelling from one side of the road to the other. When the car swerved, the bottles strewn through the car would clang together and wake Silvio for a short while.

When the wheels hit the dirt next to the bitumen, Silvio would wake and continue driving. He knew it would be no good asking one of the others to drive as they were a lot drunker than he was.

Silvio was about halfway between Glendambo and Coober Pedy. He had just had a fright. He had gone to sleep and had woken up when the car was well off the road. Luckily there was a flat area alongside of the road, so the only damage was a few stones rattling under the car.

Silvio got out into the cool night air to try and wake himself up. He had a pee and then got back into the car. Both Tom and Wombat were snoring loudly. Silvio thought very seriously of sleeping in the car but knew the Dragon would be waiting for them. He restarted the car and drove off down the road again.

There was a slight turn in the road. Silvio had finally succumbed and was fast asleep. The car drove straight on. There was an embankment around two metres high, where the road had been cut into the earth to keep it levelled.

The car drove up the bank at 130 kilometres an hour. Silvio woke up with a start, but there was nothing he could do. The car was airborne. About three metres in the air.

The car travelled around twenty metres before it hit the sandy dirt. It did so, first causing the front of the car to dig into the ground. This made it to end for end. The car finally came to rest on its wheels, after tumbling at least six times. Wombat had been thrown out of the back window and was laying on the ground with his head cocked to the side at an odd angle. The suitcase full of money was also thrown out and lay on the ground with the lid torn open. There was a trail of packages of money leading back towards the car.

Meanwhile, the bag of eggs had tumbled around in the car and had also come open. One of the eggs had broken and was lying on the floor of the car. Both Silvio and Tom were still alive but unconscious. They had been wearing their seat belts.

The middle of the egg had been full of a slimy, moist goo. There was also something else. A skinny segmented worm was beginning to stir on the floor of the car. This worm was nearly a metre long but very thin. The creature thrashed back and forth on the floor, trying to extricate itself from the bottles and other rubbish on the floor of the car.

The creature's skin was beginning to harden and dry out, very much the same as a butterfly as it dried its wings. It opened its ghastly mouth and convulsed as it took its first breath of air. The creature lay and breathed for a short while. It exercised its mouth, which was surrounded by rows of sharp serrated teeth. Almost like shark teeth.

Silvio, by this time, had regained consciousness and was beginning to moan softly. He tried to move but was pinned by the car seat, which was wedged forward from the bend in the middle of the car. The car was bent like a banana from the accident. The roof was crinkled like an accordion. He tried a little harder to shift himself, but it was impossible. He scraped his foot on the floor, trying to get some purchase to move himself. He was firmly pinned by the seat and the steering wheel.

The creature wriggled along the floor of the car towards the faint movement and waited for it to start again.

Silvio again shifted his leg slightly. The creature moved up to Silvio's foot and prised itself off the floor, entering his blood-soaked trouser leg.

Silvio felt the movement and tried to shake his leg but was too constricted to do so. His first thought was of a snake, but snakes did not usually slither around at night.

The creature moved purposefully towards Silvio's warm crotch. It stopped moving for a few seconds and then struck. The animal's row of needle-like teeth with sharp serrated edges grabbed a mouthful of Silvio's testicles and bit. Silvio screamed in terror at the pain. He tried harder to move away. The creature kept eating, finally devouring Silvio's testicles, and then it worked its way inside his body, pulsating and chewing as it went.

For a while, Silvio's loud screams could be heard, but these slowly abated as the creature chewed further into his body.

The skinny worm was getting fatter with every mouthful of Silvio it took. Finally, it started to pass casting out of its rear end, which was not inside Silvio's body yet, and was leaving a sticky trail of droppings in its wake.

Tom had regained consciousness by now. He had been roused by Silvio's loud screaming. Tom tried to move also, but like Silvio, he was also pinned to his seat.

Silvio's cries had long since died down. He was past caring what happened to his lifeless body. The creature kept eating and moving forward. Finally, the creature emerged from Silvio's lifeless body under his ribs. The creature was caught for a while in Silvio's clothes. Its razor-sharp teeth gnawed their way through the layers of clothing, allowing it once more to emerge into the cool night air in the car. The hood light of the car had come on when the doors were buckled. The creature lay on the floor of the car bathed in the dim light. It was a ghastly sight with the clotted blood and dirt from the floor of the car stuck to its wet body.

Tom sat pinned to the dash of the car, softly moaning from the pain of a broken leg and arm. He could hear a slurping sound and had the feeling that something was in the car and moving around. He thought it might have been a lizard or some other small animal.

Suddenly there was a thrashing of something large in the car cabin. Tom was a bit frightened. There was an unusual smell in the car. He wondered what it was. Tom tried to squirm around to see what was in the car but could not see the floor of the car as he was pinned hard against the dash. He felt something brush against his leg. He wriggled his leg to get it to go away, but the creature was determined to moved further up his leg. Suddenly, the creature struck at his groin and bit into his trousers. It thrashed about and then got another mouthful. This one was latched on to Tom's penis. It bit hard. Tom found out why Silvio had been screaming. He let out a blood-curdling scream and tried to writhe out of the creature's way. The creature was far stronger now and was not going to be denied its feast by Tom's feeble moving. It bit in further and kept eating.

Tom was dead and getting cold when the first rays of dawn were just starting to appear. The creature extricated itself from his lifeless body, having satisfied itself with its gory feast.

The creature was two metres long now and as thick as a man's arm. It finally cleared itself from Tom's trousers and then slithered out of the open door of the wrecked car. When it fell on to the ground, it lay and purged itself of some of its gory feast and then burrowed down under the car, swinging its head to move the earth so it could get under the car, which was half buried in the warm sand.

The creature then went to sleep.

A light breeze heralded the first rays of dawn. As the sky lit up with more light, a wedge-tailed eagle and some crows circled well above the scene of the accident.

After some time, two of the gamer crows landed next to Wombat and strutted warily around his body. They would come closer, take a furtive peck at his clothes, and then scuttle back away. Then they strutted for a few seconds to see if everything was safe and then move back. The crows were not too sure of a human lying on the ground. Finally, the greedier of the pair fluttered on to Wombat's chest and waited to see if there was any reaction. The crow was getting gamer. Finally, it pecked at his sightless eye. As there was no sign of movement, the other crow joined in, pecking with their sharp beaks at the eyes.

The wedge-tailed eagle landed and tried to hunt the crows away from their feast. They cawed loudly in defiance at the intrusion and flapped their wings. Finally, some more crows and three more eagles landed and squabbled over the carcass. The eagles tore the skin off Wombat's bare body, which was not covered by his clothes.

Some trucks were starting to move along the main road by now—heavy transports and road trains, who had obviously been camped in the parking bays off the side of the road for the night. The signs of the car travelling up the embankment were quite visible. There were also quite a few other such signs along the road, usually left by city people in four-wheel drives, who were trying to impress their passengers with their ability to drive up a steep incline in the outback, or someone who ran off the road, trying to dodge a kangaroo.

An old, hand-painted Volkswagen Kombi was kangarooing along the road, its engine revving up and then cutting out. It stopped alongside of the embankment, and then a young bearded man got out and proceeded to open the rear engine compartment. A girl got out of the passenger side and joined him. 'What do you think the problem is?' she asked.

'I think the drum of fuel we put in this morning may have had water in it.' He pointed to the glass filter bowl on the fuel pump. 'There it is. The water was visible in the glass inspection bowl under the fuel pump. I'll have to drain the tank and carburettor.' The filter bowl was taken off and then cleaned out with a piece of rag, and then the carburettor was drained. Droplets of water balled up and ran off the petrol from the carburettor. The man then got an ice cream container and slid under the bus and, with a small shifting spanner, undid the drain plug on the fuel tank and drained some petrol out of the tank into the container. He put the bung back in the bottom of the tank, having some petrol run down his arm as he did so.

He looked into the container. This also had a small amount of water in it, balled up under the petrol. The petrol was carefully tipped off the top of the water back into a plastic funnel into the fuel tank.

Charlie and Karen had met at university and had decided to travel north, chasing the warmer weather, trying to get some work as they travelled.

They had bought the old Kombi from some friends, not realising that the motor was not too sound. This was typical. Charlie always believed the hard-luck stories people told him. He had been told that the motor on the Kombi had just been done up.

Charlie got in the Kombi, started the motor, and then revved it up. 'Right, let's go,' he called to Karen.

'Wait a second. I think I'll go and squat behind a bush,' said the girl.

'OK, but don't take all day.' Karen walked up the embankment to have some privacy from the passing traffic. She called to Charlie, 'Quick, come up here and have a look.'

'What do you want now? We should keep going,' yelled back Charlie.

Karen was annoyed. 'Just bloody hell, come here.' Charlie knew from the tone of her voice that she meant what she said. He got out of the van and followed her tracks up the bank.

'Bloody hell! What a mess!' Charlie surveyed the accident scene. The crows and eagles were still arguing over Wombat's body. Charlie did not realise what the crows and eagles were fighting about until they had hopped away and then flown off before alighting a short distance away.

Charlie felt a hot wave of nausea envelop him. He crouched down and spewed on the ground. 'Don't come over here,' he warned Karen. 'There's a dead body here. It's not too good. The birds have been at it.' Karen backed off and watched from the sidelines.

Charlie peered through the car window from a distance and checked to see if anyone was breathing. Both Silvio and Tom were obviously dead. They were a horrible blue grey colour. 'There's two guys in here too. Both dead.' Charlie was starting to walk back to Karen when he spotted the suitcase. He could not believe what he saw. 'Hey, Karen, come over here, quickly. I want a hand.' Karen had no intention of coming anywhere hear the station wagon.

'I'm not coming near the car. Let's go and flag a car down on the road and let them cope with this mess.' Charlie was starting to pick the wads of money up and toss them into the case.

'Hey, have a look at this then.' He tossed one of the bundles of hundred-dollar bills the twenty metres over to where Karen stood. She walked to where it had landed and picked it up. Karen lost her fear of the dead and quickly came over. She started to help Charlie stack the money back into the case, occasionally glancing towards the remains of Wombat's body.

'There must be hundreds of thousands here,' she said. 'I wonder what these blokes were doing with all of this money.' Charlie thought for a second. 'Probably drug money. Anyhow I don't think they will need it any more.'

They finished stacking the cash into the case and were lucky enough to be able to do the catches up again. 'Right, let's get the hell out of here.' Charlie swung the heavy case on to his shoulder and walked to the edge of the embankment to make sure no one was coming along the roads. The coast was clear. They stumbled down the steep embankment and walked over to the van. Karen slid the side door of the Kombi open, and then Charlie tossed the heavy suitcase inside.

They both climbed in. Charlie turned the key. The old Kombi spluttered to life. Charlie turned back on to the road. Pebbles shot out from the rear tyres as he gunned the sick old motor to try and leave the scene in a hurry. They headed back on the road towards Coober Pedy.

'What do you think we should do with the money?' asked Karen.

'Well, I don't think those blokes will need it any more. No one went past whilst we were stopped, did they?'

'No, I didn't hear anyone.'

'So I think it's finders keepers,' said Charlie.

'How much do you think might be in the case?' asked Karen. Charlie thought for a while.

'There must be hundreds of thousands of dollars there.'

The old car bonnet signs on the highway proclaimed that they were getting closer to town. Karen did not know what to think about the money. She had heard all the stories about the drug dealers and had seen a lot of films about the Mafia. 'Do you think we should hand the money into the police?'

'Do you really think they would hand it on?' Charlie was a cynic when it came to honesty and all things good, especially the police. He had been involved in a few arguments with the police over having some marijuana a few years back. 'I reckon we should keep the money and get as far away from here as we can.'

The old Kombi was at its best speed at eighty kilometres an hour. Anything over this caused the motor to rattle in protest. It was hard keeping the speed down to this, especially with the suitcase of cash on board, but one thing was for sure. Charlie didn't want the motor to give up on them at this time.

Above the furthest hill on the horizon, there appeared a large cross. Both Charlie and Karen were mystified by this until they finally got closer and saw the tower of the wind generator, which helped augment the power supply for the town.

Charlie drove down through the town, then turned in to a BP service station, and filled with fuel and filled the old motor with oil, plus bought two more five-litre tins for the trip to Alice. Then they drove off to the supermarket to get some supplies.

'I really think we should ring the cops and tell them about the accident,' said Karen.

'Just don't tell them who you are. I'll get the groceries whilst you do the phone call.' Charlie reluctantly agreed. Karen walked along the wall of the supermarket to a group of phone boxes and then rang the police. She described the accident and the position of the vehicle in relation to the road, stating that they would be able to the skid marks from the road. Karen declined the police man's request for her name. She just said that she did not want to be involved and hung up.

Charlie had bought some cooked chicken as well as the groceries. 'Right, let's get out of town.' He got into the van. Karen slid her bottom into the van and shut the door. The old van trundled back through the town, followed by a cloud of white smoke, and then back on to the main Alice Springs road.

Charlie worked out that they had enough fuel to get to Kulgera, which was over the border. They passed Cadney Park and then Marla. The van was protesting loudly. If he exceeded seventy kilometres an hour speed limit, it had placed on itself. They camped the night just over the border in a deserted parking bay.

Chapter 9

Three police officers left the Coober Pedy police station for the thirty-kilometre trip down to the accident site. The Toyota Land Cruiser troop carrier was equipped for most emergencies that they were likely to encounter in their travels through the rough bush country in the outback.

The trip only took half an hour. The scars on the roadside embankment were easily seen. Officer Sean Murphy drove well past the scene of the accident, then put the vehicle in four-wheel drive, and drove up the embankment to check whether this was the right place.

Upon seeing the wrecked car half buried in the sand, Sean then turned back towards the wrecked car and then parked about thirty metres away. It was now one thirty in the afternoon.

The flock of crows and eagles reluctantly flew off Wombat's body and alighted nearby, crowing their disapproval at being once more disturbed. One greedy wedge-tailed eagle was loath to leave. Finally, as Sean neared the bird, it reluctantly hopped off and flapped its wings across the sandy ground, finally becoming air borne.

It did not matter how many times constable Tony Arbon had seen the results of these accidents; it always turned his stomach. Some people, such as Sergeant Sean Murphy, did not ever seem to be affected by the gore of the roadside carnage. Vince Jones was a little like Tony at these accidents; he did not like having to pick and scrape up the pieces of someone's misfortune and have to put it into a body bag.

Vince bent down, picked a branch of a tree up, and tossed it at the greedy eagle who was trying to sneak back for another mouthful of the hapless Wombat's body. He was almost tempted to take his pistol out and open up on the greedy birds.

'You blokes work around the edges from around here and see if you can find any tracks. Be careful where you step,' said Sean. 'I'll go down to the road and have a look.'

Vince and Tony worked their way around the edges of the accident, taking notice of the tracks which seemed to lead to one central place about twenty metres from the rear of the station wagon. They then studied the drag marks where the suitcase had been picked up.

Sean walked back up the embankment. 'There's some tracks down there. I'll get the camera. I think the vehicle tracks look like old Kombi van tyre marks. They are the only vehicles on the road now with the old-fashioned skinny tyres with the wiggly tread pattern, unless it was a very old car.' Sean thought for a while. 'It looks as if it was broken down from the look of the scuff marks. Someone was lying down under the vehicle.' Sean went back and took some photos of the roadside, noting that most of the footprints and scuff marks were at the rear of the vehicle. This substantiated his theory of a rear engine Kombi van. He then climbed back up the bank and rejoined the other two officers. 'I am pretty sure it was a Kombi. Someone has been lying under the rear of the vehicle working on it.'

Tony and Vince pointed out the shoe marks in the soft red sand, near the wrecked car. 'Looks like a bloke and a girl by the size of the shoe prints,' he surmised.

The trio then approached the wreck and looked inside. *Oh shit*, thought Tony. He walked back and nearly spewed. Sean was a lot more interested. 'Hey, come back and have a look. I reckon that's that bloody crooked Silvio bastard. That means the other one is probably Tom, and the other poor bastard the birds have eaten would most likely be that Wombat cove.' Sean walked over to Wombat's body and pulled the shirt down from where the birds had feasted.

'His skin is a bit dark like Wombat's.' Sean thought for a while. Then he walked back to the wrecked station wagon. 'I wonder what those crooked buggers were doing this far out of town. It's not their car. Why were they coming from down south?'

Sean noticed the bloodied sport bag lying on the floor. He bent to pick it up by its corner. One of the remaining eggs rolled out on to the floor of the car. 'Jesus Christ, have a look at this.' He reached into his pocket and got out a pair of rubber gloves which he put on, and then he picked the egg up. The other two looked reverently in awe at the black opal.

'What the hell would this be worth?' asked Tony as he studied the opal egg. 'A hell of a lot of money. More than you'll earn in the next few years.'

Tony went back to the four-wheel drive and called the station. He described the egg to the police radio operator, who informed him that they had just got a memo on these from Adelaide. The eggs had been stolen the day before. There were four. There was meant to be a large case full of money too.

A tow truck and car trailer would be sent down to move the wreck and would be dispatched straight away to the scene of the accident.

The other two eggs and some of the broken one were recovered. These were put back into the bag, then carried, and placed in the rear of the police wagon. There was no sign of the case full of money. They deduced that this might have been the scuff marks and all the tracks near the wreck.

The inside of the station wagon really smelled bad. The officers could not work out what the round bloody balls were on the floor of the vehicle were. These had a particular bad odour. Sean pushed one of these with a short twig he had picked up off the ground. He was puzzled. These things looked like minced meat. Skinless sausages crossed his mind.

Sean studied Silvio and Tom's bodies. 'I don't think these two were killed straight away in the accident. Look at all the blood coming out of their crotch areas. Plus the scuff marks in the blood on the floor. It looks as if someone or something has pulled their nuts out whilst they were stuck in the car, and they bled to death.' Even Sean shuddered at the thought of what might have happened.

'There weren't any tracks we could see really close to the car that we noticed,' said Tony. 'Yes, you're right about that, unless they brushed them out with something.'

The men walked away from the scene and sat, waiting under a small scrubby tree for the tow truck to arrive. Tony would still have liked to have had a shot at some of the eagles which were still perched in another small shrubby tree twenty metres away, as well as the crows, which were squatting on the ground some distance away, still cawing in protest, wanting to get back to their feast of Wombat.

Sean was puzzled about the accident. Things did not seem to add up. The three crooks pinching the opal were plausible but definitely out of the threesome's league. They were well-known night shifters and claim robbers, cunning and sneaky, certainly not intelligent. Plus the tracks up the embankment meant that they had come from down south. It was plain to see. There were no skid marks prior to the car mounting the embankment, so another vehicle being involved was unlikely. The main reason for the accident was plain to see. Empty bottles and beer cans littered the ground around the station wagon, as well as some still being inside the car. They were mainly VB beer bottles and cans. What happened to the men in the car, causing them to be killed so violently? And what happened to the case full of money? Also why did the people who reported the accident not want to be known?

After a half an hour, the Ford F250 four-wheel drive ute and a car trailer drove up the bank on the same tracks the police had used. Harry Francis, a part-time miner, tow truck owner, and a bit shifty on the side, got out of the big four-wheel drive. 'Everything OK for me to pick the car up?'

'Yes, I don't think we are going to learn any more around here,' said Sean.

His off-sider, Willie Brooks, got out to guide him back to the wreck. Willie was one of the town barflies. Willie was noted for his assignations with the young aboriginal girls in town, usually much to their parents' disgust. Willie was also one of the main suspected marijuana suppliers in town. He was a rough-looking character with a host of tattoos and a greasy black ponytail.

Willie guided Harry as he reversed the car trailer into the front of the car, and then Harry got out, undid the bolt on the front of the trailer, and then tipped the trailer so the rear dropped down under the half-buried front wheels of the wreck. He then walked over to the car to have a quick look. When he saw the bodies, he turned back and bent over to tie his shoelace up. He did not really care who was in the station wagon. He had seen plenty of accidents on this road before. Willie ran the cable out from the winch on the front of the trailer near the drawbar and then hooked the cable on to the front of the wreck. He had to scratch under the half-buried car to find the towing hook.

'What's that inside?' Willie asked Sean.

'That's a couple of mates of yours. I don't think they mind you shifting the car too much.' Wombat, by this time, had been slipped into a body bag, and the bag was zipped up.

'Wait a bout, we'll put the other guy in the back.' The three police manhandled Wombat's corpse over and slid it into the rear of the station wagon through the broken rear window. Everything had now been photographed for evidence.

Willie was a bit reticent about getting too close to the bodies in the car. Harry put the winch in gear and tightened the steel cable. The winch squealed in protest because the station wagon was half buried. 'Come on,' Harry chided to Willie. 'Give it a bloody push, you lazy cow. They won't hurt you now.' Willie half-heartedly pushed the station wagon to get it to move.

Harry started the electric winch going again. The car's body finally started to move. 'Give it another push to get it straight.' Willie was still not too keen to get too close to the dead men in the car but went over and pushed the side of the car so the front mudguard would not catch on the side of the trailer.

Under the car, the sleeping creature was rudely awaken from its sleep by the moving car. It was not happy. It coiled back, then sprang out from under the car, and struck up at the poor hapless Willie's crotch. The razor-sharp teeth dug in through the material of Willie's jeans, taking most of Willie's penis and the front of his trousers in one bite. It was wrapped around his leg, trying to get more purchase so it could bury its head deeper inside Willie.

Willie dropped to the ground, screaming. Sean, who was the closest to Willie, thought he must have got his hand caught. He ran around the side of the car to get a better look at what had happened. Sean noticed the writhing creature and thought Willie may have been attacked by a snake. He grabbed the writhing creature by the tail end and pulled it from Willie's leg. The creature spun quickly back, curling back over itself, latched on to Sean's other hand, and bit.

Sean reeled back and shook the creature off. Blood streamed from his hand from where the two middle fingers had been. The creature spun on the ground and tried to return under the slowly moving car. Tony had pulled his gun by now. He fired at the creature, hitting its flaccid body. He fired again and again, until the gun was empty, and the creature finally stopped writhing. It lay limp on the ground.

Harry had not seen the start of the action as the slowly rising car had partly obscured the scene from him. He stopped the winch when he heard the shots. Harry stood back. Then upon seeing the creature on the ground, he leaped nimbly on to the ute tray. 'What in the blazes is that thing?' he yelled over the noise of the idling ute.

Sean had pulled his handkerchief out of his pocket and had wrapped his hand in it. He was evidently in shock. He had started to shake uncontrollably. Willie lay moaning next to the car.

'What the hell has happened?' yelled Harry from the safety of the tray of the ute. He had been concentrating on getting the vehicle into the trailer and was more intent in watching the mangled front wheels so they didn't get caught on the trailer frame. 'What the hell is that?' he yelled again, pointing to the creature on the ground.

Tony and Vince were reluctant to even come near the creature on the ground in case it was not dead. Tony got the tree branch, which he had thrown at the eagle earlier, and prodded the creature with it.

Vince called the station on the radio and requested an ambulance for Willie and Sean. Vince, in the meantime, had removed the first-aid box from the police car and had started to treat Sean's hand with disinfectant and then applied a new bandage.

The men then cut away Willie's trousers and inspected the damage. Most of Willie's penis had been bitten off and was bleeding profusely. His testicles were also a bloody mess. Vince wound a bandage around the remains of Willie's testicles and the remains of his penis and stuck it the best he could with sticky tape. Both Willie and Sean were given a dose of morphine for the pain.

'What do you think we should do with this?' He pointed at the creature lying still on the ground and shuddered at the thought of what it had just done. The men looked around. 'What if we tip all the tools out of the big toolbox in the back of Harry's ute and we put it in there? Yuk, I can hardly bear to look at the horrible thing. I certainly don't want it in the police van on the way back home.' Harry agreed to let them put the creature in the toolbox. They stacked the tools in the front of the ute tray behind the cab.

Tony laid the toolbox on its side, next to the creature, then pushed the creature with the stick, and started to push it into the now-empty toolbox, which was laid on its side. He quickly tipped the toolbox back, then shut the lid, and put the padlock through the catch. The toolbox was carried on to the tray of the Ford tow truck.

The ambulance arrived twenty minutes later. The ambulance attendants looked at Willie's bitten-off privates after they had removed the temporary bandage. They applied some more disinfectant and gave him a tetanus needle. The whole area of the wound was re-bandaged, ready for the trip back to Coober Pedy. Willie was carefully put on to a stretcher. He had been given more morphine but was still moaning loudly. 'What in the world did that?' asked the female ambulance officer. 'It looks as if he was caught in some sort of mincing machine.' Vince tried to explain about the giant worm to the lady and finally reluctantly showed her and her assistant the creature in the toolbox on the ute. A discussion ensued as to what this creature was. Afterwards no one was any wiser. Vince could hardly bear to look at the creature. He was pleased to finally shut the toolbox again.

The bandage on Sean's hand was undone and rechecked, and more disinfectant applied and then bound up again. Sean, who was still able to walk, climbed shakily up into the rear of the ambulance, next to Willie. The rear door of the ambulance was pulled shut by the St John's officer. The ambulance drove back down the embankment and then headed back towards Coober Pedy with its light's flashing and siren wailing.

'How about giving me a hand to finish loading the car?' asked Harry.

'I'm not standing anywhere near the bloody car. There might be another one of those bloody things under it.' said Vince, keeping his distance. It was late afternoon now, and the light was just starting to fade. The shadows were lengthening.

Harry climbed on to the ute tray, then leaned over, and started the winch, sitting on the tray of the ute whilst he worked the controls. The car slowly pulled straight; then with an effort, it was towed up the tray of the trailer, the buckled wheels with their flat tyres grinding in protest on the steel floor of the trailer, finally causing the pivoted trailer to overbalance and drop down so the catch could be bolted shut. Harry still didn't climb down. He had the bolt in his pocket. He reached in, got the bolt, put the bolt through the hole, and then screwed the nut on with his fingers.

Harry still didn't climb right down on to the ground. He slid around the side of the ute tray, opened the door, and then lowered himself into the seat. The creature had brought out the sensation of fear in Harry. This was a sensation Harry was not used to. He always prided himself that he was afraid of very few things. Evidently, the creature had gone to the top of his list.

The men were anxious to leave the accident site. Neither of them wanted to be around the area after the sun went down. In case, the creature had not been alone. Having seen what its sharp teeth could do and its favourite method of attack made the men's crotch feel very itchy.

Harry unhooked the trailer at the police station, then helped lift the toolbox down on to the ground, and then headed for his home. He was more than happy to leave the car, toolbox, and bodies for the police and hospital staff to deal with. *What else might have been lurking in the wrecked car?*

Harry went straight home, which was unusual for him. Harry usually detoured into the pub on the way home each night unless he could not afford it. Harry walked through the door of his shack. His wife saw the look on his face. 'What happened to you?' she asked, knowing something strange had happened.

Harry recounted the story of the attack of the creature on Willie and the police officer. 'I don't think poor Willie will be chasing the young aboriginal girls around any more. The bloody thing bit his dick off,' he shuddered as he thought about the afternoon's events. This was unusual as Harry thought he had seen just about everything, everywhere; it took a lot to move him.

'Here, have a look at this.' Harry reached into his pocket and pulled an oval piece of opal, about five centimetres long and three across; it was a centimetre thick. The opal was curved slightly—obviously, a piece of the egg which had been broken. The brilliant colours flashed over the black background even in the dull light of the dugout. This was obviously the missing piece of the egg.

Harry's wife picked the opal up. 'I've never seen such good opal before. This must be as good as the best Lightning Ridge black opal. What would this be worth?'

'Fifteen or twenty thousand dollars, I reckon,' said Harry. He picked up the piece of opal, then walked over to the kitchen dresser, and picked up an old-fashioned square tea tin, which sat on top of the kitchen dresser. Harry prised the top off and put the piece of opal in it.

'If it had not been for the opal, today's fiasco would just about drive a man to give up the demon drink,' he said as he walked over to the refrigerator and got a long neck of beer out of it. He then lifted its lid with a dirty knife which was sitting on the sink amongst the array of unwashed dishes. Harry had no use for a glass. He tipped his head back and poured the beer straight from the large bottle down his throat.

Chapter 10

The three bodies of the accident victims were carefully removed from the wrecked station wagon, Silvio and Tom's bodies were put into body bags then, with Wombat's body loaded into the ambulance, then taken to the Coober Pedy hospital, and put into the morgue.

Willie Brooks had been operated on the next morning, and the mess the creature had left was sewn together the best the doctor and staff could.

Willie's willy was well known around town before the accident; it was more talked about than it ever was before. Willie didn't have enough penis left to even hold to pee. The other genital parts, the testicles, were so chewed around that the doctor had to remove them also.

Sean Murphy had his hand stitched up as well, where the two middle fingers had been was neatly trimmed and repaired.

Willie Brooks was starting to get a bad red rash around the bandaged area. Willie's temperature was beginning to rise alarmingly. The ward sister called the doctor. the doctor did a quick examination of Willie and was worried as to the speed the infection was starting to take hold. More antibiotics were introduced into Willie's drip.

The doctor and the nurse wheeled Willie out of the ward to the theatre and then removed the bandages from Willie's wound and were shocked as to the rapid onset of the infection. The area near the wound had started to turn a bluish shade as if a fungus was starting to grow from the wound. Dr Canopoulis had never experienced an infection of this type before and was extremely worried that the infection was not responding to the antibiotics, which he and the staff had been administering.

Vince Murphy's hand started to show signs of the same infection. Dr Canopoulis was very worried that they may be going to have an epidemic on their hands.

The doctor put in an order for the flying doctor's ambulance plane so the two men could be flown down to the Royal Adelaide Hospital, where there were a lot better facilities than there were in Coober Pedy. Both Vince and Willie's condition could only be monitored by the hospital staff whilst they waited for the plane to arrive. The doctor and the staff were not able to think of any other treatment for the infection than the one which they had tried already.

The Coober Pedy airport had never been so busy. Two chartered planes had flown in from Adelaide, carrying staff from the Adelaide Museum and the CSIRO to study the dead, now frozen creature. Two of the scientists went to the hospital to concur with Dr Canopoulis regarding the two men who had contacted the unusual infection. Some trucks with mobile laboratories and scientific instruments were at the moment on the road, the convoy having left Adelaide that morning.

The robbery and the attack by the creature had made world news. Everyone wanted to be in on the discoveries which were about to be made.

The creature in its steel toolbox had been taken off the ute when the car trailer had been unhitched. The police were still reticent about opening the box, in case the creature was not really dead. Finally, the box was opened, and the creature was tipped on to a large piece of plastic. The large worm lay on the plastic with its mouth with the rows of needle-sharp teeth open. A red liquid oozed from the open maw. The smell was revolting. The other end of the worm had purged out two stools, the gory remains of its last feast, which explained the sausage-like material on the floor of the wrecked car. The skin of the worm was a sickly grey green colour. It looked revolting as it lay on the black plastic sheet. The police took some photographs of the creature. The plastic sheeting was then folded and then the worm rolled up in the sheeting. Then the creature was taken on a stretcher and tipped off into a large freezer for the night. No one wanted to touch the plastic or get too close to the body of the now-dead worm.

Achmed and Aaron Goldstien, the American buyer who had been in Achmed's office at the time of the robbery, had chartered a light aircraft from Adelaide for the journey to Coober Pedy to reclaim the remains of the eggs and to try and find what had happened to the lost money. All of the commercial flights had been booked out for the next few days.

The trip to Coober Pedy seemed to take forever. The men wanted to be on the scene to try and find out what happened to the money and to regain the eggs.

The plane finally descended through the light cloud to reveal the almost alien-looking landscape of the Coober Pedy opal field, which was pockmarked with the thousands of white dumps, which were mainly in tight clusters, denoting one or other of the named fields.

The scene of the opal workings never failed to fascinate Achmed as he flew in to the area. It was as if this was another planet that they were going to land on—a world which was pockmarked with meteor craters.

Achmed and Aaron were met at the airport by one of Achmed's friends who had been phoned before leaving Adelaide. He drove them to Achmed's dugout.

The dugout was a far cry from the one the Kellys rented from the Dragon and his ex-mates. The front of this dugout had a room with windows. The walls of this long room was sheathed in the brown baked rocks, which had been gathered from the Moon Plain, which was situated just out of Coober Pedy towards Oodnadatta. There was a wall in front of the dugout which was sheathed and topped with these rocks. These had some of the hardy trees, which would grow in the harsh climate, growing behind the wall. Two peppercorn trees grew near the doorway.

The men took their clothes inside the dugout. Aaron went and freshened himself up by having a wash in the bathroom, whilst Achmed got the keys for the old four-wheel drive out off the kitchen dresser and then walked outside into the bright sunlight. He blinked at the glare of the sun and then opened the roller door next to the dugout where the ute was kept. He walked into the shed and then started the old ute, which was always kept at Coober Pedy. He then reversed it out of the shed and drove it to the front of the dugout. Achmed stopped the ute and then returned inside the dugout.

Aaron had a large natural history museum in Chicago in the USA and was always looking for unique items to display in the gem section of the establishment.

Rare gems and fossils were one of the main attractions of the museum. Aaron had spent most of his life travelling the world to acquire such materials.

The eggs were to have been the jewel in the crown of a lifetime of collecting. Finding and purchasing such rare objects was a once-in-a-lifetime experience.

Such rare objects were a draw card for the public. Aaron had hoped that the eggs would have paid for themselves from the extra attendance at the museum.

Achmed thought for a while and then spoke, 'We were in a business deal involving these eggs. In simple terms, if you were to buy a basket of eggs and one hatched into a chicken, you would still be the owner of the newborn chicken. Wouldn't you? So I think you should also claim that you own that monster worm. If, heaven help you, it had hatched whilst you had it in your possession, there would be no dispute at all about your rights.' Aaron had not thought of this new angle. He brightened up considerably at the thought that he may also be the proud owner of the now-dead prehistoric worm. The publicity that this creature had kindled in the last two days in the imagination of a lot of people worldwide could be worth millions.

The men drove to the police station to claim the eggs and to formally put in a claim for the now-dead monster.

There could be no doubt about the ownership, be it either Achmed or Aaron, to the opalised eggs. John Nickols had been contacted by the police and had said that he had sold the eggs to Achmed. John had described the eggs and had told what they had weighed.

Luckily John had said to the police that the eggs had been sold for an undisclosed price. There would be problems with the Taxation Department at a later date as both parties had not intended to declare the dealings. A story would have to be cooked up between John and Achmed. This would make things difficult for both parties.

The case of money, which was now missing, was another matter. The dealings with the cash in the suitcase were well documented. Achmed had told the police of the amount of cash which had been in the suitcase.

Having the eggs returned was not a major problem. They were handed over without a fuss. The three eggs and the pieces of the broken one were bought out. Achmed opened the bag and checked the eggs. He replaced all the pieces of the broken egg, trying to rebuild it. The result of this was to reveal that there was a large piece missing. The police had not tried to recreate the egg. 'There is a piece of this egg missing,' stated Achmed to the police officer.

'What about the car? Have you searched the car?' The officer informed him that the car had indeed been very well searched by the boffin brigade from the museum. They had taken samples of the stools and the now-dried fluid from the floor of the car. The car interior was being completely dismantled inside a shed at this present time. The seats had been removed, as well as the carpet and centre console.

Aaron thought for a while. 'What about the crash site? What has been done down there?'

The crash site was also well searched by the museum staff to see if there was anything extra to be learnt about this mysterious creature. They were sieving the ground from around where the car had come to rest following the accident at the present time.

This was a set back. Aaron had thought that the missing piece of egg may have fallen out of the car during the accident. If the museum staff had been looking, they may have already have sieved it from the ground around the accident site.

Achmed and Aaron left the police station. 'We'll drive down south to the accident site and ask the men working down there if the piece of opal has been found.' Achmed was keen to try and find out what had happened to the piece of egg as soon as possible. If the matter was not dealt with straight away, the missing piece of egg would probably be sold and on its way to China or another country. There was also the slight chance that the piece of egg may have fallen from the car on its trip back to Coober Pedy.

Four men were working at the accident site. The site had a circle of star fence droppers around it to keep the sightseers out. A circle of orange twine was tied to the droppers. A few curious people stood around, watching the men work.

Achmed called one of the workers over. The man reluctantly left his sieving job and walked over, obviously thinking that Achmed and Aaron were just two more tourists. Achmed explained that they were the owners of the opal eggs and a piece of the broken egg was missing. The man's attitude changed from one of indifference to a more helpful nature. Achmed asked the man if they had found the piece of opal. 'We have sieved all the ground around where the car was wrecked. The only thing which we have found is some pieces of broken beer bottles and some of the worm's castings.' Achmed thanked the man very much for his trouble. The two men walked back down the embankment, got into the four-wheel drive, and started back to Coober Pedy.

Achmed and Aaron returned to the police station and started to speak to the officer at the counter. 'Someone must have stolen this missing piece of opal,' Achmed bluntly stated to the police officer. 'Could it have been one of your men?' Achmed was noted for his lack of diplomacy when dealing with public servants. The officer was taken aback. He assured him that the three officers who were at the scene of the accident were beyond reproach. By his manner, he was evidently not pleased by Achmed questioning the honesty of his work mates.

Achmed was still deep in thought. 'Who else was at the site?' asked Achmed. 'Only the tow truck driver and his assistant.'

'Who was the tow truck driver?' asked Aaron.

'Harry the Horse,' volunteered the officer. 'Willie Brooks was his helper. Willie certainly didn't have any opal. He was stripped off at the hospital, and his clothes were checked over by the museum mob for clues.' The officer thought of the misfortune which had involved Willie's willy. It made him shudder at the thought.

'Willie was the bloke who had his dick bitten off by this monster,' added the officer. Achmed signed for the eggs, and then the men left the police station.

They drove back through the town to Achmed's dugout. The men got out of the ute. Aaron and Achmed went inside. Achmed put the eggs into the large modern safe, which dominated one wall of his bedroom. 'Right, I think we should go and put a bit of pressure on this Harry the Horse character. I have heard he is a bit shonky,' said Achmed. Achmed phoned his mate again and asked where this Harry the Horse lived.

The Ford ute was parked outside of the small iron house, which was set well back on the large block. There was an assortment of old mining machines in various stages of disrepair littered across the block. Most of these machines looked as if they had not been moved for years.

Achmed knew Harry slightly. He had bought a few good shells from him a few years before. Harry had the reputation of being a bit light-fingered.

The driveway was a circular gap between the wrecks. Achmed drove through to the house and parked next to the Ford ute. He got out of the vehicle. Aaron stayed in the ute. He did not want to be involved in these transactions. He thought he might frighten the guy off if the two of them were to be involved.

A small mousy woman answered the door. 'Yes. What do you want?' She said curtly, unsure of what Achmed was doing at their house.

'Is Harry at home?' asked Achmed. The woman looked at Achmed.

'What would you want him for?'

'I understand he has got a good piece of opal he wants to sell.' Harry had evidently overheard this conversation. He appeared at the doorway.

'Who told you that?' asked Harry, displaying a guilty look.

'We have just been to the police station and picked the opal eggs up which were stolen from us. One of the eggs has a piece missing. The museum crowd have been down at the accident site. If the opal piece had been there, they would have found it. Now the only other person we could think might have this opal was you.'

Harry spluttered and hotly denied having any opal. Achmed still kept very calm. 'Look, we are not trying to get you in any trouble with the cops. But we can get them involved if you like. The thing is that I have sold those opal eggs, and it's more in the new buyer's interest to get the other piece of the egg than anyone else. Right, here's the deal. You can sell us the opal at a more than fair price with no questions asked. Or we can do this the hard way. I will report this to the police, and the cops will become involved.'

Harry's shoulders dropped in resignation. He thought about this for a short while. 'You had better come in then.' Achmed followed them into the untidy house. Harry walked over to the dresser and got the tea tin down. He opened it up, took the opal out, and handed it to Achmed. 'Is this what you are looking for?'

'Aha, yes, it surely is,' said Achmed as he turned it to catch the light's rays so the colour flashed.

Harry had an excuse. 'It was just lying on the ground next to the car when I was looking for an easy place to hook on to the wreck before I was going to load it. I didn't even know about any opal eggs.' Achmed studied the piece of opal.

'What would you think this is worth?' Harry became cagey.

'What about thirty thousand?' he said hesitantly, not too sure what Achmed had in mind.

'I thought more like twenty thousand, seeing it's not yours for a start.' Harry dropped the bravado; his shoulders slumped in resignation. Harry's wife was about to say something. She looked as if she was going to start to argue. Harry waved his hand at her.

'Keep out of this woman.' He then turned back to Achmed. 'Oh, all right then, take the bloody opal then.'

'I will be back with the cash in fifteen minutes.' Achmed turned, walked out, and then got into the ute. As he left, he could hear the woman bickering in a high nasal voice; an argument was about to ensue.

'I've found your opal' was all he said to Aaron, and then he drove off back to his dugout to get the cash.

The dead monster was a different matter. Most of the boffins from down south seemed to think they had some sort of claim over this creature. There was even talk of the eggs being re-classed as fossils and thereby not being able to be sold to be shipped out of Australia.

Another compounding factor was the ownership of the eggs. Had Aaron just lost his money, or was Achmed responsible and should he be made to hand the eggs over?

The price that Achmed and Aaron had agreed upon just before the men had broken into the room was for five million dollars. This was the amount which Aaron had in the suitcase and had been stolen from the office.

Had the eggs been sold to Aaron and therefore Achmed had lost the five million dollars? Or if the deal was not finalised, then Achmed had got the eggs back and Aaron had lost the five million dollars? This was very confusing, especially when dealing with a good client who had bought some very expensive items from Achmed in the past.

Achmed drove Aaron back to the dugout after paying Harry for the piece of egg. He made a coffee and put it on to the table, then sat down, picked up his mug, and sipped his coffee. Achmed was deep in thought. Aaron sat opposite, sipping his hot coffee. Both men started talking about the ownership of the eggs. 'I think this matter should be able to be worked out between ourselves,' said Achmed. 'If we bring lawyers into the matter, they will make a lot of money from each of us, and they will eventually be the ones to win. Also the ownership of the eggs would be in limbo for years. I certainly don't want to be bogged down in court cases for the next five years and have the eggs held by the court, possibly to be forfeited to the crown as fossils. What would you suggest?'

'There is the matter of the museum people trying to make it so the eggs have to stay in Australia. If the eggs are held here in Australia for too long, they might get their way,' added Aaron.

Aaron was deep in thought for quite a while. 'I really want these eggs for my museum. As far as a draw card is concerned, they have received a lot of worldwide publicity, so I can see no sense in losing all of this with the eggs locked in a vault for years. I will pay you half the original sum. Two point five million dollars for the eggs on the understanding that if the money is found, I shall receive the other two and a half million back.'

Achmed thought this was a fair way of resolving the problem. The case of the claim against the different groups of experts from the various museums for the return of the monster worm was a different matter. This was Aaron's sole responsibility. If he could swing such a deal this way, this would be worth millions in extra attendance fees for his museum.

Chapter 11

Charlie and Karen wanted to put as much distance in between them and the accident as possible. They left Coober Pedy and drove as fast as they were game, towards the Northern Territory border. The Kombi was definitely on its last legs. Their speed was down to sixty-five kilometres an hour now as the rattling of the engine was getting worse.

They stopped in the first parking bay just over the border. This had taken all day at the Kombi's snail's pace. The suitcase full of money was still untouched since leaving town. Their main concern was to put as much distance between them and the accident site. The sick motor in the old Kombi van was certainly not helping their nerves.

They had eaten their lunch on the way in a deserted parking bay, when they stopped to see if the oil level in the motor was OK. Charlie had to refill the motor with oil to the full level on the dipstick. The motor had used two litres in the short distance from Coober Pedy. The Kombi was billowing a cloud of blue smoke from the exhaust as it travelled slowly along the road.

The sun was just setting when they finally did stop. The case full of money had to be shifted so they could sleep. This was put into the front seat with much effort, as it was awkward and very heavy. Even though they were very worried about the case full of cash, they were too tired from the strenuous day to check the contents to see just how much money was inside the case. They laid the table down, rearranged the cushions to make the bed, then undressed to their underclothes, and then went to sleep.

The tweeting birds woke the pair in the morning. The dawn sky was just starting to redden; the beautiful red and gold sunbeams preceding the sunrise radiated from the horizon and then shone through the windows of the van. The inside was covered with the golden light.

Karen had a bad night's sleep. She was evidently having nightmares. She had thrashed around in her sleep all night, moaning and jumping occasionally. This had also kept Charlie awake.

Charlie walked into the scrub for a short distance and had a pee. He noted that they were the only ones in this parking bay. Charlie returned, then filled a small plastic bowl with water from the large plastic water drum they carried, and then set it up on the concrete table which they had parked next to. He washed his face and hands, whilst Karen went for her morning walk to the scrub, carrying a small spade and some toilet paper; the spade was to dig a hole. Charlie then cooked some toast on the small gas stove in the camper van, then set it on some plates, which he carried out to the concrete table, and then placed the plates on the table.

The sun was just peeping over the horizon now. The clouds in the east were coloured with the beautiful reds and gold colours were even more brilliant. A spectacle that only the outback can produce.

The bed was put back down and the suitcase was stood on its side on the seat whilst they had breakfast outside. The breakfast dishes were put in the wash-up bowl and shifted on top of the stove.

Charlie lifted the suitcase up on to the table-top in the van, then opened the lid, and then set about taking the money out, putting it on the table and counting it in the half-morning light, being mindful of any traffic which might be slowing down to enter the parking bay.

Karen's dreams had involved the Mafia chasing them, and they were in the Kombi going slower and slower. The Mafia were getting closer all night, nearly catching them. The dream had seemed so real.

First one of the bundles of hundred-dollar bills was opened and counted. There was five thousand dollars in each bundle. Then the bundles of notes were individually counted. They were put into heaps of fifty, and then each heap returned to the empty suitcase. Karen wrote down a mark on a piece of paper for each ten bundles, which were returned to the case. They finally finished the job. They were jumpy every time a car slowed down. There had been one hundred bundles of notes put into the case. 'Wow,' Karen said, 'five hundred thousand dollars.' Charlie thought for a second.

'No, you didn't carry enough zeros when you worked it out. Here look at this.' Charlie took the pen from her and showed her the error. Karen was very quiet for a while.

'Bloody heck, there's five million in here.' She looked around, fully expecting a bevy of Mafia troops in their black suits to jump out of the bushes.

Charlie packed the large suitcase back on the floor of the van, walked around to the rear, and lifted the motor hood and checked the oil. 'Bring the oil tin out, please, Karen. The old girl has started to use a lot more oil than usual.' Karen walked around the side with the oil tin. Charlie filled the motor through the oil filler intake to the mark on the dipstick, then walked around, and slid into the driver's seat and started the motor. A cloud of blue smoke poured out from the rear of the old van. Karen got into the passenger seat. 'That old engine is rattling a lot worse than yesterday,' she said as they drove off on to the main road.

'Right, let's go, Gertie,' Charlie said to the old Kombi. 'I only hope this old bomb holds together for the rest of the trip to the Alice.'

It had taken all day to finally coax the old Kombi to Alice Springs. They had stopped at Kulgera and filled up with fuel. They were about a hundred kilometres from Earldunda, when they stopped for a wee break. Charlie stopped the old, protesting motor, checked the oil, and then topped it up again.

Charlie was very pleased to drive in through the Gap to the city of Alice Springs. He felt extremely exhausted, almost as if he had carried the van there himself.

They drove around the outskirts of the city and finally found a place to stay. They booked in at a small inconspicuous van park on the edge of the town for a couple of days. They were looking for a decent shower and a place to wash their smelly clothes. Charlie had kept out thirty thousand dollars from the suitcase. Karen paid a two-day fee for the site. Charlie was not too sure what the future was going to bring. His brain felt as if it were in overdrive.

Karen was the one who came up with the brilliant suggestion. 'Let's buy a van privately if there's one for sale around town. We can ditch the Kombi in the scrub somewhere around here. This would save having to change the registration over on the new van and having to leave our name, as we would have to do with a car yard and leave a trail for someone to follow us from here. We could just keep the old registration on the other van in the previous owner's name if there is enough time left on the registration to get well away from here.'

Karen minded the fort, so to speak as Charlie went over to the kiosk and bought an Alice Springs newspaper.

They studied the for-sale adds in the newspaper.

'There's four Winnebago's and three camper vans in here that I can find.' They ringed the address of each add and the name of the owners. Charlie went back to the kiosk and got a street map for the Alice Springs area.

They drove off to look at the dearest van advertised, which was a late-model Mitsubishi canter truck with a beautiful, near new, professionally built van body on its back. This was what the ad stated.

The usual cloud of blue smoke followed the Kombi out of the van park as they set off to look at the vans for sale.

The van belonged to an old couple, who, by the look of their house, were not short of a dollar. The unit looked as if it was in a new condition. It was parked in the front yard of the house, facing the street with a 'for sale' sign on it.

Charlie drove off from the house so the old Kombi was out of sight. He left Karen in the van, minding the cash, whilst he walked back to the house. Charlie had the thirty thousand out of the suitcase ready to offer for a good van. The price of the dearest on the list was twenty-five thousand dollars. The van at the old people's house—the canter truck and van.

Karen sat in the Kombi, whilst Charlie went for a drive with the old owner. Charlie had talked for a while to the owner of the van and his wife. They were selling the van because the man had suffered a mild stroke a few months before and did not think he could travel any more. Charlie really liked the van and had agreed to buy it off the man. 'I hope you don't have any aversion to cash,' he asked the man. 'This is nearly all the money we had saved for our trip,' lied Charlie. The man agreed and was more than pleased to get the cash.

Charlie counted the cash out for the man, who, in turn, checked the amount. Charlie was handed the registration papers, which the other couple had signed. He promised to take these to the Alice Springs registration office to transfer the registration as soon as they had left with the new van. There was still nine months' registration on the new van.

Charlie drove the new van around the corner to where Karen had been waiting and showed her through the new vehicle. Karen was very impressed with the fittings inside and the extra space. To be able to lie down without building the awkward bed every time was a real bonus.

Charlie drove out of town, heading south on the road they had entered the town from. About five kilometres away from habitation, he turned to the left, towards the Todd River on a narrow track. He could see the smoke trail coming from the old Kombi trailing behind it; the poor old Kombi was getting sicker by the minute. The cloud of blue smoke following behind them was thicker now.

There was a rarely used track off the main highway. Charlie turned on to the rough track and drove for about five kilometres until they came to the banks of the Todd River.

Next to the dry, sandy river bed, there were clumps of thick acacia bushes. They drove up to the nearest one about fifty metres from the track and stopped. The Kombi was cleaned out thoroughly, and then Charlie removed the number plates and also scraped the registration disc off the windscreen, making sure to pick up the pieces. They had spoken of burning the van, but they thought this would only draw attention to them and the burning vehicle. A last check under the seats for forgotten papers, which might have had their names on it, was carefully conducted.

The money in the case was well stashed in the bottom of the wardrobe in new camper. At least, they had some room to move about now.

Charlie got in the old Kombi and started the motor. He drove back fifty metres away from the clump of acacia bushes. He roared the protesting motor up; smoke poured out behind the Kombi. With a shuddering spin of its rear wheels, the van drove quickly towards the acacia bushes. The old Kombi bounced and then embedded itself deep into the clump of dense but spindly bushes. Only the tailgate could be seen. Charlie lifted the rear tailgate, climbed out of the rear of the van, and then jumped down to the ground.

Charlie and Karen poked some of the broken bushes into the rear bumper bar of the van so it was almost impossible to see, unless one was right next to it. The track being about fifty metres away, they were hoping that the van would not be found.

As they drove off in the new van, Karen looked back to see if the old van was still hidden from view as they drove slowly down the road. She could not see anything of the old vehicle. They then headed back to the main Alice Springs highway, turned left, and then drove back to Alice Springs.

The new van was filled with diesel whilst Karen bought some food. Charlie started the van. He stopped at a hardware store and bought some wood glue, saw, hammer, and nails, and some plywood and battens. They returned to the caravan park where Charlie made a false bottom for the wardrobe. There was already a place under, where the clothes hung to do this. The battens were cut and glued just under the floor level; each had small brads hammered in to hold it in place. Then the lid was fitted to the top; the money was shifted into this hidden recess. Charlie had kept out three bundles of notes. He then nailed the lid in place with four nails. This looked as it were part of the wardrobe. It was dusk by the time they had finished. They stayed the night in the caravan park.

Karen studied the road map the next morning before they left Alice Springs. The road to Darwin forked some distance up, just passed Tennant Creek. Their options then were either Darwin, Western Australia, or Queensland. She was hoping to vanish into obscurity. *North Queensland in a commune, somewhere near the beach sounded pretty good*, Karen thought.

CHAPTER 12

Two detectives flew up from Adelaide in a chartered, light aircraft. They were to help the local police to investigate the robbery. They were met at the Coober Pedy airport by Tony Arbon, one of the local officers who had been at the scene of the road accident, in a police car and taken to the police station. The detectives had a meeting with all the officers involved and were given a thorough briefing about the accident and the robbery.

After lunch, the detectives were taken down to the scene of the accident on the highway to start with their investigations. They got there just before the scientific staff from the museum, who arrived in a large van. The detectives had thoroughly scoured the scene by this time and left the scene for the museum people to start their work, looking for clues about the worm.

The car was traced to being registered in the Dragon's name. This certainly didn't surprise the police as the threesome of dead crooks usually associated with the Dragon. This type of robbery was more to the Dragon's planning than the three dead men. The finding of the car's owner tied him in with the robbery. This was as close as the police had got many of the crimes in town, which might have been associated with the Dragon. Usually, he was far more careful to not be able to be traced or have any distinct evidence which could be traced back to him. The huge amount of money and opals in this robbery must have clouded his judgement.

Two police officers were sent around to the Dragon's house. They parked their four-wheel drive, alighted, walked to the door, and knocked. One of the officers stepped back so he could get a good view of the rear of the shack.

After numerous knocks, finally, the Dragon slowly opened the door slightly and peered out at the officers. 'What do you want?' asked the Dragon warily, as he stood in the half-opened doorway of the house, trying to block the officers' view of the inside.

The news of the accident had not had time to travel all the way around town yet. Plus the Dragon had not gone out or had anyone call to see him. He was more interested in finding out where Silvio and the others were and why they had not contacted him. He had not wanted to leave his phone, in case the men rang with some news.

Not knowing about the accident was what the officers were hoping for. For if the Dragon had heard that his car had been wrecked and dragged into town on a trailer complete with the three dead men, he would have probably left town.

'We want you to come around to the police station to help us with some inquiries.'

'What sort of inquires?' asked the Dragon warily.

'We will talk about that when you get there,' said one of the officers, not wanting to give the game away before the Dragon was at the police station.

'I will drive around to see you in a minute,' offered the Dragon.

'No, I think you had better come with us in our four-wheel drive. The matter is very serious,' said the officer.

'Just wait a minute.' The Dragon shut the door of his house. One of the officers went around the rear to check that the Dragon didn't leave by the rear door.

Inside the house, the Dragon gathered up the spoils of a good night's work by one of the local night workers. This man had gone down a shaft in the middle of the night and had robbed the claim's owner. The Dragon put the opal he had bought for less than half of its value, in his safe and locked the door.

The Dragon's mind was racing, trying to figure out what had happened. *Which one,* he thought, *and who?* He had a couple of dirty deals going at the present time. *The robbery was,* he thought, *the least of his worries.* The men had rang and told him they were on their way up to Coober Pedy. They had the opal and the money. The Dragon was worried that they were late. He had thought they may have stopped and had a sleep on the side of the road or picked a couple of women up in Adelaide. The men never were very reliable. The thought that the men had double-crossed him and had shot through with the money and opals had also crossed his mind. He knew that Silvio was extremely frightened of him.

The Dragon reluctantly came out of the house and joined the officer at his door. He locked the door with a large padlock.

The other officer walked from the rear of the shack and joined his mate. One of the men opened the rear door of the troop carrier for the Dragon to get in.

The Dragon was still thinking. He had tried the phones during the night, but the men were evidently out of range with the mobile phones or had left them switched on without charging the batteries. He had rang during the next day and had one of the phones answered by a strange voice. The Dragon had hung up without speaking. He had nearly asked for Silvio but had hung up instead. His number had been noted down in the police station, as the phones were now there in the station and had their batteries recharged, in case anyone was to phone them.

The Dragon was grilled for about two hours. He genuinely did not know of the accident. His face had dropped markedly when he had heard the news, but true to his form, he had recovered quickly. The Dragon was, of course, the prime suspect. The men were in his station wagon; also the police had the three mobile phones which could be traced to the Dragon. 'Why did you try to phone one of the mobiles?' asked the police officer.

'I wondered where my car was. I knew the phones were in the glove compartment. I wanted to contact Silvio to tell him to bring my car back.'

'Why didn't you answer the phone?'

'I thought someone must have pinched it out of my car. I didn't want them to know who I was.'

The Dragon sat impassively through the lengthy interrogation, sometimes scratching the scar on his face when he became annoyed with the questioning. 'I knew nothing of the men taking my car to Adelaide. If I had known they were going to do this, do you think I would have lent my car to them? They told me that their ute had broken down and was being fixed, and they had no way of getting around. They wanted my car to go noodling.'

The police hated interviewing the Dragon. They had done it before on many occasions and never looked like making any charges stick, even for more incriminating evidence than this. The Dragon was an expert liar, and, as a lot of Asians, he could sit and not show any emotions when he was being questioned. The Dragon would just stare at a fixed point on the wall when the questions got too hard for him to lie about.

The police were sure the Dragon was involved in this crime, but through the normal lack of substantial evidence, they had to let him go. The dead trio would not have had the brains or resources to work out a job like the opal heist in Adelaide.

The two officers drove the Dragon back to his house. 'I should ring my lawyer and charge you with harassment of an innocent person,' threatened the Dragon.

'I wouldn't push my luck too far if I was you, mate,' said one of the officers as the Dragon departed through the door of his house.

All of the caravan parks and other accommodation venues were phoned and asked about a Kombi van. The Volkswagen Kombi van travellers were getting less every year. Mainly because of the age of the vans and the lack of highway speed in the old vans. They were usually driven by some of the younger people because the old Volkswagens could be bought very cheaply.

Two Kombis were found to have been staying in the Coober Pedy area on the day of the robbery. Both of these were checked out to prove they were not the van which had stopped at the scene of the accident.

The police had obtained the names and addresses of both of the Kombi owners from the caravan park proprietors and had phoned the owners who both had just returned to Adelaide. Both of these people in the vans had been heading down south and could prove that they were not near the scene of the accident at the time.

The next aspect of the inquiry was to canvass the service stations and the supermarkets to ask if anyone had seen a strange Kombi in town.

One of the proprietors of the BP service station could remember a Kombi van filling up with fuel. It was driven by a young man, with a girl with him. The time the van filled up corresponded to the phone call which the police had received about the accident. The man from the service station could remember that the old van was hand-painted with some flower motifs painted on it. The attendant could also remember the man being very edgy when filling up with fuel. He also explained about the pool of oil on the driveway and the cloud of blue smoke from its exhaust as it had driven off.

'With a bit of luck, the van may be broken down on the side of the road,' he added.

The Marla Bore police station was contacted to check Cadney Park and Kulgera to see if the old van had passed through.

The Glendambo roadhouses and the fuel stop at Pimba were also contacted. Staff could remember the two other vans at the Pimba fuel stop going south. There had been one travelling north. This had stopped, and the young couple had bought some takeaway food the day before the accident. This sounded like the one they were looking for. This van had flowers painted on its body.

Later in the afternoon, the Marla police rang. The van had been seen filling with fuel at Kulgera, just over the Northern Territory border. The service station owner could remember the van sounding very sick at the time. He was not sure that it could make Alice Springs. The police were convinced by now that this was the van that they were looking for; the time factors seemed to coincide with the crash.

The next step was to ask all the van parks in Alice Springs to check if the van had been staying the night before.

The Alice Springs police rang back. There had been a van of this description staying at a small park in town. The people had paid cash for the two days they had booked for. The park operator remembered that they had left after the first day. The park attendant had not taken the registration number and driver's licence details as they should have. The van was not entered into the books. A usual practice with some park operators when a cash payment was made. This was to save paying tax by down-stating the amount of people who stayed in the park.

This dead end was a blow. The only recourse now was to draw a facsimile of the van from the description from the BP service station man and fax this to the Alice Springs police station to be circulated through the town and in the local newspaper. A large reward was offered for information leading to the van or its owners being found.

The *Royal Flying Doctor* plane which had been called to take Willie Brooks and Sean Murphy down to Adelaide was cancelled. Sean was starting to show signs of getting the infection as well.

Dr Addams, the head doctor from the team, who had arrived from Adelaide, contacted the hospital about the other two casualties which had occurred at the accident site, Willie and Sean, to ask what their condition was like. When told about the infection, the hospital was told to cancel the *Flying Doctor* plane. Willie and Sean were not to leave Coober Pedy with the virulent infection, in case it was a new strain of a virus.

The team of specialists who had flown in from Adelaide conducted their investigations under very careful circumstances, owing to the infection that had infected Willie and Sean.

The specialists were sure that the infection and the worm were connected. Willie and Sean were transferred from the Coober Pedy hospital to the small group of demountable buildings which had arrived from Adelaide and were being quickly assembled by a team of workers who had accompanied them up from the city.

The three dead men's bodies were carefully opened up, and photographs and tissue samples taken. There was evidence of a strange fungal type of growth in the insides of the bodies of Silvio and Tom. None of the specialists had ever seen anything like it before. When studied under a microscope, the growth showed similar characteristics to the infection which Willie and Sean had contracted. Both men had been gutted from the inside by the creature.

The creature's teeth had evidently been razor-sharp. This was evident from the way the material on the men's trousers had been cut through as the creature first penetrated their clothing.

Achmed and Aaron had been talking of going back down to Adelaide in the light aircraft they had chartered. Both men had thought this a wise move because of the suggestions about confiscating the opalised eggs.

They were to work the final details of the payment for the eggs back in the city. Aaron wanted to get out of the country as quick as possible.

Before he left Adelaide, Aaron was going to engage the best law firm in Adelaide to try and claim the monster back from the boffin brigade who were studying it. If he could do this, he would more than recoup the cost of the trip.

Newspapers all over the world were carrying the story on their front pages. The robbery, the prehistoric creature which had hatched from the broken egg, and the subsequent killing by the creature of the two crooks were definitely front-page news worldwide.

The flaccid dead monster was an instant celebrity.

The day after Charlie and Karen had left the town, there were some news from the Alice Springs police. The Kombi van had been found driving around the town. There were a large group of aborigines driving it, and when questioned, they said that they had found the van about ten kilometres out of the town, next to the Todd River. They must have found the van the day that Charley and Karen had left the town.

The aborigines had been walking along the bank of the Todd, hunting for goannas for food, when they had noticed the back of the van in the acacia bushes. They had managed to find their way into the van then by crossing. The ignition wires had been able to start the van and drive it back to Alice Springs.

The police did a thorough search through the van and took fingerprints from it. The fingerprints did not have any matches on the computer. The registration plates were not on the vehicle or the stick on tag, but there was an engine number which was checked. *This was a breakthrough*, thought the officers.

The owner of the van was in Adelaide. The Adelaide police checked on him and found that he had sold the van for cash three weeks before. The registration papers had not been filled out by both parties.

The only thing the police had to go on was the hazy description tendered from the man in Adelaide who sold the van to Charlie. This could have fitted half of the young travellers in Australia.

The Alice Springs police did a check on all the car sales, both commercial and private, for the period of the van travelling to Alice Springs. There had been five cars sold, as well as the private sale of the Mitsubishi canter van. The car sales were all OK as there had been trade in vehicles; the names were all checked and found to be local people. The canter truck was a different case. The old owner had the registration number and the name of the purchaser. He had taken the papers to the registration office to do his half of the transfer, but there was no record of Charlie having done his side of the paperwork. The old man described the van and said about the names on the back with the Citizen Band radio frequency call sign. The names were Bert and Amy, and the call sign number fifteen. Bert had been a spray painter in his younger days and had customized the side and rear of the van with some stripes and some other marks to make the van more attractive. Bert had some photos of the van which he loaned to the police. At least, the police had the registration and the owner's name now. But when the check was made on the owner of the Kombi van, the name was fictitious. Charlie had used a bogus name. At least, the plates could be picked up on the Canter truck.

The canter camper van did have some different markings on the side, two names, and a radio call sign on the back. The police sent photos of the van, with the registration numbers to all the police stations further along the highway.

Chapter 13

What a delight it was to drive a decent vehicle instead of the clapped-out old Kombi! Having some room to move was another bonus.

The new van could easily travel at one hundred kilometres an hour, with plenty of extra in reserve if needed.

Charlie and Karen were not in a hurry. Now they were convinced that no one would find the old Kombi hidden in the bushes, and as their names were not on the old man's registration papers, the need for stealth and speed were not their main concern. Charley was convinced that they were home free.

Charley stopped the van at a service station at Tenant Creek to fill up with fuel. When they had finished, they drove to the local shops to have a meal and buy some much-needed groceries. When they came out of the shops and got into the van to continue their journey, a police car pulled in behind the van, cutting their exit off. Two officers got out and walked to the door of the van. Charlie's face dropped. There was nothing that they could do. The officer told them to follow the police car to the station.

'Well, that's a nice mess. I wonder what is going to happen now,' said Karen. Charlie was in deep thought. 'I'm glad I didn't change the plates for the old vans. We could be in a lot more poo if I had done that.' Charley turned into the police station driveway after one of the officers directed them to do so.

The officer asked Charlie about the money. Both Charlie and Karen could see no use in lying to the police as this could only make matters worse. Charley showed the officers where the money was and helped take it out of the false bottom of the wardrobe. He was now resigned to the fact that there was nothing to do. The money was put into secure plastic bags. Charley and Karen followed the officers into the police station. One of the officers rang the Coober Pedy station and gave them the good news about the recovery of the money. The Coober Pedy police sent an officer around to Achmed's dugout with the good news.

Achmed and Aaron were having lunch when there was a knock on the door of the dugout. Achmed looked out of the corner of the window to see who the person knocking was. He then opened the door and let the officer inside. 'I have some good news. The van with your money has been found at Tennant Creek.' Both Achmed and Aaron were extremely pleased and thanked the officer. 'It appears that the two people in the old Kombi van had broken down and had got out to fix the van, when they had found the accident. They were the ones that reported the wreck to us, but as they had the suitcase full of money, they did not want to give their names.'

'Could I go and get the money? I have a friend with a small plane here which I could hire.' Achmed was worried that the longer this amount of money was lying in someone else's care, there might be some more of the cash disappear. The office gave Achmed the number of the Tennant Creek police station. Achmed thanked the office profusely, reached into a cupboard, pulled out a bottle of expensive Scotch whisky, and gave it to the office.

'I don't know whether I should take this,' said the officer.

'Just share it with your mates to thank them all from me.' The officer took the bottle and then walked out the door and drove off.

'Well, Aaron, this must be our lucky day. Aren't we lucky we didn't leave the town yesterday as we had planned? Would you like a trip up to Tennant Creek if Tony is around the town with the plane?' Aaron agreed as he wanted to get out of Australia as soon as he could with the eggs. Achmed rang the Tennant Creek police station and said he was going to fly up and pick the money up. He also added that he would like to meet the couple who found the money.

Tony Lang was around the town. He had taken some tourists flying around the Coober Pedy area in the morning. There was a good business with the tourist trade as there was probably nowhere on earth with the scenery that this part of Australia offered. Tony was going to fill the plane with fuel ready for the next trip, when Achmed phoned and asked about flying him and another man to Tennant Creek. The plane would be able to get to Alice Springs in the late afternoon and then finish the trip in mid morning.

'G'day, Achmed. Sounds as if you have been having a bit of fun.' Tony Lang was a weather-beaten, lanky guy of an age which could have been between forty and sixty. He was very well versed with inland Australia as he had flown nearly anywhere there was to go. He did a fair amount of work to Mimili, Indulkina, and Fregon, which were aboriginal settlements, ferrying the administration staff and their ilk for inspections. Tony finished filling the *Cessna* with fuel and then started to do the normal check of the plane. 'OK, guys, get aboard.' The trio settled into the seats of the plane. Tony started the motor, then taxied out on to the runway, and then gunned the motor, and after a short run, the plane was airborne. Tony liked this sort of job. There was a lot more money in the long charters than just carrying tourists for an hour at a time. Achmed started to discuss the trip and recovering the cash. He drew Tony into the conversation.

'I would not like to think that this young couple would be prosecuted over finding the money. It was only a coincidence that they had broken down at the spot where the thieves had run off the road. I wonder what most other people would have done about the suitcase full of cash. Would they have kept it?' Both Aaron and Tony agreed with this. 'I have had a bit of a run-around regarding the money. But I think I will give this young couple a reward.' The rest of the long run to Alice Spings centred around the eggs and the Dragon and his mates. Tony had the same opinion of the Dragon as most others in the town. He had been robbed of opal from a claim he was working part time with a mate. Silvio and crew were the prime suspects.

Tony landed at Alice Springs just as the sky was starting to turn red. He taxied the plane off the runway and shut it down in a parking area. Achmed called a taxi and phoned for some accommodation. All men had each small bag with a change of undies and pyjamas.

After an interesting night at dinner and some good discussions about the problems in the world, although they did not fix any, the men retired to bed ready for an early start.

The sun was just about up when they left. The sky was a golden colour in the east. Finally, they arrived at the small Tennant Creek airport just before lunch. Achmed phoned for a taxi. Tony was going to have a look around the town for an hour.

Achmed and Aaron walked into the police station and asked at the counter about the stolen cash. Achmed also wanted to see Charlie and Karen. Achmed was asked for proof of identity, which he produced to be photocopied. He then proceeded to an office, with Aaron following. The bags of money were produced. Aaron and Achmed set about counting all the money. This took quite a while. Just as they finished counting the money, Charlie and Karen were ushered into the office by one of the young police women. The count on the money was just forty thousand dollars short.

Charlie and Karen did not know what to expect from the man who owned the money that they had picked up at the accident scene. Both were quite worried as to the profession of the two men in the room; a couple of heavies from a drug cartel came to mind. Achmed stood up and shook both Charlie and Karen's hands and then thanked them for finding his money. They both felt a lot of relief. 'You have led us on a bit of a chase to get this money back. Do you know how this money got to be where you found it?' Charlie and Karen then heard the details of the robbery and the demise of the trio in the getaway car. Both were extremely thankful that they had not ventured near the car at the accident scene when they heard about Willie and the police officer being attacked by the worm, as well as the thieves.

Achmed went on, 'I had offered a reward for the return of this money so, even though you picked the money up and drove off with it, I am prepared to let you keep the vehicle you bought and give you another seventy thousand dollars and ask the police to drop all charges related to this matter. Both Charlie and Karen were so pleased that they did not have to face any charges relating to the picking up the cash. They thanked Achmed very much. Achmed counted seventy thousand dollars out of the bag of money and handed it to Karen.

'I think you should keep this, my dear. Most women have a lot more idea about money than men. This is my gift.' Karen took the money.

The police officer said, 'You are free to go now if you wish. Just pick up all of your belongings at the counter'. Charlie and Karen walked to the counter and got the keys of the canter van.

The young police officer said, 'I think you should fill in the registration forms with your right names before you go and pay the stamp duty on the van.' Charlie picked the forms he had got out of the pile of papers he had picked up, sat down, and filled the form out in both his and Karen's names. He paid the stamp duty and the transfer fee. Then both walked out of the police station free to travel in the near-new Canter van. After they had left, Achmed said to the police officers, 'What should I have done? I do not want to see young people like that getting into trouble for doing what half of the people would have done. I am more than happy to get my money back. I consider to be lucky to ever see it again. If there had been another car other than the old Kombi van, I do not think we would have found it.' The officers agreed. One of the officers offered to drive the men back to the airport ready for the trip back to Coober Pedy.

Chapter 14

After two days in the city, Tony had driven back to the farm. Typical of most country people, he could not wait to leave the mad pace of the city. He, especially, hated driving in the crowded highways. This was totally different from the snail pace of Kimba. Most of the time when driving, Tony was lost, having been caught on the wrong lane when he wanted to change roads. He then had to stop and study the new Adelaide street directory he had brought when he had filled up with petrol. Tony wanted to get home so he could keep an eye on the sheep. He felt so proud, driving the new Ford utility, but had the horrible feeling that if he didn't get out of the city soon, he would end up in a car accident with it. City driving certainly was not Tony's forte. He hated it.

His only hope of getting a ute prior to the opal find was to have bought an old, clapped-out one and do some work on it himself. He had no intention, as a lot of young people did, of tying himself down with hire purchase, especially, when the finance situation had been so bad.

Tony had kissed Helen and then given John a big hug before he left for home. He insisted that they stay at the hotel for a few more days. It did not take a lot of convincing to get Helen to stay. The change of fortune and circumstances was most welcome.

John had read with great interest of the robbery and then the grizzly demise of the three pirates by the worm. The police had contacted John at the hotel to ask if he had sold the eggs to Achmed. He had to describe the eggs' colour and weight to try and verify Achmed's ownership.

'I reckon that if we hadn't left Coober Pedy when we did, those bloody pirates would have stolen our opal and money which was in the safe. I would bet that they were the ones who broke in to the dugout. Bert said the safe must have been opened with a key, as it had not been forced in any way. It would have been those three blokes who were killed in the accident that were involved.' Helen was so pleased that John's hunch about the eggs and cash had been right. To have been so close to getting rid of the bank debt and then to have the chance of stolen from them by a mob of thieves would have really broken her heart.

'Well, what do you want to do?' asked John as they sat in the small restaurant and had their lunch. It was still hard to let the purse strings open, as they had such a battle for the last three drought years. Helen thought for a while, *Why don't we buy a new car and then drive up through the Barossa Valley for a couple of days on the way home? I would like to go and see where my grandparents were born. My parents always used to talk of the place they grew up and where both of their parents were finally buried when they died.*

It was still hard to bring himself to finally agree to buy the new Holden. The change of fortune was still like a dream to John. He did not want to wake and find the bank was still hounding him for the money. *If it is a dream,* he thought, *at least I've had the dream of beating the Lizard at his game.* His mind came back to the reality of the moment. He had been daydreaming as the salesman got the registration papers ready for him to sign in the Holden dealer's office. John wrote a cheque to pay for the car.

The new car was left at the dealers. John had no intention of trying to drive in the city for the first time, especially in the new car, which he was not used to.

John hailed a cab, went to the bank, and redeemed the suitcase full of money. They were not sure what to do with the cash. They were going to make an appointment to see their accountant when they got back to Kimba.

What a change to be able to take their time and finally begin to relax after the ordeals of the last few years!

When John and Helen arrived back at the Holden dealers, they made arrangements for the salesman to drive the new car out of the city for them. John gave the man fifty dollars for his trouble. He felt that this was better than smashing the new car in the first day they owned it.

It was a pleasure to finally leave the city and drive up through Gawler and finally to the Barossa Valley.

The green fields of the Barossa Valley rolled before them as the leisurely drove from one small town to the next. *What a pretty country after the dismal Kimba of the last few years!* Green paddocks, with fat sheep and cattle. The wheat and barley were almost up to the top of the fences. In the lower valleys, there were the lines of grapevines all neatly trellised, with their bare black limbs pruned back, waiting for the kiss of the warm autumn sunshine to bring forth the first green buds.

Helen had never been to the Barossa before but had heard a lot of stories about her German ancestors who were amongst the early settlers in the valley.

Helen studied the road map and finally found the small hamlet where her great grandparents had settled. John followed the back roads to the ruined church. This was a very emotional time for Helen as she got out of the car and walked into the church yard. She was holding John's hand tightly as they both walked through the graveyard, looking for the family plots, which were the final resting place of three generations of her ancestors—two lots of the graves of the first German emigrant great grandparents and one of her grandparents' graves as well. 'This has been one of my dreams to visit this spot and do this.' She hugged John. They then left for the car as a misty shower of rain came over the hills. As they walked back to the car, Helen looked back towards the graves and noticed that a ray of sunlight had shone through the clouds and was shining on the small graveyard, illuminating the tombstones of her ancestors. It was as though they were saying how they were watching over them.

John and Helen were quiet as they drove back to find a motel for their last night's break before going back to the farm. The visit to the ruined church had been a very moving experience, especially for Helen.

The smell of the new car, and the lack of rattles, which had inhabited the old one, and were getting more and more as the years passed on the rough dirt roads, was a strange feeling. They had never bought a new car or tractor before in their lives. They had not been able to afford such luxuries.

Just past Port Augusta, John bought up the subject of the opal claims and the dozer. 'We had better go back to Coober Pedy and finish the cut and bring the low loader back home. We still haven't got down to where we drilled the opal from. I think we will leave the dozer at Coober Pedy. There is still a lot of work to do with the rest of the claims. We don't need it on the farm now.'

The Kellys paid them a visit the day after they returned from Adelaide. 'Come in and have a look at the new suitcase we got in Adelaide.' The men followed John and Helen into the lounge room of the house. John reached behind the old lounge suite and pulled out the case full of money. He lifted it up on to the small coffee table, then undid the clasps, and then lifted the lid. 'Christ,' croaked Bert, 'is that all money in the case or have you got the bottom padded just to make it look good?'

'All solid cash,' said John. 'We don't want the news to get around that we have got it here. It's just that at present, we don't know what we are going to do with it.'

'Spend it,' joked Harry.

'When are you going back to finish the cut?' asked Bert.

'When do you think you might go back'? asked John.

'In about a fortnight's time. That should give us enough time to get a bit more work done at Coober Pedy before harvest time.' They went to the kitchen and sat at the table.

'We bought a better dugout on the North West Ridge,' said Harry.

'What's it like?' asked Tony as he got some stubbies of beer out of the fridge.

'It's a hell of a lot better than the Dragon's. We have a front section with a lot of windows with tables and chairs. This leads into the main dugout. There is an opal room with a steel door and even a proper bathroom. The main bedroom has a big safe with a combination and key lock.' This sounded a lot better than the Kellys' home at Kimba.

This time, the evening meal with the Kellys was not the usual skinny mutton chops but good fat steaks instead. Buying meat was a new experience for Helen as they had always killed their own sheep and the occasional pig.

The sheep on the farm had improved in condition. Tony had fed a couple of bins of oats to them, mainly to empty the silo of the old musty oats so the silo could be cleaned out ready for the new season's crop, which, by now, was showing some promise of some sort of yield—a far different prospect then a month ago, when everything looked as if it was going to die.

The wheat crops were just showing the first signs of running up to head. By the look of the crops, the yield would not be fantastic—a little below average but far more heartening than the wipe-out the season looked like a few weeks before.

Helen had been in contact with the patent attorney. He had done a search on the new ripping tool and had found only one patent, which looked slightly similar to the tool they were using. He suggested to Helen that they should think of starting a provisional patent to cover the product. John phoned him back and then authorized the provisional patent to be drawn up.

John and Helen drove into the town. John felt embarrassed about driving the new car into the town. He felt as if he was trying to show his friends up. Another thing which John felt guilty about was not buying the car through the local dealer, who also had experienced the hard times with the demise of the farmers. Buying the car in the city had saved them freight on the new car and the air fares home. Old habits were hard to break.

John drove up to the bank. They walked in and deposited thirty thousand dollars into their working account. Whilst they were talking to Debbie, the Lizard peered around the corner of his office and sneered at John and Helen but made no attempt to greet them.

After doing a few days' work on the farm, John and Tony were ready to go back and finish digging the cut.

Bert and Harry came over to the farm one evening for a visit and to enquire about the forthcoming trip to Coober Pedy in the next few days. Even Bert and Harry had spruced their act up. They had bought a better Land Cruiser ute, and, by the look of them, when they arrived in the afternoon, some better clothes than they were used to wearing. These evidently came from a shop, instead of the Salvation Army store.

John and Tony followed the Kellys up to Coober Pedy. This trip did not have the desperate feel of the gamble they were taking in the last two trips. They were both looking forward to getting back to work again.

'I wonder how many people know the bloody combination and have a key to this safe,' said Bert as he showed John and Tony around through the new house. 'See it's even got a proper inside toilet and bathroom,' which was a far cry from the primitive set-up in the small outside iron room on the farm.

There was a spectacular view from the front of the dugout over the plain towards the blue mesa-type hills towards the Breakaways, which poked up off the Moon Plain like a mirage, in the far distance. The front room had a table and chairs set up so the people sitting at the table could really enjoy this scene. 'A bloody good place to have a few beers,' pointed out Harry as they looked around the new acquisition. John and Tony complemented the men on their recent purchase.

The next morning, the men drove out to the claims to check the machinery before starting to work.

The truck was the first thing which John noticed. Its windscreen and lights were broken. When the dozer was checked, all the glasses of the engine gauges were also broken. There were the small footprints of bare-footed children around the machines, even a disposable soiled nappy was tossed in on the front seat of the truck. Evidently, a large mob of people had been noodling on the claim and had bought all of their children out with them.

John was extremely worried that the dozer and truck's oil might have been tampered with. Tony went over to the dozer and checked the oil filler of the motors and transmission, whilst John checked the truck. Both of the motors still had a heavy film of greasy dirt stuck to the oil-filling plugs, as did the transmission filler with no tell-tale marks of any tampering. Both radiators were still full of water. 'Just bloody kids whose parents couldn't care less,' growled Tony.

Bert and Harry had splashed out with some more of their cash before they had left and had bought an old truck with a blower on it. The poor truck had suffered a similar fate as the other vehicles. 'I'll stuff the bloody rocks up the little sods' bums if I see them around here again,' threatened Harry as he cleared some rocks, which had evidently been thrown at the windows of the truck, out of the cab. 'Those bloody kids toss rocks through the windows in town. The rotten little sods can stay back there in town and do it to their own houses.'

Bert had another shaft drilled with a Caldwell drilling rig so the new blower could be sited near to the old shaft and have its pipe lowered down through it to the drive below. There was not enough room to have the pipe and be able to climb down underground through the old shaft past the thick suction pipe of the blower. 'Well, at least this lot haven't stolen any batteries.' The alleged previous battery thieves were well past taking any more batteries.

John stayed and helped Bert and Harry finish installing the blower pipes, whilst Tony removed the old gauges from the dozer and drove back to town to try and buy some replacements. The main worry was the oil pressure gauges for the transmission and the motor. These had been gouged at with some kind of tool, and the insides were hanging out. This would have let the oil leak out of the broken pipe if the motor had been started.

Finding parts in Coober Pedy was usually a headache. One firm would have one piece, and then you had to go to another business to look for another. Tony was able to get the engine oil pressure and ampere metre gauges at the Opal Miners coop store where they usually bought their fuel. The transmission gauge was harder to find. The firm he was sent to still had the gate shut at ten o'clock in the morning. Tony had to wait for half an hour until the sleepy-looking man finally opened his gate. There was a queue of people waiting to get into the shop. Finally, it was his turn to be served. At least, he was able to get the part for the dozer.

The Kellys new blower was belching a plume of dust out of the outlet John was waiting next to the dozer. He had seen Tony turn off the road and head towards the claim.

'Why didn't you go down and have a look at the way they worked with the blower?' asked Tony with a wry grin. John didn't bother to answer. They went on working and finally got the dozer going around 2 p.m.

It seemed as if they had been away for months, not just the few weeks. The men soon settled back into the familiar routine of ripping, checking, and then pushing the old, worked sandstone out of the cut. Only a small patch of potch was found for the afternoon's work.

Bert emerged from the shaft, carrying a bucket. He had a beaming smile on his wrinkled face. John had just shut the dozer motor down for the day. He and Tony walked over to the Kellys' utility. Bert had just tipped the contents of the bucket on to a piece of black plastic. Harry, who had just come out of the shaft, joined them. 'Have a look at these beauties,' offered Bert. There were ten full shells and a small amount of skin shell. Two shells amongst them stood out. These were black opal. 'You're not the only smart arses who can find black opal, are you?' joked Bert. 'Have a good look at these beauties!'

Back to the routine of a trip to the pub again to celebrate. Bert started in a serious mood, 'I don't know why we didn't get a blower when we got our first lot of money. Crikey, it's a hell of a lot easier than dragging those bloody heavy buckets back and forth along the floor of the drive. The more work we did, the longer the drive was, and the further we had to drag those damned buckets.' He went off and bought the first round of beers.

'What do you think the opal would be worth that we got today?' asked Harry in a low voice when Bert got back and had finished handing the beers around.

'I reckon those good shells may be worth around twenty or thirty thousand each,' he answered quietly so the men at the next table could not hear him.

'As much as that?'

'Well, do you remember the shell that Black Mick was showing off. He got twenty-five thousand for it. I reckon ours are as good as that was.'

After the meal, Tony went off with a couple of lads he had met up with when they had been up working before. 'That boy of yours has made us a bit worried. He wants to get himself a couple of sheilas to relieve the pressure.'

'That's probably what he is going to do right now,' said John with a wink and a smile.

The next three days were walk and check. There were no signs of any opal. Walking and checking by one's self soon became boring to anyone when there was no sign of opal. The sandstone was the same. The brown line of the slide showed in the floor of the cut. This was about two centimetres wide in places. There were thinner lines crossing the main fault. These were the usual places that opal or potch was found.

Tony still turned the sandstone blocks, which the ripper pulled from the solid floor of the cut, occasionally scratching at the bottom of the rock to try and hear the telltale sound of cracking glass on the sharp point of the pick.

The men had estimated that the cut was now about seven metres deep. This was approximately the depth that the first lot of opal had been drilled from before they had bought the dozer up from Kimba.

The first rip of the new day, the sandstone showed signs of changing. Small darker brown patches began to show in the floor. The old dozer was finding the sandstone harder to rip. This was the sign that the main level should be showing up soon.

Because of the harder stone, John was only able to complete one rip and push instead of the usual extra rip. The new design ripping tools were working very well, although changing the picks was difficult. The boot had to be removed from the tine, and then the broken tool belted out with a sledge hammer and long drift. John found a place on the dozer where the boot could be wedged between the track frame and the long blade arms to set the boot so it could be worked on. The picks were cooked into the hole on the nose of the boot and took a lot of work to remove. The job was dangerous, for if the rift was hit at an angle, the person holding the drift could get badly hurt.

Bert and Harry had come out of their shaft at lunch time and had looked down the wall to notice that the floor of the cut was beginning to change colour. At the end of the work, the four men had walked the floor of the cut, chipping at the darker patches of sandstone to see if they could see any traces of opal.

Bert scratched his wiry grey hair. 'I reckon that you should cut the level tomorrow by the look of this. This light brown is what we have got about six inches above the main level. What say? We give you a hand to check tomorrow as well,' he offered. John thanked him but didn't want to impose.

'Silly bugger! We wouldn't offer if we didn't want to help. When the level comes up, it's bloody hard for one man to check. Hell, you don't want to push the bloody opal out on to the dump. Plenty of people have,' Bert motioned towards the small group of people who had arrived and started to noodle that day.

'They're probably the same bludgers whose kids smashed all of our windows. Do you want to give them the opal?'

'Don't be so bloody pig-headed. I could sure do with a hand,' said Tony. John agreed. He always felt uncomfortable imposing on someone else to help.

John and Tony called in to Ivan's workshop on the way home to discuss some modifications to the new ripper boot design. John wanted to have a tapered shank on the pick to make removal a lot easier. The boot could be left on the tine when removing the tool.

They sat at a table in the workshop and drew some plans. Ivan had some very good ideas as to the retaining pin and removal tool design. Tony got two worn ripper boots from the tray of the ute for Ivan to modify to build the new tools. Ivan was very interested in helping and said that the tools should be ready in a day.

Bert and Harry had only been shifting dirt for the last few days. They were looking forward to the change of scenery. It was always exciting to see opal dug up by a bulldozer.

The dozer scrabbled down the steep ramp of the cut. John lowered the blade and then cleaned all the loose dirt from the floor of the cut. This was to make it easier to spot any opal traces if they showed up. All of the men were keyed up with anticipation of what might happen with the first rip. They wished that John would back up and start ripping. He pushed the blade over the floor to remove some small, long mounds of sandstone which had escaped the ends of the blade in the previous rip.

Finally, John reversed back along the straight wall of the cut and dropped the rippers and then started forward. The dozer tracks spun slowly and fought to get traction on the stone. The harder stone now made a cracking sound as it was reluctantly freed from the hard parent rock. The thin brown cross slips in the cut had now thickened and turned to a hard, shiny black ironstone in places.

As the stone was turned, there were plates of the dark, hard ironstone on the bottom of some of the rocks. 'Bloody good level,' muttered Harry as he turned over a stone to check for opal.

The dozer was halfway across the cut, nearly to the main fault line, which ran from one end of the cut to the other. There was a sound of breaking glass, like glass being trodden under foot. Crunch, crunch it went as the ripper tore through it. Bert turned a stone over with the point of his pick. 'Jesus Christ,' he said in awe, 'opal. Look at that.' John had felt the dozer shudder and had heard the opal cracking, even over the noise of the rowdy old dozer. He was looking over the rear of the machine and had seen the shine of the opal in the bright sunlight. He throttled the dozer off and took it out of gear, leaving it with the motor idling slowly, and then he climbed down and joined the three men who were squatting by now and separating the opal from the dirt. Tony finally took his leave and went back up the steep ramp to get the buckets and sieves.

The noodlers were trying to get a better look to see what was taking place behind the dozer.

John had a hammer and screwdriver from the tractor toolbox and was chipping the thick pieces of opal from the virgin rock. He had flattened out a piece of ground next to himself, on to which he had laid the piece of old tarpaulin to catch any pieces which fell to the ground. He was putting the large pieces of opal into a large round sieve as he took them off the virgin rock.

The sun's rays caught the pile of opal, making it look as if the heap was alight. The fire colours of the stone flashed in the sunlight. Tony transferred the opal to the bucket, which he left next to John.

The rocks were carefully checked and then discarded if there was no sign of opal. Occasionally, a particular piece of opal was shown around to the other men. A pile of rock was building up next to John, waiting for him to remove the opal. A similar pile of rock was building up in the dead area.

The light breeze wafted the not unpleasant fumes of the idling motor on the dozer,it helped to keep the small sticky bush flies away. Tony took over from John on the cleaning side of the operations, whilst he climbed up on to the dozer, reversed slowly back, and did a short rip where the opal had disappeared into the solid rock.

One of the rocks which was pulled out had the unmistakable sign of the drill hole through the middle of it. This was where they had drilled up the opal eight weeks previously. John did another short rip as the opal seam was still carrying into the rock.

The ripper had now ripped the line which was showing in the floor and running through the cut from end to end. This was now the hard black stone and appeared to be the edge of the opal find. The drill hole must have been one of the outer holes they had drilled.

Tony had to walk up and get another bucket from Bert's ute as theirs were full. A lot of the opal still had stone on it, but there was still going to be a lot of material when it was cleaned.

No one had thought about lunch, only the digging out of the opal. Finally, the men were convinced that they had picked up all the opal. The heavy buckets were loaded on to the floor of the dozer. John carefully drove out up the dump, past the noodlers, who were watching the other men intently, as they had their last scratch at the ground before leaving for the day.

The buckets were off loaded on to the ute, and then the dozer motor was idled to cool the turbocharger for a short while and then shut off for the day. Then they headed off towards the dying sun to the main road back to town.

The opal was tipped from the buckets into a two-hundred-litre drum to wait for a chance to clean and class it ready for sale. The drum had a series of holes on the rim around the top, which allowed a bar to be put through, which had a padlock fitted. This was not for Bert and Harry's sake but to be a bit of a deterrent if someone else should try to help themselves. The bulk of the material was too large to fit in the safe.

Some of the pieces of opal were studied under a bright light before the opal was finally tipped in the drum. Bert thought the best of the opal might bring as high as four thousand dollars an ounce. There were a lot of ounces in the three buckets which had been tipped into the drum. 'Money attracts money,' said Bert as he helped John fit the top to the drum and lock the padlock.

The room the opal drum was in had a very solid sheet-steel-covered door with a deadlock fitted to it and steel door surrounds, so the men felt reasonably comfortable about going to the Italian Club for a meal.

Secrets were hard to keep at Coober Pedy. The minute they walked through the door, the men sensed that the conversation had begun to include them. A lot of faces turned towards them. One of the local men, who had got to know Bert and Harry, came over and asked, 'I hear you guys have found a lot of opal again?'

'Nah, only some potch and colour.'

'Bullshit, one of the abos told me that you dug some opal out today. He was noodling your dump.'

'What were you doing chasing the abos? Chasing their women, I suppose?' asked Bert. The man laughed and walked back to his mates at the bar. 'I think we had better clean the opal soon and sell it.' John walked over to the bar and got four more beers.

'Bloody farmers, coming up and pinching our opal,' said one of the men with a wry smile. John couldn't really work out if the man was joking or having a shot at them.

'I reckon that we should get busy and clean the opal tomorrow. Everyone seems to know we have had a find,' said John as he came back to the table with the four beers.

They didn't stay at the club for very long after their meal. The fact that most of the people in the club knew about the opal meant that most of the crooks about the town would know also.

The door of the dugout was open when they returned from the club. There were marks where someone had forced the door with a round bar. 'Bloody hell, some prick has broken in.' The inside of the dugout had been shifted around. Cupboard doors were pulled out, and clothes had been tipped out of the suitcases on to the beds. Someone had scratched the paint on the safe door but had not been able to open it. The fridge was open, and all the beer was missing, as well as a new unopened carton plus some food. 'God, what is that horrible smell?' said Bert sniffing, trying to determine from where the odour was coming.

'Oh shit, here it is,' said Tony, pointing behind one of the lounge chairs. 'Some dirty bugger has crapped on the floor.'

The door of the opal room had been hit and prised at also. Something that the thieves did not realise was that the heavy door of the opal room was covered in a sheet of steel. A very unprofessional burglary job. 'I think we had better ring the cops.' The new dugout had the advantage of having a telephone. Bert rang the police.

The men made sure they didn't touch anything that had been moved. The police arrived within half an hour and checked the outside of the dugout for footprints. There were a few sets of barefeet marks in the dusty dirt outside the dugout. Evidently who had broken in had not driven in to the dugout but had walked. 'They may have only walked up from the road,' the young officer said. When they checked the opal room door, the officers looked closely at the marks on the door.

'I reckon this was done by some young blokes who have just come to town. They use round reinforcing bar when they are noodling. See the round dents. The crap on the floor is one of their trademarks too.' He pointed to where the door had been interfered with. The men could see where the reinforcing bar had been bent. 'You're lucky they didn't have a proper jemmy bar. They would probably have got the door open.'

Tony went out, got a shovel out of their ute, gingerly picked up the smelly mess left by the burglars, then took it outside, and then dug a hole to bury it. He had thought about the Kellys dogs rolling in it so he dragged a large piece of stone over the filled-in hole. He got some disinfectant from the laundry and then scrubbed the floor. The other men tidied the dugout up after the police had left and then went to bed.

The police rang the next morning just before Bert and Harry left for work to inform them that they were not the only dugout to be broken into in the area. There was a mob of young men who were in town. They had come down to Coober Pedy from past the Mintabie opal fields. The police said they were known troublemakers in their own community and had been kicked out by the elders of the community.

Bert and Harry went to work. They had offered to help to clean the opal, but John, in his normal pig-headed way, did not want to impose on their working time.

The opal was taken out of the drum, put into the concrete mixer drum in small lots, and then tumbled.

When the opal was cleaned, they noticed that there was quite a bit more potch in the cleaned material than they thought there was. There was still a lot of good quality opal.

As the mixer turned and cleaned the next lot of opal, John and Tony sat and classed the potch from the opal, cutting the dead pieces of potch from the good opal with the tile cutters. The job took all day. They were still working on the opal when the Kellys returned from work.

Bert looked at the opal under the bright lamp. 'It's a pity about all the potch, but the rest of the opal is still pretty good. Probably up to three thousand an ounce for the tops.' He shuffled through it with his horny old hands, turning the material over and over under the light. He would pick a particular piece out and hand it to Harry, who would hand it on. This was almost like a ritual amongst opal miners. No two pieces were ever the same.

John went to the supermarket to get some more beer and some groceries. He met a man who spent some time at the Italian Club. John asked if he knew of any halfway honest opal buyers in town.

'Hmm. There is one man from near Streaky Bay, who is in town at present. He makes a lot of triplets for the tourist-type trade,' Guy explained where the man lived. John offered to buy Guy a carton of beer if this man was OK.

John called into the man's house, which was quite easy to find. He knocked on the door. A woman answered the door and gave John the once-over. 'Yes, what are you looking for?'

'I was talking to a man called Guy. He said your husband is looking to buy some opal.'

The woman walked out of the door, pulling it shut behind her. 'Follow me. Bob is down in the opal shed.' The shed behind the house had a steel door and bars on the window. There was a light coming from the window. The woman yelled out, 'Bob, there is someone who wants to sell a parcel of opal.' The door opened slightly, and then Bob took the security chain off and then opened the door. John introduced himself. The three shook hands. Bob asked if John would like to see some triplets being made.

Inside the shed, there were three large tables and an assortment of opal saws and polishing machines. The tables had thin pieces of black potch lined up on to which Bob was sticking thin slices of opal with a clear epoxy glue. He then stuck a domed, clear glass cap on top of the opal. The end result was a lot brighter stone as the black enhanced the colour of the thin opal and the dome magnified the material and scattered the colour. 'Do you mind if I finish this job? I have all the glue mixed and don't want to waste it.' As he worked, he explained the process of the triplet making. John was very interested. John described the opal that they had found and approximately what value they thought it would be. Bob asked if they could bring the opal the next night.

Before leaving for work the next morning, they drove to Ivan's workshop. Ivan proudly showed the two new ripping tools and the four extra picks. The concept looked as if the picks would be a lot easier to remove. The retaining pins and the removal tool were very well built.

CHAPTER 15

Fatima drove to the Parafield Airport, picked up Achmed and Aaron, and then drove them back to their house. Aaron had been invited to stay at Achmed's house after the trip back from Coober Pedy. They had a lot of things to work out, following the robbery and Aaron's subsequent battle for the remains of the prehistoric worm.

Fatima had a friend stay with her whilst Achmed had been away. She did not feel happy being in the house by herself whilst the children were at school during the day. The children themselves still woke during the night with nightmares about the robbery. The house was securely locked each night.

Fatima served up lunch for the men. They discussed what the next mode of action should be to try and get the cash back and to have the worm returned to Aaron.

The next problem was the worm. Aaron wanted to engage a solicitor to handle the matter of having the now-frozen remains of the creature returned to him so he could display it in his museum.

Not having much experience dealing with legal firms, Achmed phoned a friend to ask about the various law firms in the city to try and find the best person to represent Aaron about his claim for the return of the worm. Achmed had been given the names of two men who worked for two different legal firms. One name was the name of a radical politician, who had been dumped by his party. Achmed had never liked the way this man had conducted himself whilst he was in politics. He suggested that Aaron ring the other man who was already making a name for himself in the news, representing some high-profile clients.

The trip into the city to see the solicitor at the law firm took all the afternoon. The whole story of the robbery, the subsequent hatching of the worm, and then the killing of the three men was recounted to the solicitor.

The solicitor had been following the story as most other people were in the newspapers. The solicitor assured Aaron that they could see no reason why the museum staff should not be made to return the remains of the worm. He would get started on the matter straight away. Aaron thought, as the solicitor was talking, that he would not like to have to hold his breath whilst all of this took place. A solicitor was like a spider; they sucked all the goodness out of the client before they were finally finished toying with them.

Aaron always recalled a mural in the law court building in Budapest, which depicted two farmers and a cow stuck in a hedgerow. One farmer was pulling on the halter to try to get the cow over to his field. The other farmer was pulling the cow's tail, trying to get the cow back in his field, whilst the lawyer calmly sat at the side of the cow with a bucket and milked the cow. The worm was now the cow. Both men felt quite exhausted when they left the office.

'I think they would probably be as big a robbers as the men who took the opal in the first place,' offered Achmed as they got into the car to finally drive home.

Aaron took Achmed, Fatima, and the children out for a meal at a bistro to try and relieve the tension of the last few days, as Fatima and the children were still very upset and still having nightmares over the robbery.

Aaron and Achmed had buried themselves in their work for the last few days and had not had time to brood on the previous few days' events. If the men had not gone straight to Coober Pedy, the missing piece of the broken egg would not have been recovered, and possibly more of the pieces would have been missing by now. There was also the advantage of being in Coober Pedy when the cash had been found. Achmed was pleased that he had met with Charlie and Karen. If the police had dealt with the matter, things might have been quite different. Achmed still did not trust the authorities when it came to resolving the money issue. There may have been a lot more of the money missing and Charlie and Karen blamed. They would not have been able to prove that they did not still have it secreted in some safe deposit box or somewhere else.

Achmed drove Aaron to the Adelaide airport to catch a connecting flight to Melbourne on the first leg of his journey home.

Aaron was really in a hurry to get back home with the eggs and put them on display in his museum to try and capitalise on the publicity of the last few days. His mind had been working hard on how to maximise the publicity of the broken egg and worm. He had talked with Achmed about this for a long time and had decided to make a mock-up of the worm and display this with the eggs.

Chapter 16

Inside the mobile laboratory, the creature's flaccid body was laid out on a table covered by a disposable sheet.

Because of the infection which had almost claimed the lives of Vince Murphy and Willie Brooks, the lab was sited a long way from town.

The lab was situated about five hundred metres from the airport terminal on a deserted area of the opal fields. This was an area which was banned from mining as it was close to where the planes landed—an area without any unauthorized people nearby.

A prefabricated fence had been erected around the buildings, inside which was the trailer-mounted alternator as well as the buildings. A long plastic airlock was joined on to the doorway of one of the buildings. This had a facility to completely disinfect anyone coming or going from the lab.

Another van, a small freezer van, was situated inside the yard. This held the bodies of the three men killed in the accident. The infectious material in the two bodies of the men, which the creature had killed, was a real worry. The men had been manhandled from the car by the ambulance officers before anyone had any real idea of what they were dealing with. Any person who had contact with the accident site or the subsequent handling of the creature was put into a quarantined area and monitored by a special staff who had been flown in from Adelaide. People were worried that the new-found infection may escape into the township.

One major worry was the men who were to be transferred by the ambulance plane to Adelaide. The hospital was contacted, and the plane cancelled. Willie and Vince were taken out to the facility and installed in one of the buildings, which had been set up as a hospital ward. How easily this infectious material could be dispersed through the community!

Security guards monitored all the facilities which had been erected around the town.

Before entering the lab, all the scientific staff donned the overalls and a clear plastic head cover with its own air supply. The scientists looked like space men in their suits.

The body of the creature was starting to thaw out after its stay in the deep freezer. Liquid was oozing from the bullet holes in its ghastly body. The creature's mouth was agape, showing the double rows of razor-sharp teeth, which had inflicted all the damage to its victims. A stool protruded from the creature's rear.

The creature's grey rubbery skin appeared soft when prodded with an instrument, belying the strength the creature really had. Other than the head, the creature looked just like a giant grub. There were even a few stiff hairs protruding from its skin. There were no sign of eyes on the head. Most of which was taken up by the mouth with the rows of teeth. The creature must have found its victims by sound, heat, or movement. A discussion was held between the chief scientist Alan Matters and the pathologist Sue Pentagast about what size this creature would have been at maturity from the size of the eggs. They estimated at least five metres. This would not have been a very nice creature to have sliding around. It would have been a real killing machine. It was Probably a creature which had evolved in the oceans or lakes of one hundred million years ago when the opal fields were inhabited with marine life. 'Maybe this creature was a marine creature, which breathed air, such as seals, dolphins, and the like. It could certainly move well in the water with its shape.'

Sue answered after some thought, 'I agree. If it were at Coober Pedy at the time of when this country was under water, this was the more probable explanation.' The discussion continued throughout the afternoon.

Some sort of eel without a skeleton was another suggestion. 'I certainly would not like to run into one when I was swimming,' said Allan.

Small samples were taken from the creature to get some DNA samples to try and match this monster with any which were still living today.

All persons who had been in contact with any part of the accident were questioned over and over about what they had been doing and what they had touched at the accident scene. Had they cut themselves or had they any open sores before the accident? One by one, they were questioned, over and over, to try and make sure there was nothing they had missed in their first statement. Harry the Horse was very glad he did not cut himself on the piece of opal egg he had found.

Two factors which were extremely worrying to the scientists were the fact that the eggs had been taken from the town, and as far as the scientists knew, they may have already left the country for their trip to America. Were any such other creatures present inside any of the other eggs? To have any more of the eggs broken and more creatures released was a real concern.

The worm was finally rolled back into its shroud and relegated to the cold room again. Tom's body was brought in to replace it on the slab.

Tom's body was carefully cut open from the chest to the hole where his penis had been located. A curious-looking green fungus had started to grow on the moist parts of his insides. There was not much left of his insides. Tom had been very efficiently gutted from the inside out by the creature, nearly all of his organs had been consumed. Only small scraps remained.

Jenny Mayfield and her assistant Brian Cain had thought that they had just about seen everything. They had conducted autopsies on nearly all the weird accident and murder cases in the country. Jenny, in particular, enjoyed her work; nothing had ever fazed her.

Jenny was a plain-looking woman who had mousey-coloured hair. Her whole life was tied up around her job. Her long-time partner and assistant Brian looked the part of the typical nerd, complete with the heavy horn-rimmed glasses, sallow complexion, and thin, wispy beard, which seemed to always be a badge worn by his ilk.

This case was extremely different—far different from any that they had ever encountered before. At first, Jenny had viewed the monster with a great deal of wonder. But after seeing Tom's body, she had changed her opinion to one of a feeling of fear and loathing for it.

The bodies of the two men also created problems. To bury their bodies in the warm Coober Pedy earth could exacerbate the infection problem. The green fungus would probably still keep growing inside their lifeless bodies. Would it remain underground? What the outcome of this would be was only a guess. The worst-case scenario was an epidemic similar to the spread of the Aids virus. There were so many unknown factors which they were dealing with in this case.

A special cremating unit was ordered and was being sent up from Adelaide to deal with this problem after the autopsies had been completed. Tom and Silvio were to be cremated with a special extra hot cremation, similar heat used to dispose of dangerous chemicals. There were too many loose ends regarding the infections, as it were.

Other units arrived during the next day. A mobile office was set up inside the fenced yard as well as the crematorium. So far, there only seemed to have been problems with anyone who had been attacked by the creature and had been bitten, thus having their skin broken and the pathogen distributed through their bodies. By that method, Aaron and Achmed were the other two people who were not under quarantine. Achmed and his family were contacted in Adelaide and were checked by a doctor at their home for two days. The children were kept home from school.

Aaron was back in Chicago. He was contacted and told of the infection which had broken out on the victims of the creature. All pieces of the broken egg as well as the other ones were to be thoroughly disinfected. It was made very clear to Aaron that if he were to cut himself on any of the broken egg, this would probably cause the infection to invade his body. The symptoms of such a happening were explained to Aaron. There was now hope as the cure for this affliction was almost ready.

Aaron could feel that the chances of finally obtaining the body of the worm for his museum were getting slimmer by the moment. After hearing what effect the pathogen had on its victims, he was not so sure that he really wanted it.

There was not much chance that a source of such a dangerous infection would be allowed to be imported into the country.

After two days of no one showing any signs of any symptoms of the infection, the quarantined people were allowed to return home. They were to visit a special clinic for the next week daily to check on their progress.

The future of the worm's body was still uncertain. It would probably end up in a sealed glass case in a place where no one could handle it.

Three days had passed since all the people who had been detained in quarantine had been let go home. Willie Brooks and Vince Murphy were still in the quarantine unit. Up until now, their condition had been stabilised. Vince, in particular, was healing well with no apparent new symptoms.

A nurse was attending Willie Brooks. She removed the dressing on the remains of his penis to discover a new green mouldy growth starting to grow. Willie's temperature was beginning to soar. The nurse quickly called the doctor.

A doctor and a scientist in their protective suits attended to Willie. Drastic steps were being taken to finally halt the spread of the infection. After Willie was stabilised, he was taken back to rejoin Vince in the makeshift ward. The doctors had tried a new treatment which had seemed to work on the pathogen when it was grown in a Petri dish in the lab. This new treatment had been tested at least ten times and had worked on all occasions.

<h1 style="text-align:center">Chapter 17</h1>

John and Tony fitted the new tools which Ivan had fabricated to the bulldozer. The performance in the hard sandstone of the opal level was similar to the other pointed tipped tools. They were hoping that changing tools was going to be far easier and safer. John had nearly bee-hit by the heavy sledge hammer on one occasion when the drift had shot out from the hammer head.

The Kellys were still walking with Tony. There was the usual good-natured banter as they turned the rocks and scratched. After the dozer had ripped back and forth four times, the glass-breaking noise was heard again. One part of the large rock was kicked up by the ripper to reveal an edge of opal approximately two centimetres thick. A brilliant green orange colour flashed as the sunlight hit it. John had heard the noise through his earmuffs and stopped moving and then turned on the seat. Just looking from the seat of the dozer, he could see that this opal quality was superior to any other seam opal that they had found. Tony had already set off to get the buckets and sieves.

The rocks were being checked for opal and the barren rock discarded. There were two rocks close to a metre across, one which had been turned on its side and its adjoining mate. Tony came down the steep ramp and slid on a loose rock. He landed heavily on his behind. He very gingerly got up and walked over to the men and the new opal seam. 'Hell, my bum landed on a small round rock. It hurts like hell.' He squatted, got comfortable, and started to chip the opal off the rocks which Bert and Harry were tossing to him.

'Now you know why some of those TV wrestlers walk about on tiptoe after they have been lifted and jammed down on the other guy's knee. You've hurt your coxic bone. It'll be sore for quite a while.'

A large hole over two metres across had been excavated. This opal did not have the potch pieces in it that the other find had. It was a very clean material. 'Well, you have outdone yourselves today. This is the best yet other than the eggs.'

Finally, after three hours' chipping and sieving, the opal had all been removed from the rock and put into the buckets.

'I think I would like to go home now. My bum really hurts now.' Tony started to hobble carefully up the ramp of the cut, looking where he put his foot, in case he had another slide. Very carefully, he slid into the utility and slowly wriggled his bottom until he found a comfortable spot to sit. John had received a few of these bumps in the rear region when he had played football in his younger days. These were usually a payback for a black eye or some other sore wound he had given his opponent.

The opal was started to be tumbled in the concrete mixer. Bert and Harry were doing the work. Tony had had a very hot shower and was sitting in a padded chair with his pillow under his bum. It still hurt like hell, but the pain had abated a little after the shower.

John picked up the opal from the previous find and headed off to see Bob. Bob's wife opened the door. Bob yelled, 'Come in if you are good looking.' John walked in with the bag of opal. 'Sit down and have a cuppa coffee.'

'White with one,' said John as Bob's wife set three mugs on the table. Bob rose and picked up a desk lamp from a box on the floor. He put it on the table and then turned it on.

'Let's have a look at the opal.' John slipped the large plastic bag over to Bob. The buyer sorted the opal into different grades and then reached over and picked a set of balance scales from the box where the light had been. The heaps of opal were weighed, and the weights and numbers of each heap were noted on the pad. After some more considering and adding on a calculator, Bob started to write down the prices.

'What does 260,000 sound like?' This was about the price they had been working on. So John agreed. The men shook hands on the deal. 'Do you want more coffee?' asked Bob's wife.

'No, thanks.'

'As you probably realise, I haven't got that much money here at this time. Would you take a bank cheque or do you want cash?'

'I can have the bank cheque tomorrow, or the cash will be here in three days.'

John said he would wait for the three days. The opal heaps were bagged up, and the numbers, weight, and price were written on each bag. John took the opal and left for the dugout.

Tony was feeling a bit better. He was walking slowly to try and get some exercise to the affected part. 'How did you go?'

'Two hundred and sixty thousand dollars.'

'Shit, that's not a bad price. I reckon we should see this guy, Harry,' said Bert.

'I have been thinking about the dugout security. We don't want any more unwelcome visitors in here. Seeing Tony has a sore bum and would not be too good walking, we should clean your opal. I will go and get a strong bolt and padlock for the door, as well as some sheet of steel to cover it with, plus some builders reinforcing mesh so we can make some guards to fit over the windows. We could have a building day whilst the opal is tumbled.

Bert and Harry returned with a sheet of builders mesh tied over the top of the ute. There were new tools and fittings to complete the job, plus the sheet of steel for the door. He had also bought two other heavy bolts to fix to the top and bottom of the opal room door.

The outside door was removed and planed down to allow the iron to be bent around the edges of the door. Wood glue was smeared all over the door, the iron fitted, and the edges of the iron carefully bent over the edges of the door, leaving the hinges and lock cut out. 'What about some paint to make it look better?'

'No, I like the look of the silver finish,' said Harry. The door was refitted, and then the bolt was screwed in place. It shone in the sunlight like a dull mirror. 'See I told you it would look OK.' The opal room was then fitted with the new bolts on the top and bottom of the door. The two like keyed padlocks left in the bolts without the bolts pushed in place.

The next project was to cut the mesh with an angle grinder to fit the windows. The edges were bent to make a box for each window; the box sections were screwed into place with some tabs which had been drilled.

The door and window protectors made the dugout entrance look a lot more secure. Bert had at least bought some galvanized paint which they had used before fitting the boxes.

The opal had been cleaned by the time they had finished. Tony had tried to help but had to admit that the sore bum was still giving him some serious problems. John rang Bob and asked if he would come and class the opal the next day. He agreed to come after lunch.

Tony did not want to come to the Italian Club because of his bum problem. John called in to the bottle shop and bought a carton of beer for Guy on the way to the club. He was standing at the bar of the club, ordering a round of beers, when Guy walked over. 'How did you get on with Bob?'

'Really well. I have a carton of beer in the ute for you.'

'You didn't have to do that.'

'Do you know how hard it is to find out about opal buyers? I think a carton of beer is very cheap.' Both men walked out as the beer was transferred from John's ute to Guy's car.

'I often wondered about that spot where you and the Kellys found the opal. It's funny how everyone shoots through to a new find and leaves more money back where they came from. It's happened lots of times.' When they arrived home Tony said that one of the Greek opal buyers had called. He was snooping around where the mixer was. Tony had walked out and asked what he was doing.

'Have heard that the tumbler has been going a lot today. You must have found a lot of opal.'

'No, we have used it to do a bit of concrete work inside the dugout,' Tony lied. He had met this man before and did not like him.

'I think you have a big parcel of opal for sale. Let me have a look. I will give you top dollar for it.'

'We have not got any opal for sale.'

'Are you sure?'

'I'm sure, mate, and if you do not leave, I will let the dog out that lives inside. You would not want to meet him.'

'Ha, I don't hear no dog.'

'This dog does not bark. He bites. Now piss off.' The pushy Greek walked down to his car and drove off.

'I reckon that if you shot that crook, he would push his fingers into the bullet holes and keep talking.'

Bert and Harry had gone to work. Tony's affliction was improving, but he did not think he could walk behind the dozer yet. John had made some sandwiches, which they were eating when Bob knocked on the door.

Bob was studying the new additions to the security. 'Have you had some unwelcome visitors?' John explained about the break-in a few days before.

'That's why I have such a strong door and bars on my windows. I was broken in a few years ago and had sixty thousand dollars stolen. That was a bit more professional than the job you had done.' Bob walked into the dugout. He was carrying a parcel with him. 'I have been able to get your cash for you.' He handed the money over. Tony walked out with the opal from the recent find. John introduced the men.

'You had better go and get the other lot of opal from the safe as well. Bob has got the money.' John started to count the money as Bob had a quick look in one of the large bags of opal. John finished counting.

'Is all of the opal in these bags the same?'

'Yes, we have just randomly bagged it up, straight out of the tumbler.' John explained about the visitor that had been sneaking around the concrete mixer the night before.

'That man is a real con merchant. Never sell any opal to him. He would be worse than the Dragon.'

It took Bob three hours to finally get the opal sorted out ready for sale. The bagging, weighing, and pricing was all finished. 'This is exceptionally good opal. There is not much difference between the top grade and the lower grade. The final price was totalled up on the calculator.

'Six hundred and eighty thousand dollars,' said Bob.

'Bert and Harry said it should be worth over a half a million,' said Tony.

'I cannot afford to buy a parcel like this,' said Bob. 'There is a Greek who visits during the year, or two buyers in Adelaide I would recommend.'

'We have sold two lots to Achmed Farrah.' 'I would stick with him'.

'Yes, we are going to give him a call,' said John.

Bert and Harry arrived home. They were introduced to Bob. The men talked for about two hours on the state of the opal field, some of the crooked deals that had happened and also about a few men who had disappeared down some of the deep exploration mineshafts over the years. There was no need for lawyers and courts in this multicultural community. Some of the nationalities had their own way of dealing with thieves and paedophiles. Bob was very interesting to listen to. 'Hell, I had better go home. My missus will kill me. We are going out tonight.' Bob left with the opal he had bought. John phoned home and told Helen about the new sale and the valuation of the new find. She was very excited.

John phoned Achmed and also the patent attorney and made some appointments to see them on Monday. He was going to fly down to Adelaide on the *Commercial Airline* flight. Helen was flying to Adelaide to meet up with him

000 OOO 000

The End

BIOGRAPHY
OF JAMES CALDERWOOD

I was bought up on a farm near Port Lincoln South Australia.

I attended a small school with about twelve pupils, which was near our farm . From seventh grade, I was sent to Adelaide to boarding school Prince Alfred College. I learnt stick up for myself and fight. I returned home to work on the farm. After leaving my parents farm, I worked in a few jobs. I got married to Glenys, then bought a small property near Elliston. The price of wool dropped by 50% in the first year. We tried to crop some of the rough stony country, but the crops were attacked by the kangaroos and emus.

We sold this farm and bough a farm in a better area near Port Lincoln. My wife and I developed a lot of good farming land. I spent a lot of time rebuilding machinery to handle the development stage of the farm.

After visiting our daughter and partner in Alice Springs we called into an opal mining town Mintabie. This was probably a mistake as we had never seen so much cash being thrown around in our life. We got ripped off a couple of times. I broke my leg working on the farm and was laid up for a long time. Then graduated to Coober Pedy on a part time basis .We purchased a medium sized bulldozer.

We started to find some good opal but as the rock was very tough, I used some of my farming experience to develop a new tungsten tipped ripping tool. This worked very well and we patented it.

I started to work with a multinational firm to develop this tool, but when the Financial Crisis hit worldwide, they walked away from the project.

This book has been around for a long time, but I could not seem to be able to get the last few chapters right.